HIDDEN

HIDDEN

Karen E. Olson

This first world edition published 2015
in Great Britain and the USA by
SEVERN HOUSE PUBLISHERS LTD of
19 Cedar Road, Sutton, Surrey, England, SM2 5DA.
Trade paperback edition first published 2016
in Great Britain and the USA by
SEVERN HOUSE PUBLISHERS LTD.

British Library Cataloguing in Publication Data

Olson, Karen E. author.
  Hidden.
  1. Hackers–Fiction. 2. Suspense fiction.
  I. Title
  813.6-dc23

ISBN-13: 978-0-7278-8532-6 (cased)
ISBN-13: 978-1-84751-636-7 (trade paper)
ISBN-13: 978-1-78010-696-0 (e-book)

All Severn House titles are printed on acid-free paper.

Severn House Publishers support the Forest Stewardship Council™ [FSC™],
the leading international forest certification organisation. All our titles that
are printed on FSC certified paper carry the FSC logo.

Typeset by Palimpsest Book Production Ltd.,
Falkirk, Stirlingshire, Scotland.
Printed and bound in Great Britain by
TJ International, Padstow, Cornwall.

ONE

I went missing fifteen years ago.

And now the only person who knew where I was is dead.

I fold the newspaper in half, then in half again before putting it in my recycling bin. There is no indication that I've read any story more than once, running my finger along the print so many times it's now black with ink.

Some said *I* was dead. Some said I was still alive – there were 'sightings' of me in Sicily, Miami, Hong Kong, even Havana. Exotic places. Good places to hide. Those people spreading the rumors might find it funny to learn that I'm giving bicycle tours on Block Island, just off the coast of Rhode Island. Not exotic, not hiding. Just existing.

When I first arrived here, I knew this was where I wanted to stay. I'd never been to Block Island, didn't even know it existed until someone on the bus told me. Which meant others might not know about it, either. An island shaped like a pork chop in the Atlantic, a little more than an hour's ferry ride from Point Judith, population less than 1,000 year round, although surging to about 20,000 or more during the summer. What really struck me was how I felt when I stepped off the ferry: as if all my worries had been stripped away. I could breathe here, the air heavy with saltwater and fog but light as the clouds that skipped along the horizon.

I live in a small white Cape just up the road from the farm where they've got the llamas. The furniture came with the place; it's a little worn but not worse for wear. The front porch and living-room bay window overlook the ocean – and the dock at Old Harbor where the ferries come in. I've got a telescope set up inside so I can see them.

My name's Nicole. It's not the name I was born with – not even close. But I've always liked it and figured since I needed a new name I might as well pick one I liked. I could have it for the rest of my life. As long as it might be. Or might not be.

My last name's Jones. Not exactly original. But no one's ever questioned it.

I didn't change how I look. At least not then. Now I look a little different, but it's just that I'm getting older. My hair's starting to get some gray streaks – I cut it short to keep it out of my way – and I wear glasses. I wore contacts back then, but I like the way the glasses look, like I'm a college professor or something more distinguished than I really am. The biking has made me leaner. I was always comfortable in my body, but now I feel better, more alive.

I still look over my shoulder when the door opens in a restaurant or a shop, but now the person coming in is usually a friend or a tourist looking for some clam chowder or a painting of the island. I paint a little, too, when I'm not out on the bike. I have an easel that I can set up wherever I like and some empty canvases that I fill with the bright colors of the ocean and the sky and the cliffs. People buy them, wanting them as souvenirs of their stay here. I'd never done anything creative before. Didn't think I could. My hands had never held a paintbrush. It felt heavy to me the first time, that thin little stick.

I started the bike tours because of my friend Steve, who owns one of the independent taxis on the island. Taxi drivers here are also tour guides, and I took Steve's tour not long after I settled here. He told me everything I know about the island: its history, its landmarks, where the dead bodies are buried, so to speak. He tried to talk me into driving a hack, but I can't get a license so the bike thing was a fallback. I run the tours through one of the rental places; I bring in the business, split the takings forty–sixty. I get the forty, but I'm not complaining. I take home cash.

I didn't tell Steve why I couldn't get a driver's license, and he didn't ask. It's that New England Yankee thing: they keep to themselves and let strangers in selectively. For some reason, I passed Steve's test. We meet every Friday for happy hour at Club Soda up on Connecticut. It's where the locals hang out. There's foosball and pool and darts and usually music of some sort. The beer is cold, and if you want to be left alone, no one will bother you.

I go sometimes without Steve and have a burger if I don't want to cook. I am doing just that now, minding my own business, when Steve comes in with the paper. Not the *Block Island Times*, but the *Providence Journal*. He'd gone to the mainland today to pick up his new LCD TV. I didn't think he was back yet; otherwise, I would've invited him along.

'Hey, Nicole,' he says as he shifts his heavy frame onto the tall chair across the table from me.

I look up from my plate and nod, my mouth full of beef and bun and lettuce. Steve is about sixty-five, the same age my father would be today if he were alive. He's tall, with a big barrel chest and bushy white hair and a nicely trimmed beard. He plays Santa every Christmas for the kids at town hall. Steve was a geologist in his other life, that's how he ended up here, studying the island's rock formations. But when he'd spent all his grant money, he stayed, writing up his research, buying his first cab and settling into island life. He married a local girl who died twenty years ago of breast cancer. He swears he will never love another woman again. And then he asks me again to marry him, because I'm the only woman left who will tolerate all of his tired old stories. It's a joke almost as old as the stories now, but we keep it up just because we can.

Steve perches his reading glasses on his nose.

'Interesting story in the paper today,' he says, his voice low, a tone in it I haven't heard before. 'They're doing a series on cold cases. You know, police cases that never got solved?'

I swallow, but it feels like the burger's too big for my throat and I have to take a swig of my Bud Light to force it down. 'Yeah?' I ask, although I don't really want to go there.

Steve puts the paper on the table and turns it so it's the right side up for me. I push my glasses higher and squint through the bottom half of the lenses. Immediately I want to laugh. Not because the story is funny, but because I'm relieved. The story is about a series of rapes that occurred twenty-five years ago. The rapist wore a mask, never spoke and always entered through a window and left the same way. None of the women could ever identify him, even though there had been a couple of suspects. But with no hard evidence, the case stayed open.

I concentrate on the story, reading each word as Steve wants me to. When I'm done, I take another swig of my beer. 'Interesting.' It's all I can think of to say.

'He could be anywhere,' Steve speculates, flagging down Abby, the waitress, and asking for a beer.

'It's creepy,' I say. 'I don't want to think he's here, living among us.' *Not like me.*

Abby returns with the beer, sets it down, and Steve orders a burger just like mine. No tomato. No ketchup. Just lettuce, mayonnaise and mustard. We're like an old married couple. Abby is used to us. She winks at me as she leaves.

'Just think about it, though,' Steve continues, even though I want him to stop. 'He was never caught. What's he doing now? Is he married? Does he have kids?'

'Maybe he's dead,' I say flatly, taking another bite so my mouth's full and I can't respond to Steve's expression.

'You're heartless,' he says after a minute.

'He's a rapist,' I say after I swallow. 'It would be better if he's dead. Then he's no longer a threat.' I think for a second. 'Maybe the reason the rapes stopped is because he's dead. Maybe he died, so he couldn't rape anymore. The case will always be open, then, won't it?'

Steve admits he hasn't thought of that. He prefers to think of this animal as living among regular people, trying to be like one of them but always fighting his demons.

'You should write for TV or something,' I say when Abby brings his burger. By now I've finished mine, so I order some onion rings for us to share. I don't like anyone to eat alone. Except for me.

I pull my sweater around my shoulders and shiver. It's the beginning of May; the island's getting ready for tourists, but it's still chilly as the breezes sweep off the ocean and envelop the island. It's always windy here; I'm always wearing a sweater or a fleece or a windbreaker. I don't think I've put a bathing suit on the entire time I've been here.

'You've got to be from Florida,' Steve starts up again. Another old argument. 'No one can be as cold as you are all the time.'

I don't answer. I have no history, no life before Block Island. Steve teases me, but he respects that and doesn't ask me anything about it. It's why we're friends.

I busy myself reading the paper placemat. 'We're All Here

Because We're Not All There.' It's Club Soda's slogan. When I
first got here, it struck me as something I could have as my own.

The onion rings arrive. Steve has moved onto the sports section
of the paper, speculating about the Red Sox and if they'll win
the Series again.

'They've become the Yankees,' he says somberly, because
that's a bad thing. But I know at the same time it's a good thing
because they've stopped disappointing. Baseball was new to me
fifteen years ago; now it's a bond I've got with my new friends.
I've surprised myself in many ways.

'Getting ready for the season?' Steve asks, folding the paper
up, finished with it. He takes an onion ring, dips it in ketchup
and brings it to his mouth. I take the biggest one off the top and
nod.

'They'll be here soon,' I say, meaning the tourists. Just a few
weeks now until Memorial Day weekend, when they'll file off
the ferries into our lives. 'I've been mapping out a couple of new
routes.'

'You can still find new routes after all this time?' Steve is
teasing me. Every year I change up the routes, just in case I've
got repeat customers. I don't want them to think it's been there,
done that.

I take another onion ring and suck the onion out of the fried
breading.

'That's so gross,' Steve says, but then he does it, too. We go
through the rest of the onion rings and leave their skins, like
shedded snakeskins, on the plate.

When we walk out of Club Soda, the night air pierces my
face and I wish I had more than my sweater. I walk around to
the bike rack and start undoing the lock.

'I can take you back,' Steve says, nodding toward his Explorer
in the lot.

I'm not one to argue. We get the bike into the back of the
SUV with no problem, and as I start to climb into the passenger
seat, a sleek black car skids around the corner and slams on its
brakes. Steve takes a step out of the Explorer, ready to give the
guy a lesson on how to drive here. I lean around in my seat to
watch, but the dim light inside means I can't see very well.

I hear raised voices, Steve's and another man's. I see a shadowy outline and hope he doesn't take a swing at Steve, who isn't in the best of shape. But then it's over, and Steve is back, getting into the Explorer and shutting his door, which means the light goes out abruptly.

I can see outside now. I can see the stranger's face. But the problem is he's not a stranger after all.

TWO

Missing women are all the media rage. It seemed to have started with Laci Peterson and morphed into Natalee Holloway in Antigua or Aruba or Antilles, one of those 'A' islands. The Runaway Bride wasn't missing too long, and the poor thing looked like she'd stuck her finger in a light socket – in more ways than one. That Elizabeth Smart was still a child when she went missing. Too bad she wasn't when she finally turned up.

All of these women were victims of men; isn't that such a cliché?

I watch these cases picked apart on the twenty-four-hour news channels. Maybe I would've been one of them, too, but when I disappeared it wasn't like those other women. I was a story that faded as the days and weeks went on, one of those cold cases that might show up in the papers fifteen years later. By then everyone would have forgotten about it. If it weren't for that FBI agent, who took it personally that I managed to lose him.

Shame that he'd found me.

Steve drops me off at my house, helps me get my bike up on the porch before giving me a kiss on the cheek.

'Good night,' he says, and even though it's dark, I can see him smile.

'Don't stay up too late hooking up that new TV,' I say.

'What do you mean? It's already hooked up.' He laughs as he heads back to the Explorer. He pauses at the door, just before getting in. 'You could come over and watch, if you want.'

This is as much for him as it is for me. I used to think he asked me over all the time because he worried about me being lonely, but it's him. Since Dotty died, he's the lonely one. But tonight I can't. I need to be alone.

'Thanks anyway. I'm beat,' I say, my keys in my hand.

'Suit yourself. See you tomorrow,' Steve says, climbing into the SUV.

I wait until the engine roars, he puts it in gear and I watch its back end disappear down the road, toward the llamas. In my head, I map out his journey home as I would one of my tours. He lives over near the Great Salt Pond, which once upon a time was the island's only entrance point – before Old Harbor and the ferry. A little historical tidbit I offer on my tour.

I stick the key in the lock and open my door, stepping into the little mudroom off the kitchen on the side of the house. I slip off my sneakers, my socks allowing me to move quietly into the silence. I flip a switch, and the light over the stove comes on, a dim glow that bathes the room in yellow. I've changed all my light bulbs over to those energy-saving ones. I want to get solar panels for hot water, but the cost's too prohibitive. I do have a wood stove, which heats the whole house, except on especially gusty nights when the cold air creeps through the cracks in the old window frames, its frigid fingers touching every surface.

The clock tells me it's still early, not even nine o'clock. I put on a kettle of water to boil and stick a teabag in a mug that I take from the cupboard. While the water begins to heat up, I go into the bedroom, taking off my jeans, sweater, and long-sleeved T-shirt, replacing them with flannel pajamas and a fleece bathrobe. Maybe sometime in June I'll put the flannel and fleece away and take out the cotton.

I still haven't turned on any light except the one in the kitchen. I tell myself it's because I like the cozy feel, but I know in my gut that I'm afraid that black car followed me here, that he knows where I am and is just waiting for the right moment.

I go into the bathroom and close the door, trapping the light inside. I stare at my reflection in the mirror. If he shows a picture of that long-ago woman to anyone, will they recognize me? I trace the lines in my face near my eyes, around my mouth. When did these show up? The glare of the bulb in the lenses of my glasses hides my eyes, so I take them off. The lashes are black with mascara. I pick up a cloth and wash my face with soap, wiping away the day but not the years. There is even more gray in my hair than I thought, leaning closer to take in the short curls, the wisp of bangs covering a high forehead.

I have not seen that younger face in so long. I cannot say for sure that I won't be recognized, or that I will.

The TV lends its own blue film to the darkness that envelops my bedroom. I don't keep a TV in the living room, only here, where I can pull the covers up and prop myself up on my soft, goose-down pillows. They are my only luxury, a piece of my past I cannot let go of no matter how much I have tried. My green tea is on the nightstand, the doors are locked, I am alone watching a movie about a boy who was taken hostage and held for ransom. It is based on a true story.

I decide the next morning while making my oatmeal that I have to go out today. I woke up in the night wondering if I had imagined him. It was possible. At first, I thought I saw him everywhere, but soon his numbers diminished to nothing. When I close my eyes and force myself to see that face from last night again, it's not the young, beautiful man I remembered. This man was handsome but older, his hair receding, his jaw settling into a looser jowl, his middle thicker. He was a man I might notice at Club Soda and play a round of pool with after a few drinks. I try to conjure what had been familiar about him: his stance, the way he held his head, his back stiff and straight, his arms at his sides.

The image plays over and over in my head like a movie marathon. With each showing, however, he becomes more and more a stranger. Like any other tourist wanting a getaway before the crowds show up.

I chew a raisin, stirring a handful into the hot cereal as I walk out onto the front porch. I pulled my dingy wicker chair out of the garden shed last week, and now it waits for me. I sit, eating, staring out at the water. A gray strip of fog hovers on the horizon, but I spot the ferry, a pinprick in the blue cloth laid out in front of me. Some days I never move from my chair except to get another cup of tea or a sandwich, wrapped in my fleece cocoon, the angle of the house such that the wind misses this spot. I watch the ferries come and go, the top of an occasional car or bike that passes below the green strip of grass that slides down over a small hill to the road.

Today, though, I don't stay. I finish my oatmeal and carry the empty bowl into the house, to the kitchen, and rinse it out in the sink. I get dressed in my usual uniform of jeans, T-shirt and fleece pullover and put on the sneakers that I'd shed the night before. I grab my backpack and go outside. My bike is propped up next to the back door. I don't lock it up. Steve tells me I'm too trusting, that bikes can go missing even here.

I know what happens when something goes missing.

So far, though, no one has ever taken it.

I throw my leg over the seat and shift a little so I'm comfortable, pushing the pedals until I'm flying over the hill and down toward Old Harbor. The National Hotel is open, advertising lunch and dinner, and many of the shops are hanging out their shingles and waiting for the big summer business that's on its way. I think about stopping in at The Beaches Gallery, where my paintings are on sale, but I'm not in the mood at the moment to talk to Veronica, the owner. She is a bit high maintenance, and I'm in a hurry. So I continue down past the Surf Hotel, slowing as I go around the corner, and there's the building. A small, squat clapboard house with a long deck overlooking the water. Sunswept Spa. Next to the Mohegan Bluffs, it is possibly my favorite place on the island.

I lock up the bike in the rack next to the parking lot and make my way up the steps. The soft tinkling of a bell sounds as I push the door open, and the scent of cloves hits my nose. I breathe deeply, all the stress of my nighttime wonderings melting out of my shoulders.

'Nicole!' Jeanine leans in and kisses me first on one cheek and then on the other. Very European. She is wearing a short-sleeved, lacy top and a long knit wraparound skirt. Her blonde hair, piled on top of her head and pinned with chopsticks, smells like strawberries. 'What a surprise!' She takes a step back and assesses me. When I first met her, this bothered me – the way she studies me every time I see her. But this is what makes her good at her job, owning this spa. 'You need stones today,' Jeanine says matter-of-factly, going around the dark wooden counter and checking the appointment book. 'I have an hour before my first client.'

'I really just wanted to take a yoga class.' The class starts in five minutes; I checked the schedule before I left the house. I have yoga pants and a mesh shirt in my backpack.

She frowns. 'That's not what you need. Your energy is off, you need some balance.' With that, she takes my hand and leads me down the hall, through the waiting room and a door that leads to the private rooms. She gently pushes me into one, the dim light making it seem as if it were twilight instead of early morning. 'Undress. I'll be back in a few.'

The door shuts gently behind her, and I stand for a moment. I am used to Jeanine's way but I am still a bit thrown because this is not what I've come for. I am not used to asserting myself anymore, however, so I shrug off the backpack and begin peeling off the clothes I'd just put on not twenty minutes ago. When Jeanine comes back, I am face down under the sheet, the warmth from the padded table soaking into my skin. I'm still a little tense, but the anxiety starts to ease. She doesn't say a word, but I hear the stones clicking against each other, the water in their bath sloshing. In moments, a heavy stone is sitting on my lower back. The heat penetrates my body, and I sigh before I can stop myself.

Jeanine chuckles and puts two more stones on my spine. I welcome them and want to be covered completely. I want to crawl into their bath and feel their smoothness all around me.

As my eyes droop and close, I realize she is right. I need this.

My muscles feel like Jell-O as I dress. Jeanine has left me alone again; my body is warm and tingly. I will need a shower to wash off the oils she's used, but for now I relish the slick feeling of my skin, drink in the aroma. I glance in the mirror and smooth my hair back into a short ponytail, tendrils framing my face. I don't look nearly as old as I did earlier. When I'm dressed, I leave the room, squinting as the brighter lights outside stab my eyes. Jeanine is at the counter again, and she smiles at me.

'You feel better now, don't you?'

'You just like to rub it in.'

She laughs. 'Oh, rub it in, yeah, I get that.'

I don't even realize that I was making a joke, but I go along with it.

'Plans today?' she asks as she rings up my bill. She gives me a discount because we're friends.

I shrug. 'Not sure yet,' I say. I have a flashback to a time when I always had plans. I shudder, wondering where that came from.

'Must be nice,' Jeanine says, but it's not in a jealous way. She loves her job and knows how hard I work during the season. 'Want to meet for dinner tonight?'

I nod. 'I'll call you later.'

'Four-ish would be good,' she says, looking at her book.

The door bell jingles.

'That's my next appointment,' Jeanine says, rising.

I pick my backpack up off the floor and swing it over my shoulder, turning. But I'm not watching where I'm going and I crash into Jeanine's client. I back away quickly and look up, ready to apologize.

He smiles, but there's a question in his eyes. 'Do I know you?'

THREE

A chain around a tree holds my bike securely as I make my way down toward the rocky beach, the wooden staircase twisting and turning to accommodate the terrain. The way down is easy; my feet fly as they maneuver the slats so familiar that they barely register what they're doing. Every once in a while I look down to make sure they're on the right track. My hand skims the railing, and I scan the Mohegan Bluffs that drop a hundred and fifty feet.

When I reach the bottom, I look up and revel in the craggy cliffs. I make my way across the beach, stopping occasionally to pick up a smooth rock that's caught a glint of sunshine and is winking at me. I have glass jars full of these rocks all over my little house, reminders of these days when I wander without purpose. The jars mark my time here, dated carefully: my first visit to the Bluffs; my first, fifth and tenth anniversaries on the island; the day I started my bike tours. I don't just come here on special days, but I only make a jar for those.

Today is a jar day.

The wind slides up my sleeve and touches my elbow, my shoulder, my chest before slipping out the other side. My backpack is heavy with stones, and I take deep breaths as I climb the wooden stairs back up to my bike. This is the hard part, going back up.

I have a message on my answering machine when I get home. I don't bother with it right away. Instead, I unload the stones and take one of the sparkling, empty jars out of my pantry. Carefully, I slide the stones inside. There aren't enough to fill it, only about three-quarters of the way, but I seal it anyway and take my marker and write the date on the bottom. I know where this one will go: on the bookshelf in the bedroom just next to the jar from my first visit to the Bluffs.

'Meet me at Bethany's for lunch.' Steve's voice echoes through my kitchen, bouncing off the tiles over the stove when I finally hit 'play' on the machine. The clock tells me it's almost noon; the clouds tell me rain is coming. I'm not sure I want to take the bike out now. I have a can of tuna for a sandwich. I pick up the phone and dial.

'Storm,' I say abruptly. 'Why don't you come here for lunch? I have tuna.'

'Too late. I'm already here, waiting for you. Where have you been?' He pauses. 'Forget about it. I'll get a couple clam chowders to go and you can make a couple sandwiches. I'll be there in a few.' He hangs up.

I make the tuna methodically, spooning out small dollops of mayonnaise until it's just like Steve likes it. I'm not fussy about my tuna, but he is, so I accommodate him. I find some rye bread in the freezer and stick four slices in the toaster oven to unthaw. Again, I wonder if I will tell Steve. I have wanted to, lately, more than ever. This need to talk about it has caused me to wake in the night feeling as if something heavy is sitting on my chest. But there is no guarantee that if I tell him the feeling will go away.

The knock is quickly followed by the sound of the back door opening and Steve's hearty 'Hello, hello!' It is always the same greeting. He comes into the kitchen, puts the bag with the chowder in it on the counter and peers into the toaster oven. 'Rye?' he asks.

'I've got lettuce, too,' I say, showing him the leaves I'm rinsing in the sink.

He nods appreciatively.

'Slow day?' I ask.

'It's always slow until they come,' he says. 'And then I won't have time for lunch.'

'And I won't have time to make lunch,' I say.

Our summer days skip along so quickly, however, that it barely registers with either of us, and in September we will find ourselves at Club Soda wondering where the season went. The routine is comfortable, as is the sight of Steve chewing his tuna sandwich and taking alternate spoonfuls of chowder. I have managed to find some diet soda for him. I drink seltzer, and we don't talk again until we have only crumbs on our plates. I pick them up and put them in the sink, throwing out the Styrofoam containers slick with remnants of chowder.

Steve has gone into the living room and is standing in front of the bay window, watching the raindrops slide down the glass.

'It's started raining,' I say flatly, handing him another soda.

He takes it and turns to me, a frown on his face. 'Nicole, there's something I've got to ask you.'

I feel as if he's hit me in the chest. I wait.

'I mean, don't take it the wrong way or anything, but I realized it yesterday when I went over to get that TV.'

I let out a little breath, like you do when you're swimming underwater for a long time and you want to make sure you've got enough air until you can reach the surface.

'Do you ever go to the mainland?'

My lungs can't take it anymore, and I exhale. I shake my head. 'No, no, I guess I don't.'

'Have you ever gone? I mean, since you've been here?'

He has never asked me anything like this before, and I know he believes he can trust me to tell him the truth. I give him what I can.

'No.'

Steve's face scrunches up as he registers this. 'Why not?'

I shrug. 'I guess I just don't feel I need to.'

'Is it because you don't have a car? You can't get around over there? I can take you, you know.'

I think about what it would be like, taking that ferry back across the water. I know if I do that, I will never return. So I shake my head again. 'I don't need to go, but thanks for offering.' I try to make my voice light, like my behavior isn't odd. But I know it is, and I know he sees it like that. I begin to wonder if anyone else has noticed I never leave, then dismiss that thought. Steve is the only person who sees me regularly and would notice. I am surprised it's taken him this long to figure this out, but I chalk it up to the fact that even though we're friends and we do see each other frequently, I still maintain a distance.

Steve is understandably confused; it's all over his face. But to his credit, he doesn't press it. 'How about a game of Scrabble?'

he suggests, and I rummage through my closet and set up the board on the kitchen table.

The rain continues for the rest of the afternoon. Steve wins two games, I win one, and he reluctantly bids farewell and heads back home. I know he wanted me to invite him to stay for supper, too, but I tell him I have to call Jeanine. When he leaves, I do just that and make an apology: I am tired after getting up so early, hiking the Bluffs and then spending three hours with Steve. She offers to pick me up so I don't have to take the bike out in the rain, but I beg off, repeating my excuses. I am not in the mood to see anyone else today. I have gotten used to my own company and enjoy the solitude.

I watch the gray clouds shifting back and forth. Flashes of lightning appear, followed by claps of thunder. I revive the fire and soon the house is cozier, the light from the sky reflecting through the window onto the flickering flames in the stove. I forget about supper and instead have a cup of tea and microwave a bag of popcorn. I doze a little on the sofa under an afghan I bought in the shop next to Veronica's gallery.

I think about Steve's question when I wake up in the dark, go into the bedroom, put on my pajamas and crawl into bed. I stare at the ceiling, for a fleeting moment wondering what it would be like, stepping onto land that is not an island for the first time in years. Would it be as if I've been on a boat and I'd have to find my land legs? Would I stumble, dizzy and uncertain about where to turn? The comfort of the island, knowing all its roads, its paths, its secrets, its boundaries, would be ripped away, leaving me exposed. I'm not ready to take that wall down, but I cannot ignore the feeling in my gut that something is about to change.

FOUR

In the days when I wasn't Nicole and the sun was high and the sky was its clearest blue, I slathered baby oil on my skin and baked on a multicolored blanket on sand as soft as a featherbed. But today, a day just like that, I put on bike shorts and a T-shirt, cover my head with a helmet, fit my socks over my calves and tie my sneakers tight. The coconut scent of the sunscreen I use mixes with the honeysuckles and roses I pass as I fly along the country roads. It's hard to believe that the island is only seven miles long and three miles wide when with each turn I see another long line of stonewalls, another pond, another lighthouse. Even though I believe I know each landmark, every inch of this island, I can still see things that are new. As I make one more turn, I see what it is today: the shad is in bloom, the delicate white flowers dancing across their branches. I stop to admire it, allowing me to catch my breath and take a drink of water from my bottle.

Another biker is approaching, and I raise my free hand in a greeting. I expect him to continue past but he slows down, comes to a stop next to me. Under the helmet, I recognize the man at the spa yesterday. I offer a tight smile.

'Fancy meeting you here,' I say.

His grin is broad, reaching across his face and into his eyes. 'Love this island off-season,' he says enthusiastically, and his tone is infectious. I feel my smile relax a little for a second before I reel it back in.

'This is the best time to come,' I say in my best tour guide voice. 'May and September. The shops and restaurants are open, but the tourists haven't arrived yet.'

He cocks his head at me and studies my face for a second. 'Are you heading anywhere in particular?'

'I'm going up to North Light. Have you been there?'

'I've only seen it in a picture. Lead the way,' he says.

'You don't mind a woman taking the lead?' The flirtation is an instinct that comes back without warning, startling me.

His eyes twinkle. They are a deep chocolate, with laugh lines dancing around them. 'I prefer it,' he says softly, and I find myself staring at his lips. He notices, and his tongue flicks out for a second as he licks them.

I swallow hard, trying to ignore the warmth that's flooded me, especially between my legs. It's been a long time since a man has affected me like this, and desire rushes back and clutches me. My legs feel heavy, my breasts tender. I wonder if he sees it, if he can feel my longing without touching me.

'I thought that was you at the spa, but you left so quickly, without saying hello. The woman there said your name's Nicole.' He's challenging me, but I merely nod.

'Nicole Jones,' I tell him, thinking about that other name, the one I haven't uttered for years. 'And what are you calling yourself these days?'

'Zeke,' he says. 'Zeke Chapman.'

I tighten my grip on the handlebars of my bike, steadying myself as I struggle to breathe.

It is all I can do to pedal up the next hill. When the lighthouse comes into view, I jump off the bike and walk it across the grass; he is keeping up behind me. He is in good shape, with just a hint of exhaustion that comes with the island's terrain. I wish he wasn't. I try to sprint forward, but he is there again, at my side. His name is swirling around in my head. I don't have to ask why he chose that one. I know why. He means to unnerve me in every possible way, as if just showing up here isn't enough.

'So you live here year round?' he asks, not interested at all in the history of the lighthouse that I recite.

I nod.

'How long have you been here?' he asks.

While I am tempted to lie, it would be easy for him to find out the truth, if he doesn't know already. 'Fifteen years.'

'All that time?'

I can see him doing the math in his head. 'Yes.'

'And you make your living by giving bike tours?'

'I paint a little, too. People buy my paintings.' I don't mean to tell him this; it sounds like I'm boasting.

But he's unfazed. 'Really?' He seems impressed.

It's as if we were at a cocktail party, so I ask the next logical question: 'What do you do now?'

The smile vanishes for a second and then is back, but his eyes have narrowed and he shrugs. 'Same as before.'

It's been so long that I can't imagine doing what I did before.

'Where are you living now?' I ask, my curiosity getting the better of me.

'The same place.'

'Really?' My incredulity must show, because his grin broadens.

'Not all of us run away,' he says.

I think about this for a second before saying, 'Some of us didn't have a choice.'

His eyes narrow as the grin slides off his face, his jaw tenses. 'There is always a choice.'

I sigh, shrug, kick a pebble with the toe of my shoe. I don't want to get into it right now.

'Do you want to have lunch?' he asks after a few seconds.

This is not the question I'd been expecting. 'Like a date?' I raise my eyebrows.

'You probably know the best places to go here,' he says, teasing me, his eyes dancing across my face, moving down my body, lingering.

'Yes, I do,' I say, trying to keep my tone light. 'I'm not sure I want to have lunch dressed like this,' I add, indicating my bike shorts.

He assesses my legs thoughtfully. 'I don't mind, but I understand.'

'I'd like to take a shower and change first,' I say, aware of his penetrating eyes.

'So would I,' he says suggestively.

I cannot reply, but I start walking my bike back to the road. This is the first time I have not looked across the water from this spot.

I let him into my house, our bikes parked outside. We are in the kitchen when he reaches for me. Even though I expect it, it happens so quickly, the long, deep kiss. It is so familiar I feel a catch in my throat. I am not Nicole now. I am who I was before.

His fingers move to my breasts, between my legs, and despite myself, I want it – I want him. I force myself to pull away, aware that my face is hot and flushed. He reaches for me again, but I take another step back. I can't do this. I don't know what I was thinking, bringing him back here.

'You never played hard to get before.' His voice is gruff with desire, but to his credit, he stays where he is.

'It's not the same.'

'That felt the same.'

'You know what I mean.'

'You mean, you, here, Miss Bike Tours? You're all settled in this little house.' He scans the small, outdated kitchen with its white wood cabinets and Formica countertops. 'This isn't how I remember you.'

'I'm not that person anymore.'

He stares at me a long time, then a slow grin spreads across his face. 'You've fooled them all, haven't you? Does anyone here know?'

'No. And I'd like to keep it that way.' I fold my arms across my chest, pushing him even further away.

'You would, wouldn't you?' he asks.

The threat in his tone lingers, like an uninvited guest who won't go away.

But then he leaves without another word, or another look behind him. I close the door, sliding the deadbolt and slipping on the chain as I watch him ride his bike down the hill until he is out of sight.

I shut my eyes and wish for the first time that I did not live on an island.

I don't answer the phone when it rings. Instead, I take my painting things – the easel, the canvas, my box of paints – and walk to the beach. Not the public beach, but the one near my house, the one that no one can see from the road. The clouds have moved in; the waves crash against the sand that slides underneath them. My brush strokes are long and fat, gray with hints of blue and purple. It doesn't really look like that, but I see the colors anyway.

I paint until long after lunchtime, when the clouds suddenly part and a streak of sunlight shines down on the water, which shimmers under its touch. I try to capture that, but it's impossible, and then it's gone. I decide I have to get something to eat, but I'm nervous that he will be waiting for me. My stomach growls. I pack up my tools and make my way back.

No one is there. The house is alone, like me, and I let myself inside. There are three messages on my machine.

'Call me when you get in.' Steve's voice soothes me, and I relax.

'Stop by if you get a chance.' It's Jeanine. It seems like weeks since I saw her, but it's only been a day.

'Someone wants to commission a painting of the North Light. Call me, and I'll give you the number.' Veronica, her business-like tone hiding the usual insecurity that hovers beneath her surface. I think of the painting I've started today and how I want to finish it soon and get it into the gallery.

I make myself a salad and worry about him. He is not the kind of man who will go away that easily.

He falls in step with me just as I'm about to go into Veronica's gallery. He touches my lower back lightly, and a fire moves through me before I take a step away. I look up at him as we walk through the door. His eyes are smiling, although his lips are not.

'Nicole!' Veronica swoops toward us, dressed in a green cotton pullover and a pair of Levis, Birkenstocks on her feet. Her short hair frames her face, which is straining with her forced smile. 'And Mr Chapman! I'm so glad you're here together.'

I am confused, and it must show on my face, because Veronica says then, 'Mr Chapman is the client I left the message about. He wants to commission a painting of the North Light. He came in earlier and really admires your work.'

A small pilot light inside me ignites with anger, but I force myself to look at him. 'Is that so?'

'It's a beautiful spot, and your paintings are impressive,' he says, moving around the gallery and stopping at each one to show me how he's memorized where they are. 'And the North Light has some sentimental meaning to me. Perhaps you could put a biker in the picture.'

I feel my face flush. 'When would you want the painting?'

'How soon can you get it done?'

I think a minute. 'It could take a few weeks. How long are you on the island?'

'I'm staying a few more days. I could leave my email address, and you can let me know when it's ready.'

Veronica laughs, a high, twittery sound. 'Oh, Mr Chapman, Nicole doesn't have a computer! I've offered to have my nephew design a website for her work – I think she'd do a lot more business with that – but she refuses.'

He studies me with a curious expression, and I know what he's thinking.

'No computer?' he says, the smile tickling his lips. 'Really?'

'Oh, I don't know if she even knows how to turn one on!' Veronica cannot keep her mouth shut sometimes.

He takes a pen out of his pocket and waves it at Veronica, who finds him a piece of paper. He scribbles on it and hands it to me. 'Here's my cell phone number.'

I take it and stare at it a long minute before Veronica pipes up again. 'We need a deposit.'

'How much will it cost?' he asks me.

My eyes stray to a painting behind him of a stonewall and apple trees. It is listed at $500. It's not one of my better efforts. 'A thousand,' I say.

Veronica's eyebrows shoot up into her forehead. I have never charged a thousand dollars for any painting before. But he is pulling cash out of a billfold and handing it to Veronica. 'Is five hundred enough for now?'

She spits out something that sounds like 'That's plenty' and takes the money. I am afraid she may not want to part with it, even though I am owed most of it, if not all of it. I am on consignment here, although no one has ever commissioned a painting, so I am uncertain of the protocol. I suppose it could be under the auspices of my consignment contract, but part of me wants all of the money. Especially since it's from him.

Veronica peels back four of the hundred-dollar bills and gives them to me. I shove them into the front pocket of my jeans.

'Thank you,' I say, not meeting his eyes.

'Since I'm here a few days, how about dinner?' he asks.

I can feel Veronica's stare. She has never seen me with a man, even though she's tried to fix me up with several through the years, and now she's witnessing someone asking me on a date. I want to tell her that it's not what she thinks.

'I'm afraid I have plans.' It is, fortunately, Friday night and my standing date with Steve. I look at Veronica. 'I'll talk to you tomorrow,' I say, and turn to leave.

I can feel the heat from his body as he follows me closely. Once outside, he shuts the door. I don't slow down but begin fumbling with the lock on my bike, my hands shaking. He takes it from me, his eyes again making my heart skip. Together we manage to unlock it, and I wrap the chain around the seat.

'No computer?' he asks softly, the chuckle in the back of his throat. This is not the question I'm anticipating, but as I shake my head, I am telling him, in a sense, more of my story.

I mount my bike and pedal away from him, my chest pounding. Once I get home, I lock the door and curl up in bed, the comforter around my neck. When the phone rings, I ignore it, burying my head in the pillows.

FIVE

I feel like a prisoner in my own home, no longer just on the island. I am afraid to run into him again. I cannot afford to have him popping up everywhere. It's bad enough he asked me out in front of Veronica. That is probably already all over the island. It is for this reason that I force myself to get dressed, get back on my bike and ride to Club Soda to meet Steve.

He kisses me on the cheek as I slide onto a stool across the table from him.

'How was your day?' he asks, handing me a menu.

I don't even look at it. I get the same thing every time, but every time Steve offers me that choice. 'Uneventful,' I say, although I am lying. The cell phone number crackled and called to me from my backpack, and when I finally took it out and tried to rip it up, I couldn't. I put it on the refrigerator, stuck with a magnet in the shape of the island.

Steve peers into my face. 'You look different.'

I shrug, running a hand through my hair, hopefully nonchalantly. 'How?' I ask.

He shakes his head. 'I'm not sure. You're just a little different tonight.' And then he grins. 'Maybe it's that guy who asked you out today.'

I sigh. As I suspected, Veronica has successfully spread the news. 'Did she tell you I turned him down?'

'Why? Just because of me? I would've understood.' He is so sincere, wanting me to be happy.

'Men are a dime a dozen,' I say. 'But you're my friend, and I wanted to see you tonight.'

Abby, the waitress, approaches with two beers in hand. We are about to say that we haven't ordered them when she cocks her head toward the bar. 'Compliments of the guy over there.'

I know without seeing him that he is here.

'Is that him?' Steve whispers conspiratorially.

I don't even turn around. 'I'm not interested. Isn't that enough?'

I hear the annoyance in my tone. I have never snapped at Steve before, and he leans back in his chair, his arms folded in front of him.

'If I didn't know better, I'd think the lady doth protest too much,' he says.

I cannot laugh at his joke, because he's right. Instead, I take a swig of my beer. Abby returns, and we order our hamburgers and onion rings.

'So you're not even going to go over and thank him?' Steve asks.

'No, and you aren't, either,' I say, suspecting that's what he's about to do.

'It would be the polite thing to do. He's a nice-looking young man.' He is staring pointedly over at the bar. I still have my back to it.

'That doesn't mean anything,' I say, although it does. It is what attracted me to him in the first place.

'You're blushing. I've never seen you blush before.' Steve is not teasing me now. He is genuinely perplexed. I try to think of something to say, but my mind is a blank. 'I think you do like this guy. Why are you resisting? You shouldn't lock yourself up the way you do. You're still a young woman. You should fall in love.'

I snort. 'That's easy for you to say. You had Dotty. You had twenty years of romance with the woman of your dreams. Sometimes it just doesn't happen that way.' This is not a new conversation. But it is the first time we are discussing it when there is someone who wants to date me sitting within a few yards. Someone who is viable, in Steve's opinion. And then he surprises me.

'Why don't you just take him home with you for the night?'

I am not sure what to say. We have talked about love and lifelong commitments, but we have never talked about sex. I just assumed that he's very old fashioned about it.

'I mean, Nicole, unless you're leading some sort of secret life up in that house of yours, you might need a night with a man.' His expression is so sincere, his words slice through me and I want to cry. He sees me brush at my eye, and he clears his throat. 'Of course, I've never asked you this, but maybe you're, well, maybe you—' He is so uncomfortable he has to stop, and it dawns on me what he's implying.

It makes me laugh. 'Oh, no, it's not like that,' I say quickly. 'I definitely don't play for the other team, Steve. I just haven't met anyone I want to take home.'

He looks so relieved that I can't stop laughing. It's contagious, and he joins in until we are both heaving with laughter, tears trickling down our cheeks.

'What's so funny?' Abby puts our plates in front of us and we look up, try to speak but can't, falling into even more hysterics. 'Don't choke on it,' Abby says flatly as she leaves us.

The quiet hum of the chatter around us serenades us as we eat. I can almost ignore him as I chew thoughtfully, picking up one onion ring after the other, this time eating the whole thing, leaving nothing but a couple of crumbs on the plate. Steve glances up every once in a while, his eyes skipping past my face and toward what's behind me. I shake off the gaze that has settled in the middle of my back.

A nagging feeling tugs at my stomach. Now that there is some distance between seeing him for the first time and now, my thoughts begin to line up in an orderly manner. He didn't show up here by accident. And there is only one way he could have known where to find me. I have no credit cards, no driver's license, no bank account. I pay with cash for everything. I have no Social Security number. My utilities are in my landlord's name. I do not pay taxes. I simply do not exist.

'Earth to Nicole.' Steve is waving the last onion ring in front of my face, and I force myself to smile. 'Where are you?'

I sigh. 'It's been a long day.'

Steve gets up from his seat. 'I have to hit the head,' he says, and walks away.

I count to six before I feel his hand on my shoulder. I twist around to see him looking down at me.

'Why are you ignoring me?' he asks playfully, his eyes twinkling. 'It's as if you don't want me in your life.'

'No one ever accused you of being stupid,' I say, wishing there were more onion rings so I would have something to do with my hands. An overwhelming urge to light a cigarette consumes me, and another flashback assaults my brain: a thin glass containing a clear, chilled liquid surrounded by a dusting of smoke, fingers – my fingers – curled around the glass's stem. It is gone as quickly as it came, and I blink as if someone has pointed a bright light in my eyes.

He is not to be dissuaded. He slips into Steve's chair. 'I'm hurt,' he says, pretending to pout. 'I thought you would be happy to see me.' His eyes grow smoky and dark, and I feel his heat.

Steve is coming back, and I shake my head. Before I can introduce them, he is standing, shaking Steve's hand. 'Zeke Chapman.'

'Steve McQueen.'

'Really?' He shoots me a glance. 'You're pulling my leg.'

'No, my name is Steve McQueen.'

He snorts. 'Do they call you Bullitt? Have you ever lived in San Francisco?' He is acting like a jerk.

Steve raises his eyebrows at me as if to say, *OK, I understand now why you might not want to go out with this guy*. He has no idea he's helping my cause.

But he takes this as an invitation and pulls another chair up to our table, getting comfortable. He waves Abby over and orders another round.

'I don't have time,' I start to say, and he holds his hand up.

'Where does a pretty lady like you have to go on a Friday night? Just one more.' He is coming on too strong, but I don't want to cause a scene.

'OK,' I agree.

'You're hard to track down,' he says then, ignoring Steve. 'But I asked around, and folks said you'd be here tonight. You come here every Friday.'

'You were asking about me?' A bubble of panic rises in my throat. 'Why?'

'I wanted to talk to you.'

Steve clears his throat and moves his head in a way so I know he's indicating he thinks we should leave. I am about to tell him that we have to go, but then he jumps down off his stool. He flashes a grin at Steve. 'My turn,' he says, and disappears toward the men's room.

Steve waits until he's safely out of earshot. 'Wow, he's pushy, isn't he?'

'Now do you understand why I don't want to go out with him?'

'He's borderline stalker.'

'It's certainly looking that way.' This is easy now. Steve's protective instincts are taking over, and he will help me escape.

Steve is already on his feet. He has left a pile of bills for Abby on the table. 'Let's go,' he says, and he waves at Abby as we leave. Steve lifts my bike into the back of the Explorer, and we jump in. We are down the hill before we know it. I don't even look back to see if he has followed us.

'Thanks, Steve,' I say, putting my hand briefly over his, which is on the steering wheel. 'I didn't want to deal with him.'

'No problem.'

We are silent the rest of the way to my house, which is dark. Only the light over the back door is on.

'You'll be OK?' Steve asks. 'Want me to come in?'

I don't want Steve here when he comes. I shake my head, open the door. 'I'll be fine. He doesn't know where I live.' The white lie trips off my tongue, and I feel bad lying to Steve. The irony of that strikes me as funny, and I stifle a nervous chuckle.

'Call me tomorrow,' he says. 'Maybe another game of Scrabble?'

'Sure,' I say, slamming the door shut and making my way around the front of the SUV to the house. I lift my hand in a wave as Steve drives away.

I put the key in the lock, step out of my shoes in the mudroom. I go into the kitchen and flip the light on above the stove. I take the bottle of cognac down from on top of the refrigerator and pour myself a short one, taking it into the living room, where I sit in the dark, waiting for him.

SIX

When I met him, I knew. I knew I would never fall for anyone else ever again. It was one of those take-no-prisoners types of feelings, the kind that wraps itself around you like a straitjacket and you can't breathe for days, weeks, maybe even years, as long as he's in the same room.

I am not sure I have the same feeling now, while I sit in my living room with a glass in my hand. Because it has been over an hour, and he has not shown up. He is playing games with me, just as I did when I took off with Steve. This is not unusual for us. It was cat and mouse for a long time, a power play to see who would crack first. Only that first time had it been completely equal between us.

I am not used to this anymore. I am out of practice. I have forgotten how to play the game. I panicked in the bar. I should've stayed, continued the banter, stayed in control. Instead, I ran. Just like I ran fifteen years ago.

I feel bits of myself melting away – the self that I've created. I am afraid of that other self, the other person I used to be. Him showing up here has brought her back. Even though the reports of my demise, as they say, were premature, I have in fact died and been reborn as Nicole. But now, sitting here, drinking my cognac in the dark, I know that no matter what name I've chosen for myself, no matter what existence I've managed to carve out, I am still that other person when it comes to him. I am twenty-five again, despite my aging eyes, the lines in my face, the gray hairs.

I try to distract myself, going into the kitchen and washing out my glass. I don't need another drink. I put the glass in the dish drainer to dry, wiping my hands on a towel. I look around my kitchen and it feels strange to me, as if I've never been here before. Where did that crack in the wall come from? Has it always been there? The light is too dim; maybe I should use regular light bulbs again.

I am standing there, studying the coils on the electric stove, when the knock makes me jump.

Eyes peer through the back door window at me. He backs away slightly, and I can see him clearly now in the light I've left on outside. I undo the lock and let him in.

'I've been worried about you.' Steve is wearing sweatpants and a fleece pullover. 'I wanted to make sure you were OK.'

'Come on in. Want a drink?'

Steve follows me into the house. 'How about some of that brandy you've always got here?'

I take another glass out of the cupboard and the one I've just washed out of the drainer. I pour us each a glass, and we take them into the living room. I turn on one of the table lamps, just enough light emanating to make it cozy. We settle in, me on the couch and Steve in the rocker across from me.

'I thought he'd find you,' he says.

'Me, too,' I admit. 'He has been very persistent. But so far, no sign of him.'

'I stopped back at Club Soda and peeked in. He's not there. Do you know where he's staying?'

I shrug. 'No idea. He didn't say when I saw him at the gallery.' The light does not allow me to see outside, only the reflections in the window, our silhouettes. We look relaxed, drinks in our hands, as if we are having a regular evening together and not waiting for the boogeyman to show. 'You know,' I say, 'I can take care of myself.' But even as I say it, I know I'm wrong.

Steve suspects, too, and he says nothing. Just drinks his cognac and smiles sadly at me.

Finally I stand up. 'He's not going to show up here,' I say. It has been twenty minutes. 'I think you can go home. I'll just lock the doors, OK?' I am feeling claustrophobic suddenly; I need to be alone. I am afraid that if he stays, I'll tell him everything. It's on the tip of my tongue. I cannot risk it.

We go into the kitchen, and I take Steve's glass. He leans over and kisses me on the cheek, his beard scratching my face, but not in a bad way. I hold onto his shoulder for a moment, letting his concern wash over me, knowing he is just being a friend. I open my mouth, but before I can say anything, Steve pulls away.

'See you tomorrow,' he says gruffly. 'Lock up.' And then he is gone, out the back door, letting in the crisp night breeze. It sweeps through the mudroom and clasps my legs, wrapping itself around me, spinning upward until I feel it on the back of my neck. I shiver. I close the door and lock it, turning out the light when I see Steve's Explorer heading down the driveway.

The morning is bright, the sun peeking through my curtains. I roll over, not sure just when I went to sleep, but I feel refreshed. I don't allow myself to wonder why he didn't come. It's no longer my problem, I think, tying my bathrobe around me, shuffling out toward the kitchen in my socks.

I stop in the doorway. On the table is a box. A cardboard box that I know was not there last night. It is about the size of a shirt box, but deeper. Its seams are covered in duct tape, which makes its way in a circle around the top and the bottom. There is writing on the top. I slowly make my way over to the table, put a finger on the corner of the box and turn it slightly.

'Open me,' it invites.

I pull my finger away as if I've gotten a shock. I don't want to open it. I listen carefully but hear nothing inside. Of course, bombs inside packages might only tick in movies, not in real life.

I don't know how long I've been standing here, in the same spot, my heart pounding, but the phone's ring crashes into my head and bounces off the wall, making me jump. I rush across the room and grab the handset, as if the sound of it will set off whatever's in the mysterious box.

'Open the fucking box,' I hear, and then a click. He's hung up.

I forget about the box as I realize he's watching me. I shrink back against the kitchen counter, wishing I could disappear inside it, change colors like a chameleon. For the first time I wish I did not have as many windows, because I cannot figure out which one he might be on the other side of.

Just as suddenly as the fear shot through me, however, I am no longer afraid. It is as if a switch has been flipped, and the anger sweeps through me. I take a step toward the box, and with only a second of hesitation I pick it up. It is fairly light, but something jostles inside it. Instead of ripping the tape off, I take it to the mudroom and open the back door, heaving the box out. It rolls across the grass before I slam the door shut again.

I wait for the phone to ring, for movement outside. I stand statue-like, my muscles frozen, the fear replacing the anger that had replaced the fear. I have not had so many quick emotions one after the other in a long time. I am not sure my body can handle it. I begin to shake with the realization of what I've just done. I sink down to the floor, my head against my knees, and tears slip down my cheeks. I don't know how long I stay like this, waiting for something but unsure of what.

After an hour, I unfold my legs and stand. My feet are partially asleep, and pins and needles prick them as I head to the bathroom. I turn the hot water on, making sure to lock both the window and the door, even though I know locks won't keep him out if he wants to come in, before stepping under the stream. The heat rushes through me, scalding me, but I barely notice.

The big towel covers me completely, and I tiptoe into the bedroom, pulling on my clothes while trying not to expose my bare skin. I should get mini-blinds, something I can pull shut and no one can see through.

My old, worn jeans are comfortable, the soft T-shirt smooth against my skin. I am feeling more like myself again, more like Nicole. I wear thick wool socks as I venture to the mudroom and look out the window. The box is out there, upside down and on its side, where it landed when I threw it. Curiosity tickles my brain, and I try to think logically. If it did not blow up when I threw it, perhaps there isn't anything like a bomb inside. Maybe he had just left me a present – something he found on the island and wanted me to have.

I know I am rationalizing, but I've begun to really want to know what's in that box. I open the door slowly and put my foot out on the step. The chill of the stone seeps up through my sock, but I ignore it as I take another step. I am soon standing in the yard, the dew on the grass saturating my feet. I cannot feel it. My eyes are glued to the box.

I take a deep breath and don't let myself think. In one move-ment, I pick up the box and run back inside, the door slamming behind me.

I grab a sharp knife out of the drawer and slice through the duct tape, pulling up the flaps of the box.

There is a lot of paper inside – packing paper – and something that's Styrofoam. I have to hold the box just-so and let it slide out.

It's a laptop computer.

SEVEN

I run my hand across its smooth surface, feeling its skin, hypnotized by its pureness. I lift the lid to expose the pristine keyboard, the dark screen. My fingers dance across the letters, the numbers. They bounce slightly under my touch, as if cringing. Like they know.

I rummage around in the box and find a power cord. There is no manual. I can't stop touching it. I cannot help myself.

I am sitting at the table, staring at the blank screen, when he comes in. He doesn't knock; he doesn't ring the bell. I hear the door creak open, then slam. Heavy footsteps in the mudroom.

'What do you think?' he asks from behind me, his breath tickling the back of my neck.

I do not turn around. 'It's beautiful,' I say.

'Turn it on.'

'No.'

He laughs, comes around the side of the table and sits across from me, the laptop between us. 'It's not going to bite.'

'You have no idea.' I am clutching the power cord in my hand so tightly it's made an indentation in my palm. I have been struggling with this for an hour. I need a twelve-step program.

'It's like riding a bike.'

'I fell off that bike, remember?'

He leans back in his chair and stares at me. 'You have to get back on.'

This is what I expected when I first saw him here on the island. When he first told me his name.

'I've got a job for you.' His voice is low, curling around each word like a snake.

I have not heard those words in a long time, and something moves through me: revulsion followed by a clammy fear, and then the adrenaline of desire sticks in my throat. Not desire for him – the desire to do what he wants, to get that rush again, to feel that power. I force it down, force myself to lift my hand and put the power adapter on the table, close the laptop. I get up and push my chair in.

'No,' I say simply, going to the kitchen. I can't let him see my face. I know he'll see it there. I pour myself a brandy, my hand shaking slightly, spilling a few drops on the counter.

His hand reaches around me, takes Steve's glass from last night out of the dish drainer and sets it down next to mine. 'I'll take one, too.'

I pour it, and we drink.

'Good stuff,' he says, draining his glass.

I nod, trying to ignore his hand that's settled on my back, his fingers that are gently rubbing my spine. I wriggle away from his touch and back up against the counter.

'I'm done with all that. Anyway, I haven't touched a computer in fifteen years.'

'Excuses, excuses.'

'I don't have an Internet connection.' I am grabbing at straws, but he's right about making excuses. An Internet connection is as easy as sitting in a coffee shop with wireless. I may not have owned a computer in fifteen years, but I do know about wireless. 'Even if I did, how do I know it would be secure?'

He leans back in his chair and gives me a long, slow smile. 'There are ways.'

I know. But I let him tell me anyway. I am leading him on. Despite everything in me that's saying no, I want to know what the job is.

'Virtual private network. It's not the way it used to be, when we had dial-up. It *wasn't* as secure then – you know that. But it's changed, like everything about the Internet. Now it's usually for companies to let their employees work remotely, but anyone can use it, too, and be virtually invisible. It's how the Chinese can get on Facebook.' He sees my expression. 'Social media. You hook up with old high school friends—'

'I saw the movie,' I say curtly, but I'm still thinking about VPN. How it reroutes the IP address so no one can trace where you are and logs are cleared every twenty-four hours. 'What about subpoenas?' I know about how the law works. How someone can get caught.

'There's no data retention law here in the States.' There is something in his expression, though, that I can't read.

'What?'

He sighs. 'Some surveillance. Some server raids.'

That's how it happened before. He knows what I'm thinking.

'It's not the same. It's safer,' he says again. 'You were doing your thing during the dark ages, and see what you were able to do. It's easier now, you won't believe it.'

'If it's so easy, why do you need me? Why don't you do it yourself?'

He snorts. 'You know I can't. Besides, you don't exist, remember? No one can trace it to you. Anyway, you used to be good at figuring out how to keep from being traced.'

'Until I wasn't.' The words hang between us.

'It took a long time to find you. You're pretty good at disappearing.'

I wonder exactly what he's referring to and think about the implications of what he's saying. It also reminds me of something else. 'I don't want to be that missing person who's discovered dead,' I say softly.

His face clouds. 'Don't worry,' he says, but the way he says it makes me worry. We are both remembering.

He cups my chin, stares into my eyes, and for a second I am transported back.

'I can't,' I say, moving away from him. 'Not again. I have a life here, a good life.'

'A lonely life,' he says flatly.

I shake my head. I have friends, I have a job, I have a house. I chose this. I didn't choose him.

'But if all this is really what you want, then maybe you should think about it. This' – he waves his hand around in the air, indicating my house – 'can disappear as quickly as you can. So think seriously about it.' He again diminishes the distance between us. His eyes are dark, and a chill travels down my back as I hear the threat beneath the seduction. This is what he planned all along.

'OK. I'll think about it,' I say, putting my hand on his chest to keep him from coming closer. I am lying, though. I can't think about it, despite his threat. But it is the best way to get rid of him.

He smiles; his eyes twinkle. 'That's a good girl.'

I want to slap him for that, but I keep my face neutral. 'Where are you staying?'

'Blue something—'

'Blue Dory Inn,' I say. 'Beautiful place. You can afford it?'

'I get by. Same as you. I doubt you can make ends meet just on those paintings and bike tours.'

I let him think what he likes. 'So he told you?'

'Who told me what?'

'You know. Where I was.'

He looks around my kitchen, at the brass colander hanging on the wall, the backsplash tiles with the little rosebuds painted on them, the white lace curtain over the window. 'This is a nice place,' he remarks, ignoring me, looking up toward a shelf near the back door. 'What's in the jars?' He goes over to them and picks one up, shakes it. 'Rocks?'

I stiffen, although I know those jars are not dated. 'Beach stones,' I try to say lightly. 'We've got great stone beaches here.'

He puts the jar back. 'You're just one fucking tour guide, aren't you?' He flashes me a grin. 'I'll see you later.'

And then he is gone, out the door, and I watch him stroll across the lawn, over the hill and out of sight. Again, it seems too easy to get rid of him. Which means that I have not.

I turn back toward the table, where the computer sits. Waiting for me. If I can get in wherever he wants me to, it would be a cinch this time. I read the papers. I watch the news. I see the possibilities every day. It's not like I haven't thought about what it would've been like with the technology today. He is right about one thing: the Internet was just in its infancy fifteen years ago. Now it's a toddler, growing faster and faster every day. Everyone seems to have a computer. Even Steve has one; he's offered to let me use his. I always tell him I'm not savvy with things like that, that I don't want to learn.

He has no idea.

I leave it where it is without touching it again. Within minutes I'm straddling my bike, racing away from my house, in the opposite direction of Old Harbor, and soon I'm on Cooneymus Road. I abandon the bike at the trail entrance to Rodman's Hollow, a two-hundred-and-thirty-acre glacial outwash basin where the shad creeps around me like the lace curtains on my bedroom windows. I am barely thinking, concentrating on the trail as I bear left at the split and go up the knoll. Even though I have been here hundreds of times, I am struck by the stunning view, and I sit. No one is here; I am alone. I hear birds calling to one another and close my eyes, my heart still pounding from the ride, the hike, the computer.

He asked me to do a job for him before. And I did, because he wanted me to, because I was crazy in love with him and would've gone off the edge of the world for him. Which I did, in a way. It's how I ended up here.

But what he didn't know was that I hadn't been lured by the money. It had been the power.

I had no idea someone would die.

I stare out across the water, envisioning the mainland. I barely remember the ferry ride out here. I wonder what happened to the car, abandoned in the terminal parking lot. I only had a duffel bag with two days' change of clothes and a toothbrush on me when I stepped onto the island. I walked along the beach in Old Harbor; a small yellow boat was upside down on the sand, resting against a rock. When I close my eyes, the image is still so vivid. I shed my identity before arriving, but this is where I first told someone my new name. The first time I spoke it out loud. This is my haven, the place I could heal. The place I call home.

What bothers me now is not what he has asked of me, but that I'm considering it.

EIGHT

When I return home, the answering machine winks at me with its red eye. I hit the button to hear Steve asking how I am – he's worried, he hasn't heard from me all day. I should have called him, so I pick up the phone.

'You're OK?' he asks.

'I went up to Rodman's Hollow,' I say. 'It's a beautiful day.' Not that I have really noticed.

'You know, you can't take your tour there. No bikes on the trails,' he reminds me playfully.

I force myself to concentrate. 'Maybe I'll offer a bike and hike tour.' For a moment, I wonder why I haven't done this before. My head starts spinning with the idea of it, until I turn around and see the laptop still sitting on my table. Immediately my brain shuts down again, paralyzed.

'So you haven't seen him?' Steve asks tentatively.

'The guy?' I ask. 'No.' The lie again trips off my tongue with no effort. I wait for the guilt to settle in, but it doesn't. I blame him for this. I had no guilt for a long time, until the end. I try to make up for it by asking, 'Dinner again tonight?'

'Sorry, Nic, but I'm going to the mainland. Sox game tonight.' He pauses. 'Want to come with me? I could rustle up another ticket.'

I chuckle. 'I won't have you paying two hundred dollars for a baseball ticket. I know how much those tickets cost, especially from scalpers.'

'We could make a day out of it in Boston,' Steve tries again.

'Sorry,' I say. 'Like the ladies used to say, I'm going to stay home and wash my hair.'

But I don't stay home. I call Jeanine and make a date for dinner. I put the laptop into its box and place it carefully on the floor in the pantry, under the shelf that holds the pots and pans, next to a bag of potatoes. I hear nothing from him all day, and as I dress for dinner in a pair of slacks and jersey top, I can only hope that he does not show up anywhere tonight. I know he is waiting for my decision, which I am not yet ready to make.

Jeanine kisses me on each cheek as she greets me just outside the Beachead on Corn Neck Road. It is a comfortable place, cozy and warm. My mouth is salivating for chowder and Thai curry shrimp. We are seated at a window table, near the bar, and we both order glasses of Pinot Grigio.

She leans toward me, her elbows on the table, a conspiratorial smile tugging at her lips. 'So, tell me about him,' she says.

'Who?' I ask, trying to postpone the inevitable.

She shakes her head. 'That guy, Veronica told me, the one who commissioned your painting and asked you out.'

'I didn't go out with him.' I fold my arms across my chest.

'Abby saw you with him at Club Soda.'

'Steve and I ditched him. He's a jerk,' I say.

The waitress brings our drinks, and I take the glass and sip. Suddenly I wish I'd ordered something stronger. We give her our dinner orders, and she walks away. As soon as she does, Jeanine continues.

'How do you know that he's a jerk?' Jeanine asks.

'He was really pushy. Arrogant. Obnoxious.' I try to think of more adjectives to put him in a bad light, but instead I drink more wine. 'Steve came over to my house to make sure he didn't follow us or anything. He was worried.'

Jeanine's expression changes slightly at that. Steve is known for his easygoing personality. 'If Steve was worried,' she says, 'then I guess, well . . .' Her voice trails off.

'You guess that it's not me,' I finish for her, swallowing the last of my wine. It has gone down too easily, and I want another. I gesture to the waitress, who nods.

Jeanine is staring at me. 'I don't want to pick a fight.'

'Then don't,' I snap, immediately regretting it. Her face falls, and she looks as though she might cry. I reach across the table, pat her hand. I have to do something. I am not acting like Nicole. 'If you want to know,' I say, my voice barely above a whisper, 'I did find him attractive. But it's just been so long . . .'

Jeanine's face brightens as if she understands. I have let her believe that I came here after a bad divorce. I have never said anything about any man or my past, but she has just assumed that because I don't date it is because I've been burned. 'Oh, Nicole, it's so understandable. But maybe you should just take a chance. He might not be that bad.'

She sounds just like Steve now. 'I don't know him,' I say. 'I don't really want to fall into bed with just anyone.' Although as the words fall off my lips, I think of the kiss the other night and I feel my face flush.

Again, she misinterprets me. 'Sometimes a good fuck is what we all need,' Jeanine says candidly.

The waitress has come back with my second glass of wine and overhears this. It is her turn to blush as she turns away.

I chuckle. Jeanine really is divorced, and we've been down this road before. She is dating a guy on the mainland she met through one of those Internet dating services. 'Is that the way it is with Bob?' I tease, knowing she's not serious about him.

She shrugs and winks.

Our relationship has been fairly one-sided. She talks about her relationship woes, barely registering that I never talk to her about my love life, or lack thereof. Despite her concern about me, that my 'karma is off,' she doesn't seem to notice that she does all the talking. I am very good at listening, agreeing with her when she wants me to.

Our meals arrive, and I am happy to immerse myself in the shrimp and even more wine. By the time we are finished, I am slightly drunk, Jeanine slightly less than me. She tells me about Bob, gives me some details I'd rather not hear. She talks about the spa, and we gossip about some of her clients, the tourists who are regulars every season. I've had some of them on my tours, and we compare notes. Soon we pay our bill, and we wander out into the chilly darkness. I had not expected to drink so much, had planned to ride my bike home. Jeanine helps me put it in the back of her car, but we can't find anything to secure the trunk, so the top flaps open and bounces up and down noisily as she drives up to my house.

As we approach, I see a shadow in the back, around the side of the house, that does not belong there. I don't think Jeanine notices.

We haul the bike out of the back of the car, slam the trunk

shut and say goodnight. I tell Jeanine to drive safely home, but she doesn't have far to go. I roll my bike up the hill to the house and lean it against the side as I unlock the door. Before I can go inside, however, I see him out of the corner of my eye. I turn to face him.

'Why are you hovering around my house?' I demand, my voice too loud from all the wine.

Even in the dark I can see his white teeth as he grins. 'I didn't realize Nicole Jones drinks that much,' he says. 'Four glasses?'

A sick feeling surges up through my chest. 'Where were you?' I hiss.

'Oh, no need to get all upset. I need to eat, too. It's a small island.'

'There are a lot of restaurants,' I point out, not even trying to keep the anger out of my voice.

'How would I know you'd wander in there?' he asks, cupping my chin and lifting my face to his. 'I never stopped thinking about you,' he whispers.

I feel my face trembling in his hand.

'You're cold,' he says, taking his hand away and pushing open the door. I lead the way inside, shedding my jacket and hanging it on a hook in the mudroom. He follows me into the kitchen, where only one light over the stove illuminates the room. The rest of the house is as black as the night, and it's here that he takes me, and I am helpless.

I think of Jeanine's comment as I stare at the ceiling, his breaths short and loud. I remember this about him, how he snores. How I couldn't sleep when I stayed with him. I can't sleep now.

I can blame the wine for this, the fact that I did not say no, but I would be lying to myself.

I stare at the ceiling, but instead of the white sheetrock of my little house, I see the dark wood paneling of the houseboat. It is so real at this moment that when I close my eyes, I can almost feel the gentle rocking in rhythm with his snoring, hear the crackle of the small transistor radio we kept by the bed. I find myself humming, the words in French swirling through my head.

My eyes snap open. It has been a long time since I've thought in French, dreamed in French. At first, it was every day, every night, but soon it faded like an old movie. He has brought it back. He has brought everything back.

I roll over, pulling my soft pillow over my head, the sheets caressing my body. I am sore and sated; it is almost dawn. He shifts a little, his fingers brush my thigh, and it is as though I am on fire again. I am embarrassed that it takes so little for him to affect me this way, that I have been thinking about this ever since that day at the North Light. It was one thing when I was younger. My judgment was that of a woman barely out of her teens, feeling invincible, confident in her sexuality, the power she held over him. The hunger I feel now is that of an older woman who has lived without his touch for so long that to have it again is like a drug. Yet even through the haze of desire, I know what he is really here for, and the thought of it makes me shiver.

I need to get away from him. I cannot sleep, so I slide out of bed, careful not to wake him. I put on my glasses, grab my fleece robe and wrap it around me, slipping into my slippers and tiptoe out of the room. I carefully close the door, glad that I'd oiled the squeaky hinges.

The box is where I left it, in the pantry. I lug it out and set it on the table again. I open the folded leaves and take out the laptop and the power adapter. This time there is no hesitation. I don't need a manual to know where to plug the adapter into the machine. I do that, then fit the other end neatly into the outlet next to the table. A small light is illuminated, indicating it's powering up. I sit, staring at it.

He finds me here, his hair ruffled, his face scratchy when he kisses me on the cheek. He says nothing, goes into the kitchen. I hear him putting water on to boil, pulling dishes out of the cupboards. I smell coffee, hear the sounds of eggs being turned, butter scraped on toast.

He puts the plate and mug down next to me, goes back in the kitchen and fetches his own. We eat, the only sound our chewing and sipping. When we are done, he nods at me.

'I take it this is a yes.'

NINE

I t's simple, he tells me. Even though I don't have an Internet connection, he tells me the library has wireless twenty-four hours a day.

'No password needed,' he explains.

'Why don't you just use your laptop, then?' I ask.

He gives me a long, lazy grin. 'You should have your own.'

'But it's a one-time thing.' I have no idea whether it is or not.

'Don't worry. You're worrying too much. It'll be a piece of cake.'

I chew the inside of my cheek, dubious. 'It's not going to work.'

'Don't worry,' he says again, but he misunderstands.

'We can't use the library. It's Sunday.'

'OK, then we wait till tomorrow.' He gives me a leer. 'We can find something else to do today.' He reaches for me, but I push him away.

'It's closed Mondays, too.'

He sighs and rolls his eyes. 'So then we find a coffee shop or something. There's got to be a place with free wireless, right?'

'I don't trust the VPN. How do I know it'll do what it's supposed to?'

He shakes his head slowly. 'Trust me.'

I'm stalling, although as I speak my fingers are caressing the pad, moving the cursor around the screen, getting used to it again. It's like the sex: Even though it had been a long time, there was no awkwardness; I knew what to do. As natural as breathing. Or riding a bike.

The idea of going to a coffee shop with him – or anywhere else – makes me uncomfortable. There will be witnesses. And I want to be alone this first time. But I don't tell him that.

'Loosen up, why don't you?' he teases. 'Your friends want you to have a boyfriend. Why not me?'

'I've already rejected you. I've talked about how obnoxious you are.'

He laughs, a great, big sound that echoes through my living room and bounces off the walls. 'Women like obnoxious men.'

'I don't.'

'You didn't seem to mind me last night.'

'We're complicated. Our relationship. But no one knows.'

He stops smiling and stares at me for a few seconds, his eyes dark, his jaw set. 'You really did disappear, didn't you?'

I know what he's saying. I didn't just leave, move somewhere, change my name. It wasn't just superficial. I left it all behind, my whole identity.

He waves his hand around, indicating my house. 'All this, the house, the island, that bike gig, the way you dress, the glasses, the whole package. If I didn't know it was you, I wouldn't know it was you.'

'I didn't want to be her anymore,' I say softly.

He leans toward me, touches my face, runs his finger from my cheekbone down across my jaw and traces my lips. 'But you're the same in one way,' he says hoarsely, and he reaches further and kisses me. I do not push him away this time. It is a deep kiss, as if he is searching my soul, and with one movement his hands wrap themselves around my waist and pull me onto his lap.

My robe is around my waist when I hear the knock, the 'Hello, hello!' and the door being opened. Quickly I jump up, tying the sash, making wild hand gestures to indicate he should go in the bedroom, out of sight. But it is too late. Steve is in the doorway, his eyes taking in our disheveled appearance. It is obvious we are not just having a cup of coffee.

'Oh, sorry,' Steve stammers. 'I thought, well, the door was unlocked, and I thought—' He is visibly uncomfortable, embarrassed.

I take a step toward him. 'That's OK, don't worry about it.'

His eyes then land on the table behind me. He frowns. 'Did you buy a laptop?'

I think fast. 'Yeah, I did. It just arrived.' I twitter, a sound I haven't heard come from my throat before. 'Veronica was on my case about a website for my paintings. I figure I might as well get with the program. Twenty-first century and all that.' I am babbling.

I can't tell whether Steve is more surprised to see him or the computer.

'Do you want some coffee?' I ask, slipping past him to put on a fresh pot, leaving them in a standoff.

'So where are you from?' Steve asks politely.

'New York,' he says. Interesting. He'd said he was living where he'd been before, which was not New York but Miami.

'What sort of work you in?' Steve is digging for more information.

'I dabble in a little of this, a little of that.'

I cringe as I spoon out the coffee into the French press. He could come up with something more original than that. I guess I wish Steve would think I had better taste, pick a man who was more solid professionally. I remind myself that Steve is not my father.

He excuses himself and goes into the bedroom, where I wish he'd gone in the first place. Steve comes and stands next to me as I pour the boiling water into the press.

'I guess persistence paid off for him,' he says softly.

I don't look at him. 'He's not as bad as we thought,' I say.

'I hope not.' His voice is laced with his concern.

'I'm just taking your advice,' I say.

'What advice?'

'It's just a fling, I guess,' I say. 'Long overdue. He's going to be gone soon.'

'I guess I never realized,' Steve says, and I look at him then. He is scratching his beard as he does when he's thinking.

'Realized what?'

'You never seemed to be lonely before,' Steve says. 'You always seemed to like being alone.'

He is right. This is out of character for me, and he is justifiably confused.

'Jeanine talked me into it,' I say, wanting to blame someone else for what I've done. 'She said it might be good for me.'

'Jeanine's a nut,' Steve says. 'All her talk of the spirit and chi and all that crap. You never took her that seriously.'

'But I let her rearrange my furniture according to feng shui,' I remind him. It was an odd experience, Jeanine fluttering around my house in her long flowing skirt, pushing furniture around so I'd have more 'balance' in my life.

'You only did that because you're a nice person,' Steve said, and tears unexpectedly well up in my eyes. Steve puts his arm around me and squeezes as I press the coffee.

I am pouring Steve a cup when I hear his footsteps behind us.

'Hey, Tina, got any razors?'

'Under the sink in a basket,' I say automatically, not even looking up. His footsteps disappear back where they came from.

I hand Steve the cup, the steam wafts up toward his face. He wears an expression of sheer confusion.

'What did he call you?'

I manage to convince Steve that he has made a mistake; I didn't hear him call me Tina so it didn't register with me. I feign surprise, then dismay that the man I've obviously slept with doesn't even know my name. Steve pats my hand and drinks his coffee, obviously seeing me as pathetic. I feel pathetic, lying to him about everything. But I've gone too far now, there's no turning back, and I have to keep up the charade.

He comes out of the bathroom showered and shaved. He looks as though his clothes have been pressed, too, but I had smoothed them out when I couldn't sleep and folded them over a chair after finding them in a heap on the floor.

He leans over and pecks me on the cheek. 'Later, right?'

I nod, and we watch him disappear out the back door.

Steve frowns. 'You're going to see him again?'

I shrug. 'He's not that bad,' I say again.

'There are a hundred other guys who would be better for you.'

'Name one,' I challenge him.

'Chip Parsons.'

I laugh. 'Chip? The guy who hangs out at the Yellow Kittens? You're kidding me, right?'

'He's a well-respected fisherman. Makes a good living. I also know for a fact that he's always been sweet on you.'

'Sweet on me? Oh, Steve, you're so old fashioned.' As soon as I say it, I'm sorry, because his face clouds over. I smile and sigh. 'I'm sorry. I know you're just looking out for me.'

'You could marry me, and we could live happily ever after,' he says.

'How about next Thursday?' I say, continuing our long-standing joke, but something about his expression makes me stop smiling. 'My God, Steve, you're not joking, are you?'

He starts pacing. 'Maybe I'm not,' he says. 'Maybe we should just do it.'

'But you're—' I don't want to say it.

'I'm not too old for you.' He anticipates my argument. 'There are plenty of women who marry men twenty years older or more.'

I put out my hand and touch his arm, which stops his pacing. He looks at me so sincerely that I want to cry again. I shake my head. 'I love you, Steve, you know I do, but not that way.'

It should not be a surprise. We have never ventured here before, and it's not as if we'd never had the opportunity if we both felt that way. I know he is just reacting to finding me here with another man. Somehow he is threatened.

'He's just a fling,' I say lightly, although something heavy is weighting down my chest. 'He'll be gone soon.'

'By Friday?'

He wants reassurance that our Friday night date is still on. That I won't abandon him like Dotty did by dying. I think about what I'm about to do and suddenly regret it. Things might not be the same afterward. They have already begun to change. 'By Friday,' I promise, glancing toward the laptop. I have no choice. If I want to reclaim my life, I have to learn how to use it quickly, get the job done and him off the island.

TEN

Steve didn't want to leave me, but business was starting to pick up, and he had to get down to Old Harbor to meet the next ferry. Some people like to come to Block Island in early to mid-May. The hotels and restaurants are open, but they don't have to contend with the crowds. Steve takes advantage of the situation and waits next to his Explorer, offering his services to anyone lugging a bag off the boat.

I am relieved when he leaves. I take a long shower and take my time getting dressed, thinking about what he's said. After a fifteen-year drought, I have two men vying for my attentions. I know Steve will get over it, but it might hang between us for a while and make our easygoing relationship a little uncomfortable until it wears off.

He has left me a laptop case that's a backpack, so I shove everything inside it and climb onto my bike. It looks as though I'm just taking one of my normal rides, but instead I fly down Spring Street and into Old Harbor. The bakery here has wireless; I remember seeing the sign announcing it when I was here recently for a latte and a muffin. As I dismount, I eye the small storefront and wonder about that wireless Internet. There is so much to learn.

I glance around, checking to see if he is lurking somewhere, but I see no one. I lean my bike against the rack and lock it up, the heavy backpack tugging on my shoulder.

The scent of coffee overwhelms me so that I momentarily forget my mission and order a medium latte. A croissant also seems like a good idea, and I take my cup and pastry to a small table in the corner. I position myself so I am facing the door, the laptop screen not visible to anyone but me. He has given me a URL for a VPN, but I ignore it. I would rather find my own, which I do, easily enough.

Once I'm connected and hopefully safe, I pull that other URL out of my brain, the one that's been in hiding as long as me. My fingers are trembling as I type it in, wondering if it's still the same, if I'll find anyone I know there.

I know better than to use my old screen name, so I create a new one: BikerGirl27. It sounds like I ride motorcycles, not bicycles, which is the whole point.

I go into the first chat room and have a total déjà vu moment. The first time I was here, I was fourteen. One computer class at school had opened a door for me that I hadn't known existed. I was fluent in French even then, but this was a language that came even more naturally. It made sense when so many other things didn't, but in my youth and ignorance, I made a lot of mistakes. I was an anomaly: a girl hacker, and I didn't know enough to keep that a secret. I left portals open that should've been shut tight behind me, and my father caught me hacking into his business files. That's when I found the chat rooms full of other kids just like me, computer geeks who had a special gift of making complete sense out of what looked like gibberish to most people.

It's where I first met Tracker.

He's not going to be here, it's been so long, but I find myself scanning the names, looking anyway, following threads and getting my sea legs back, so to speak, until I force myself to stop. I am not here to rekindle old relationships. I am here to get help.

This is the thing that he doesn't know. I didn't do it alone.

I glance out the window and see him walking toward the cafe. Quickly, I shut down the laptop and shove it into the backpack. When he comes in, I am waiting in line for another coffee.

'You've got an early start,' he says.

'Thought I'd get a coffee first. Do you want one?' The barista raises her eyebrows at us, and he orders two lattes to go.

'I'm not sure a coffee shop is a good idea,' he explains. 'Wireless has no boundaries, and you're right. Maybe we shouldn't be seen too much together. Let's go to my room.'

The implication is intimacy, but I know better. We pay for our coffees and head outside.

'I've got my bike.' I indicate it, locked up outside.

'Meet me there,' he says, already crossing the street, both of our coffees in his hands, and I unlock my bike, riding behind him, the backpack slapping against my back.

When we get to the Blue Dory Inn, instead of going into the main building, he veers to the right, toward an outbuilding. He pushes the door open and waits for me as I lean my bike against the building just outside his door. There is no place to lock it up, but it's so close by it shouldn't be a problem. I hope.

'Nice room,' I say as I step inside and he closes the door behind me. It *is* a nice room, cozy with a queen-sized bed covered with an old-fashioned patchwork quilt and small throw pillows, the windows covered with lace curtains like the ones I have in my house. I drop the backpack on the bed and peer out the window at the water shimmering under the late morning sun.

'You called me Tina,' I say quietly.

His eyes grow wide. 'I did not.'

'Yes, you did. When you came out of the bathroom looking for the razor.'

'What did you tell him?'

'I said I didn't hear you say anything. He thinks you don't know my name.'

'He lost some respect for you, didn't he?' His tone is kind. 'I know you've made friends here, but I wouldn't be here if it weren't important.'

'I know.' But as I say it, I wonder, *do I*?

I am sitting on the edge of the bed, and I reach across it to pull the laptop out of the backpack, but he puts his hand out, takes it from me. He stands in front of me, placing the laptop on the dresser. Gently, he pushes me back and leans over me. 'I'm sorry,' he says softly. I put my hand on his neck and feel his pulse quicken, and he smiles at me. I remember how it was, in the beginning, when my heart raced every time I saw him. I see it in his eyes now, the way he used to love me, and I let him kiss me.

The lesson starts two hours later. We make a feeble attempt to discuss how we can't keep our hands off each other; we try to laugh about it. But there is an undercurrent of desperation, as if each time we think it will be the last. As if it is a second chance we must cling to before it's over again.

There is some truth to that.

I throw on one of his shirts, and he pulls on a T-shirt and a pair of running shorts as we turn on the laptop.

'We can get access to the library's wireless from here, since it's just across the street and the signal is pretty strong,' he explains. 'We could technically use the inn's wireless, but I would need to register, and we can't have our names attached to anything.'

I think about his name and how that could be a red flag, unlike Nicole Jones, who is a ghost living on an island.

'Why Zeke Chapman?' I ask him.

He shrugs. 'I needed a name. So did you.'

'Have you been using it all this time?' My throat feels as though it's about to close up, and the words skitter through hoarsely.

'If I didn't run into you, and you found out someone named Zeke Chapman was here, you'd know it was me, right? I wanted to get your attention.' He is staring straight at me, as if daring me to keep protesting.

I swallow the lump in my throat. 'Well, you got it.'

'Come on,' he says, indicating the laptop. 'Let's get to work.' He gives me a wink. 'I know you want to.'

I don't let on that I know what he's doing as he shows me how to activate the Internet. Even though I have already done this, a surge of adrenaline rushes through me.

'It's addictive,' he warns, but the smile playing at the corners of his mouth indicates he knows too well my addiction and he is teasing.

He shows me YouTube and Facebook and other things that I hadn't even dreamed about before. This *is* new, and I am amazed at how much more there is now. He explains podcasts and I am in awe of the video quality.

I look up at one point to see him smiling at me curiously.

'What?' I ask.

'You. It's like a kid with an ice-cream cone. You should see the look on your face.'

I feel my neck and face grow hot, embarrassed. He reaches over and touches my cheek. 'It's cute,' he says.

Another flashback to the same touch, the same words. I catch my breath, look back at the laptop and, wanting to keep my hands busy, put my fingers on the keyboard.

His hand covers mine, stopping me. 'VPN,' he reminds me, and he explains how to get in, how to set it up. I am ahead of him, but again allow him to think otherwise.

I don't need him, my fingers flying, old passwords cluttering my head. I can't use them, who knows who found them, who tried to track me down with them. Instead I remember a newspaper story about passwords, how to keep hackers away. Like me.

I chew on my lower lip as I put together letters that are gibberish to anyone except me. I am careful not to let him see my fingers as they move across the keyboard. He is smarter than he looks.

When I feel safe, I look up at him. A small, amused smile tugs at his mouth.

'You look like you used to,' he says.

I shrug, shaking him off. 'Now what?'

'I've got a username and password for us to use.'

'Whose sign on are we using?' I ask, immediately wary.

'Not important.'

'Yes, it is.' He is setting someone up.

He shakes his head. 'You have to forget about before. It's the same this time, but different. You'll see.'

'So tell me.'

His face grows dark. 'Tell you what?'

'The username and password.' This is not what he was expecting me to ask, but I can't figure out what else he is thinking of. 'Can't do anything unless you tell me.'

His face brightens. 'Oh.' He recites both for me.

'Write it down,' I instruct.

'Nothing in writing.'

'So where do I go from here?'

He looks confused, as if I should already know, but the username and password are both useless unless I know which site to go to. I wonder if it's the bank again, but when I start to ask, he gets up suddenly, jostling the bed, and I steady myself, watching him cross the room and look out the window toward the water. A sliver of blue sky peeks through the space between his silhouette and the curtain, beckoning me. I suddenly want to go outside, climb on my bike and ride around the island, visiting my favorite places, my friends. They are slipping through my fingers with each keystroke.

'Did he tell you where I was?' I ask his back, pushing aside the reason for being here.

He turns to look at me. 'No, he never told me.'

'He didn't know,' I say. 'Really.'

He gives me a funny look. 'I saw the postcard.'

I gather the courage to look him in the eye, pushing up my glasses as I raise my face toward his. I'd bought the postcard when I'd seen in the newspaper that he was dying. I picked out the nicest one I could find, one with the North Light on it, the sea shimmering behind it, the hues of the sunset illuminating the lighthouse. I didn't sign it. I didn't write a message. I just mailed it to him, wanting to send the peace I'd found to him.

'How did you know it was from me?'

'I didn't.'

'Why did you think it was?'

He smiles. 'I've never stopped looking for you.'

'But you really just want my help. Help that you, for some reason, think only I can give you.'

The smile disappears. 'If I just wanted your help, you wouldn't be in my bed.'

'Maybe you're in my bed because you want more.' I cannot stop being cynical, unsure of my standing with him.

He makes a small sound that's not exactly a chuckle. 'Still difficult, aren't you? This place hasn't changed you.'

I stiffen. 'Yes, it has.'

'Then walk away.'

'What?'

'Leave. Now. If you do that, I'll know you've changed, that you won't come back to me, that you don't really want to help me.'

'*Help* you? You keep using that word. Help. I know this isn't anything noble, so why are you pretending that it is? A man died because of us. Because of what we did. And you want me to do it again.' My voice has started to shake. My heart pounds beneath the thin shirt.

'Then walk away, if you feel that way.' He is challenging me again. And then he adds, 'Or maybe this time we can go some-where together.'

My legs begin to shake, bare against the chill of the room, the shirt only coming down just above my thighs. I am exposed. But I cannot walk away. I am frozen in this spot as I think about what he's saying.

I might have to flee again. I might have to give up this life as well as the other one. My breath catches in my throat.

He touches my face, running his fingers down my neck, tracing a line over my breast, pausing a moment to caress my nipple, then continuing down to my waist. He pulls me to him and kisses me deeply, quickly, before sensing my hesitation.

'You're going to have to leave anyway,' he says, reading my mind. 'Even if you don't help me.'

'Why?' I manage to whisper.

'I'm not the only one who knows about that postcard.'

My body feels like a spring, ready to bounce. 'What do you mean?'

'I'm not the only one who's on your trail. I just got here first.'

ELEVEN

I don't need money. I have enough saved up that I could leave the island and find another place to hide. It is not money from before. That money is gone. I carried some with me on that ferry fifteen years ago, but there is none left now.

'The accounts were all frozen,' he tells me now. 'All I had was what we had on the boat.' His eyes grow dark with the thought of my betrayal.

I had a feeling they'd freeze the accounts if they found us. I'd routed the money to several places, and they found them all. Except one. The only person who knew about that one was Tracker. Tracker took what was owed him and the others, left the rest for me.

'I don't have it. It's gone.'

'But you don't deny taking it.' His tone is flat.

'I didn't take much. It didn't last long. It was gone before I got here.'

He stares at me, unbelieving.

'Really. I left you mostly everything.'

'And they took it. I couldn't get any of it.' He is angry now, and I take a step backward, away from him. The movement causes him to stand up straighter; his eyes do not let go of mine.

I wonder now what happened to him after. I have not asked him. He knows about my life but I know nothing of his. Is he really still in Miami, or is it New York, like he told Steve? What has his life been like for the past fifteen years?

'Did they catch you?' I whisper, wondering if a fifteen-year sentence would make sense.

It is as though a light switch has been flipped. His face lights up and he laughs out loud, reaching for me, pulling me to him. I tense slightly as his arms wrap around me. 'No, Tina. They didn't catch me. But that doesn't mean you don't owe me.'

It has gone from helping him to owing him.

'It's not my fault they froze the accounts.'

'But if you'd stayed, we could have gotten more. I wouldn't have been left with nothing.'

He believes I have to pay my debt to him. He has already made a subtle threat, and he could destroy me if he wants to. But as I listen to the beat of his heart beneath my ear, I realize that it might not be so easy for him. That my friends here might not believe him. After all, I am a respectable citizen. I do have odd habits, but everyone on the island is a little bit odd in their own way.

As I think this, though, I know better. I know a phone call to the police would uncover my secret. But would he do that? He would be putting himself at as much risk as me.

'You owe me,' he says again, and this time I see him as if for the first time: a man who has been harboring anger for so long that he will break me because I left him with nothing. He was hiding behind the one whose hand caresses my cheek and looks deeply into my eyes. Fear rushes through me as I realize how quickly he switches from one to the other.

I have never been afraid of him. Our relationship had its ups and downs. We are both opinionated and strong-willed. The attraction is deeper than looks; we always found our way back to each other after an argument, and our feelings were always even more intense than before. Later, there was an undercurrent of unraveling despite our best efforts to pretend otherwise. But I have never been afraid. Until now.

He pushes me away for a second before he pulls me back and kisses me and then abruptly lets me go.

I watch him out of the corner of my eye. He goes into the bathroom and I hear the shower. He is waiting for me to join him, but instead I put on my own clothes, close up the laptop and go back outside to my bike.

He told me to walk away, so I am doing just that.

But as my feet hit the pedals and I fly past the hotels and restaurants, up past the llamas and past my house, I realize I am not just walking away. I am trying to escape.

I need the Bluffs; I need to see them, to feel their power, and soon I am there. I tuck my bike behind a bush, haphazardly locking it in place. I want to leave the backpack with the laptop, but I can't. I shift it onto my back as I descend the wooden stairs, my hand gently touching the railing now and then, a grounding.

I reach the bottom and look up behind me, the stairs climbing as if to the sky. The rocks are hard under my sneakers; I stumble a few times as I get my bearings. I walk along the bottom of the Bluffs, the water dancing toward me, the sound soothing my troubled thoughts.

How could I do it again? Before, it was different. We were young and crazy and in love, and he had a plan that would make us rich. I wasn't in it for the money. I was already rich; it was my father's money, I had earned none of it. But I wanted him to have what he wanted, and I wanted to make it happen. To show that I could. I didn't think of the consequences. So I hacked into the bank's system and wire transferred money to accounts I'd set up all over the world. From there I transferred the money again and again. He gave me usernames and passwords – I never asked where he got them, didn't want to know – and Tracker gave me the way in to the system; he still thought that part was all me. I kept Tracker safe, or so I thought.

It was when the FBI showed up that we had to run.

I shiver in my fleece, a brisk wind sweeping across the water. I spot the ferry in the distance; it's on its way. Steve is probably at the Town Dock now, waiting.

He said there are others who are coming. But he's been here for five days now, and I've seen no sign of anyone else. He always had a habit of overdramatizing. It's possible he's just saying that because he wants me to do the job.

He is as vulnerable as I am, so if they really are on my trail, they will find him, too. He can't afford to stick around, and it doesn't seem as though he is in a hurry.

I am rationalizing. I am talking myself out of it. But as I do, I feel the weight of the laptop in the pack against my back. Its lure is beyond anything I have felt, even here. I have tried so hard to stay away from it, but disappearing for fifteen years to an island has not meant I do not still dream about it, my fingers on the keyboard, the codes, the passwords, the elation of knowing I've gotten past a firewall, through a portal, cracked a system.

He is right. I am like a kid with an ice-cream cone. And I have not completely changed.

I am embarrassed about this. And now I find myself tempted to go back to where I started: huddled in front of a computer screen.

I hear voices carried on the wind, and I turn to see an older couple wrapped in fleece coming down the steps. It's time to go, but something bright catches my eye. I lean down and pick up an iridescent white stone. It is smooth in my palm, and I close my hand over it, feeling its magic.

I shove the stone in my pocket as I make my way back up the steps, past the couple, giving them a nod and a quick hello, but not stopping even though they seem as if they want to ask me something.

I don't have time. I need to give him back his laptop and send him away. I just hope he'll let me.

I am not prepared for Veronica. She is pacing in front of my house, her arms hugging her chest, her hair flying in the wind. I was not going to stop, but I have to when she sees me and lifts her hand up in a short wave.

I ride up to the house and lean the bike against the side. 'What's up?' I ask. 'Why are you here?'

'Can we go inside?' Her usually bright face is dark and drawn; her eyes skitter around behind me. Something has her rattled.

I open the door, drop my backpack on the table and offer her a cup of tea.

She shakes her head. 'No, not now.'

I am even more perplexed and worried. I lead her into the living room and indicate she should sit in the rocking chair, which she does. The squeak of the chair echoes against the walls as I settle on the couch, my legs crossed. I am wound as tight as she is now.

'Your friend,' she starts, then swallows hard and smooths her hair back as though she has just realized that it's windblown.

I wait.

'He came by. Your friend, I mean. Came by the gallery. He was looking for you.'

'We had a fight.' I figure it's easier to lie a little.

'He said so.'

I'm not surprised. He can't tell anyone, either.

'He was a little desperate. Wanting to find you, I mean.'

I force a smile. 'It was a bad fight.' I try to look apologetic. 'I'm sorry he bothered you.'

She worries the cuff of her sleeve, unplaced.

I lean forward, closer to her. 'What is it, Veronica? What's upsetting you?'

She leans forward, too, so our heads are almost touching. 'He had a gun.' It is whispered, frantically.

I sit back, trying to be nonchalant. 'A lot of people have guns, Veronica.'

'He had it under his arm, in like, a holster. Like on TV or something.' Her voice is trembling.

I try a small smile on to alleviate her worry. 'It's OK. He's with the FBI.'

I don't mean to tell her this, I immediately regret it but it seems the only way to calm her down. It works. Immediately, she straightens up, the worry no longer etched in her face, a curious smile beginning.

'FBI?'

'That's right. So there's nothing to worry about.'

She takes a deep breath. 'I thought he might do something to you.'

She might not be wrong. I shrug. 'It's OK. I don't think he's like that.'

'Are you sure? I mean, how can you know so soon?'

I have to keep up the facade that I have just met him. 'You're right, I guess, but he doesn't seem like that.'

'You're sure?'

I nod, and I must have finally reassured her because she relaxes as she smiles.

'I think I'll have that cup of tea now, thanks, Nicole.'

I don't want to have tea, but I can't tell her no, so I go into the kitchen and put the water on to boil. She follows me and watches me take two mugs and the box of peppermint tea out of the cabinet.

'Steve says you got a computer.' It is said matter-of-factly, and she doesn't seem to notice that I tense up.

I smile. 'Yes, that's right.'

Her face lights up. 'Will you let me help you set up a website for your paintings? We can work it out so you can sell them through the gallery, if you like.' It's what she would like, to have the opportunity to make money off me even though my work might not be in her gallery. She realizes that I have her number, and she gives me a sheepish look. 'It would make you look more professional to go through a gallery,' she tries. 'I've done this for a couple of the other artists.'

I think about the word *artist*. I've never really thought of myself that way, but Veronica has always referred to me as an artist. I should be used to it by now.

'Anyway,' she says awkwardly when I do not answer, 'it's up to you.'

'It's OK,' I assure her. 'Let's set it up. Why don't we plan to do it sometime next week?'

'That would be great, but can we do it after hours? I'm trying to get everything ready for the season.'

'Sure. I'll let you know which day.' She doesn't have to know that a website for my paintings isn't at the top of my priority list at the moment.

The teakettle whistles, and I pour the water into our mugs, the peppermint scent sudden and strong.

Veronica takes her mug and sips. 'So what is he like?' she asks then.

I know what she's looking for: the same thing Jeanine was.

'He's nice,' I say, hoping I sound enthusiastic enough about him. I surprise myself by conjuring up an old memory: holding hands as we walked through the gardens at Viscaya, the scent of roses and a spring rain hanging in the air. His smile playful as he snapped pictures with an old Polaroid camera, waving them in front of my face as they developed, teasing me that they would come out perfect because I had a special magic power to make everything more beautiful.

Veronica is talking, and I shake myself out of the memory.

'What did you fight about? I mean, it seems that maybe you two—' Her voice trails off, and she gives me a wink.

I shrug, taking a sip from my own mug, the hot liquid burning my tongue. 'Just a little disagreement. No big deal.' But as I think about it, it is a big deal. He is no longer that boy with the camera. He is looking for me. I glance out the window and see nothing but the sea and the horizon, white clouds dancing in the sky. Even though I left his room, I can't really escape. I am trapped here.

My hand holding the mug shakes slightly, the tea spilling a little, but Veronica doesn't notice.

TWELVE

After Veronica leaves, I pace my living room, my heart pounding. He must have seen her leave. He must know I am here alone. So when the knock comes at the door half an hour later, I actually feel relieved that the waiting is over, except I then hear the familiar 'Hello, hello!' and Steve comes in.

'Are you OK?' Steve asks, the worry etched in his forehead. 'I ran into Veronica.'

So word is already out that he is FBI. Not something he'd want advertised, but what did he expect me to tell people, carrying the gun?

'I'm fine,' I say, patting his arm. 'Don't worry.'

'Is he really with the FBI?' A tone of incredulity laces his words.

'That's what he says.'

Steve makes a face and strokes the side of his beard. 'Not what I would have expected.'

'Why?' I can't help but ask.

'Doesn't seem the type.'

He says this so seriously that I chuckle. 'And what do you know of FBI agents, Steve?'

He raises his eyebrows and gives me a grin. 'You'd be surprised.'

Nothing about Steve should surprise me after all this time, and my first instinct is to think he is teasing me. But there is something in his expression that makes me ask, 'Were you FBI in another life or something?'

'Now, Nicole, you know I was a geologist.'

I think now that I have been wrong, that this is our usual banter, so I say, 'A geologist who is really MI5? A British agent who comes to Block Island to track down a wanted man?'

'Who says it has to be a man?' Steve teases.

His words catch me off guard, and paranoia spreads through

me. I have been living here under the radar, or so I've thought. What if someone has been watching me all this time? What if he had help in finding me?

Steve notices I have grown quiet, and he laughs. 'Don't look so worried,' he says. 'I was not an FBI agent, although it would have been a lot more exciting than being a geologist. At least from what I see on TV and in the movies.' His laugh dies down, however, and his expression shows concern. 'Why is he here?'

He has no idea how loaded a question that is. I have to clear the fear out of my throat so I can speak. I pick up the mug off the kitchen counter and take a sip of the remnants of peppermint tea that lay in the bottom.

'I think he's just here on vacation,' I say after a few seconds.

Steve comes closer, puts his hand on my arm. I am reminded of his marriage proposal, and the awkwardness of that moment returns. He realizes and pulls his hand back, stuffing it in his pocket.

I want to make it better. I want to tell him. The urge is so strong I don't think I can fight it. And I find myself opening my mouth, the words rushing out.

'No, no, that's not right, Steve. I'm so sorry I didn't tell you, I feel so awful about it. But I know him. From before. Before I came here.' The relief that comes with the words is palpable. It is as though I have had a balloon inside me and it's popped.

He is staring at me, his expressions changing as fast as my breaths as he struggles to comprehend. 'What are you saying, Nicole?'

'He and I, we were lovers. A long time ago.'

'Is he your ex-husband?'

Jeanine has been talking, as usual. For a second it annoys me to think that they have been talking about me behind my back. I shake my head. 'I was never married. But—'

'He broke your heart,' Steve finishes for me, his face softening as he believes he's right.

And he is. In a way. He broke my heart into a million little pieces and left it on that houseboat on the Seine in Paris, along with my old life. I nod, although as I do, I know I have made a big mistake. This is the first clue to my former life that I've told anyone here. Who is to say I won't spill everything? This is all I can allow myself to tell.

'Did he know you were here?' Steve asks.

'No. It was a fluke.' I reach into the cupboard for a glass and the bottle of cognac. As I pour a finger, I raise my eyebrows at Steve. 'Want one?'

He frowns. 'It's only a little after lunch.'

'It's been a long day already,' I say, realizing I have not eaten since my croissant at the coffee shop, but I knock back the drink anyway, the warmth coating my throat and settling in my shoulders and back, relaxing me.

Steve is confused. This is something I would have done before. Before I was Nicole. When I was Tina. He is bringing her back too quickly. I glance at the backpack, where the laptop is hidden. After Veronica left, I spent the hour trying to convince myself that it would be fruitless to take it out, since I don't have wireless here.

It only took a phone call to the landlord to ask if he could add wireless to the cable contract; I would cover the whole cost, no problem.

I put the glass in the sink and lead Steve into the living room. I settle on the sofa; he perches at the edge of the rocking chair across from me. He waits for me to tell him. I shuffle through all the things I can say and settle on something.

'We had a fight. He wants me to go back with him. I told him I can't do that. Not after all this time.' The lies slip off my tongue easily. Too easily, like all the others.

Steve rests his elbows on his knees, his hands folded between them. He waits a few seconds, then, 'Are you sure?'

He is asking me if I'm sure it's been too long, if I really don't want to go. His expression tells me he is hoping to hear exactly what I say.

'I can't go.' My tone is firm, because this is the one thing I know for sure. I will not leave this island and my life willingly.

'So you're not in love with him?' His tone is so plaintive, I give him a smile.

'No. Not now. I was, once.' As I say it, I remember. The way he would look into my eyes, his kisses consuming my whole soul. It *is* different now; there is too much behind us.

'Where did you know him? I mean, where did you live?'

'Miami,' I say, but I am thinking of Paris. It didn't start in Paris, it ended there, but when I am lying in bed late at night staring at the ceiling, that's what is stuck in my head. We'd thought we'd gotten away. Until that night.

'I've always thought you were from the South,' Steve said, as though I have confirmed all his beliefs about me.

I chuckle. 'Miami isn't "the South,"' I say with air quotes. 'It's full of displaced northerners who think it's paradise.'

'It isn't paradise?' Steve is careful about asking me these questions. I know he wants to know everything, but he must tread lightly. It makes me want to tell him more.

'I grew up there,' I say, getting myself in deeper. I should stop. I tell myself that this is safe, that it isn't the whole story, that if he tries to find out about Nicole Jones in Miami, he won't have any luck.

'Why don't you ever talk about it?' he asks, getting braver.

I shrug and bite my lower lip. 'It's not paradise.'

He gives a short nod, as though he understands. I have given him the impression that something bad happened to me there, and that's not too far from the truth. However, he keeps going.

'Your parents, are they alive?'

I shake my head. This is not a lie.

'No brothers or sisters?'

'No.' Again, not a lie. It feels better to tell the truth about something, a vindication in a way that my life isn't all smoke and mirrors. I smile more broadly now. 'You are my family, Steve. You and Veronica and Jeanine. I've never been happier in my life than I have been here. I like to pretend that I've always been here.'

These truths buoy me. It makes him happy. He grins back, the worry gone, pleased that I have told him about a little bit of my past.

'I feel that way about the island too, even after losing Dotty. But we had some good years here,' he shares.

'Do you want to get some food? I'm starving. Bethany's? Clam chowder?' I ask, although I am wound as tight as a rubber band. I don't think I can eat anything, but I have to let Steve think everything's OK, that I am the same as always.

But he gets up, shaking his head. 'I really just wanted to make sure you were OK,' he explains, looking at his watch for the first time. 'I've got a tour scheduled in about fifteen minutes. Couple who're here for the first time.'

Steve and I have always liked first-timers, to see the beauty of the island through their eyes. To be able to show them this little piece of what truly is paradise.

I walk him to the door. 'Tomorrow, then?'

'How about dinner tonight?'

I hesitate. He is going to show up here sooner or later, and I have to deal with him. Steve sees me struggling with myself over this, and he guesses right what's going through my head.

'Don't worry about it. Lunch tomorrow.' He gives me a small salute and a wide smile as he goes out the door. I watch him go down to his Explorer, waving his hand over his head at me, but he doesn't turn around.

I shut the door and go to the pantry, where I pull out the laptop. I do it without thinking and put it on the table, turning it on. I know I have no Internet access here, but I need to feel the keys beneath my fingers.

When it is booted up, I have a thought. I go into the systems folder and find the Internet access. I don't know why I haven't done this before, because I see that there are wireless networks to choose from. All of them are locked, but a locked portal has never stopped me before.

THIRTEEN

I have no idea whose wireless I'm stealing, but it doesn't matter. I have used a VPN, so even if he or she discovers someone poaching, they won't have a clue where I am. It only took me ten minutes to get in. I am getting my legs back, so to speak.

The first thing I do is a search, something simple that anyone can do. I scan the information I find. It has been so long now that I manage to find only a couple of news stories about what happened. My name is there, my real name, and how the FBI was looking for me, but there is nothing about Paris. It is as though Paris never happened.

The username and password he gave me earlier are imprinted in my memory. I'd asked him to write them down, but I didn't need him to. I didn't want him to know that I would remember them as clearly as my own name. I go to the bank site and type them in, my heart pounding in my chest.

Despite my instinct that they would belong here, they don't. The site tells me that either one of them or both are wrong. I have no idea where they belong or what exactly he wants me to do with them. I hadn't stuck around long enough to find out.

By walking away, I have told him I won't do what he wants, but being here, now, makes me want it. Not for him, not because I owe him or want to help him, but just to prove that I can still do it.

I push away my frustration, go to the chat room and sign on. Even though I don't know any of the names here, it feels more like home than Miami ever did.

I long for Tracker, his wisdom and skills. He was better than me, even though he denied it. But without Tracker, I would know nothing.

I follow some of the chats and discover that someone named Angel seems to be a leader. He is involved in several discussions, dispensing advice. It doesn't take me long to know that Angel is the new Tracker here, someone I might make use of. I invite him to a private chat.

Me: I'm new here.
Angel: I noticed. What's with the privacy?
Me: I need some help. Thought maybe you could give
    me some tips. It's been a long time for me.
Angel: I'm not sure what I can help with.
Me: I may need to get through a very secure portal
    and firewall. But like I said, it's been a long time.
Angel: I don't know you.
Me: I know that. But I used to know someone named
    Tracker. Do you know who he is?

Several minutes go by, and I am afraid that I've scared Angel away. Before, I was a part of the community. When I needed help, I knew who to go to and how to ask. I am rusty at this, but time is not on my side if he is right about others being on my trail, so I have to be more aggressive. Dropping Tracker's name, though, seems to have been a mistake. Angel is still quiet.

My fingers hover over the keyboard, ready to let Angel off the hook, when he finally responds.

Tracker doesn't know anyone named BikerGirl27.

My heart jumps into my throat, and I cannot breathe for a second. He has checked with Tracker. Tracker is still here somewhere.

Tell him it's Tiny. My fourteen-year-old self had thought it clever to replace the last letter of my name with another to create what my forty-year-old self now realizes is a stupid nickname. But Tracker will know it. He will vouch for me. And maybe, even, if I dare to hope, he will emerge and he and I can join forces again.

I have no idea who Tracker is outside this world. I have always thought of Tracker as a man, but he could be a woman, too. There aren't too many girl hackers, but they do exist, most with androgynous names to hide their gender. I had fantasized about meeting Tracker someday, but when I suggested it, in my naivete, he dissuaded me from pursuing any sort of physical contact.

'You and I can never be associated together,' he'd written me. 'It will be one of the biggest regrets of my life, but it's safer. For both of us.'

My imagination regarding Tracker was vivid: he was young, like me, or he was older and married and had a family, or he was a criminal on the run, or he was some IT guy who was bored and wanted to see what he could do outside the perimeters of his job. Or none of the above.

Angel is quiet again.

The idea of Tracker has me nervous. Will he come into the chat? Will he be the same? Can I still trust him? The cognac has made me a little lightheaded, so I get up and fix myself a cheese sandwich and pour a glass of milk.

Angel still has not returned.

The sandwich tastes like cardboard, but I force myself to finish it, washing it down with the milk. I have not been this anxious in a long time, even when I knew he was on the island. This is a different type of anxious. I touch my hair and wonder if Tracker has gray streaks in his, too. If he has crow's feet around his eyes and at the corners of his mouth.

It's possible that Tracker is younger than me. I was twenty when I first 'met' him online. It's possible that I have at least five years or more on him; hackers get early starts.

My brain is in overload, just thinking about it, when I see that I have a message. My hands begin to shake as I read.

It is Angel. **Tracker says to meet him tomorrow morning at seven EST.** He then gives me a URL, a place where Tracker and I can meet privately, away from the chat.

I know what's going on. Tracker is going to try to find out if I am really who I say I am. I smile to myself, knowing he will be as thorough as he can be, but his search will turn up no more than my search just did.

Thank you, I write back to Angel, but I see he has already disappeared.

I log out of the chat room, shut down the laptop. My whole body is shaking now, but I don't know if it's from the excitement of knowing Tracker is still out there or nervousness that I am getting back in the game. Because for the first time I am sure that I am. I wrap my arms around my chest and squeeze tight, forcing myself to calm down. I eye the glass with the remnants of my cognac from earlier and without a second thought find the bottle and pour myself another short one. Steve would be horrified, but I need to relax. Especially since I realize that he still hasn't come around. It has been a long time since I left him alone at the Blue Dory Inn, since he went looking for me while I was at the Bluffs. This worries me.

I cannot stay here and wait. I feel as though I will jump out of my skin. I put the laptop back in the pantry, under the potatoes, then find my paints and easel. I pick up the case with the paints, put my easel under my arm and lock up my little house, walking down the road and then to the beach. There is no one here today; the breeze is cool and the skies have clouded over.

I unpack everything and set up, mixing some paint on a palette, sweeping the brush through it, eyeing the canvas. It is bright white, empty. I have painted the water and sky from this place before, but the colors are different today: gray with hints of purple, tiny whitecaps dancing on the water. I sweep the brush across the white background, the color bold and soft at the same time.

I stay here for a long time, the painting taking shape, a mirror image of what I'm looking at. Veronica will love it, I think, and maybe she will hang it in a prominent place in the gallery.

As I work, I spot the ferry coming toward the island, and with a few more brushstrokes it is there, on my canvas, just off to the left.

I am calm again; the nervousness I felt earlier has dissipated with the normalness of what I am doing. I have pushed everything that's happened out of my head, and for a short time I am Nicole, bike tour operator and artist with no past, only a present.

When the painting is done, I glance at my watch and see I have been here for two and a half hours. I glance up at the road above me. A few cars have gone by; I have more heard them than seen them. Where I am, I am out of sight. Someone would only see me if he came down to the beach. This has not been by accident.

I am delaying the inevitable. If he has been looking for me, he is probably even angrier by now because I have disappeared. I study the painting, see that I can add nothing more and know it's time to go back. I pack up the paints and the easel and carry the painting carefully up the hill and to the road. I hear voices, and there is a family – mother, father and three children – laughing at the llamas.

As I approach my house, I see that something is wrong.

The door is open.

FOURTEEN

I stop, put down the easel and paints' case and gently lay the painting next to them. Every instinct is to run, but I am frozen here, staring at my house. The windows are dark; I can't see inside. But someone is there – or has been there.

I should call the police. Call nine-one-one. But what would I tell them? Someone, possibly – probably – my lover, has broken into my house and is waiting for me. It would sound crazy, and I don't want to bring any more attention to myself than he has already brought me.

I think about his gun.

I have no idea if he would hurt me. Physically, anyway. He never had before, but there are fifteen years between us since then and now, and I have changed, so who's to say that he hasn't, either? He is angry with me, for so many reasons, and I cannot guarantee my own safety with him anymore.

I stand there for ten more minutes, watching. There is no movement inside my house – at least, none that I see. The door is gaping open, letting in the cool breeze. My feet feel as though they are stuck to the ground, but I finally take a step. And then another. And another. Until I am at my doorstep, the paints left behind in the grass.

I peer around the door and see nothing but my mudroom. A fleece and sweater hang from the hooks, a pair of rain boots and heavy clogs are beneath the wooden bench. Everything as it was. I let out a breath, unaware that I had been holding it in. I move closer now. The door to the kitchen is ajar, and I push it gently so it opens further.

The kitchen is a mess. Drawers are open, dishes and glasses broken on the floor. The refrigerator door is open, too, and milk and honey and coffee grounds make a sticky mess.

Now I really cannot breathe.

I force myself to swallow, take in a couple of deep breaths. I go inside, keeping the door open behind me, just in case.

The glass crunches beneath my sneakers as I go into the living room, where the cushions have been slashed and their white cotton innards tossed around the room. My books have been tossed on the floor, pages ripped out and scattered.

The destruction is so extreme that it feels almost unreal.

The bedroom is next. The closet door and dresser drawers are open. My clothes have been cut up and left in a pile on my bed, the goose feathers from the pillows making a halo around them. I go to the closet and see the empty hangers, bare like skeletons. I glance at the floor of the closet. My shoes and sneakers are in a messy pile, but they are unscathed. I drop down and slide my hand along the wood floor underneath them. If I didn't know what I was feeling, I wouldn't know about the compartment. I lift up the top and peer underneath. A sense of relief rushes through me momentarily, until I drop the secret door, getting up and turning back to the scene on the bed.

I cannot take it all in. But I have one more room.

My jars are shattered in the bathtub, the stones everywhere, covered with body lotion and shampoo.

I sink down on the toilet seat and put my head in my hands, waiting for the tears as my shoulders heave. But what I thought was sadness is actually anger. It bubbles up inside my chest until I feel as though I am going to explode. It would have been better if he'd shot me with that gun. If he'd just come in during the night and shot me while I slept.

This, well, this is worse than anything I could've imagined.

As I sit, I realize I'd forgotten something. I jump up and go to the pantry, which is in as much disarray. I know without moving anything what is missing.

The laptop.

He has taken it away, not knowing what my decision was. Not knowing that I had changed my mind after I left him in the shower.

He didn't even give me the chance to tell him. He just came here and destroyed my house, dismantled the life that I'd created here.

Or maybe that was the point all along.

But more logically, I know what has happened here. He thinks I have money stashed away. He thinks I still have it, from back then – money that is owed him, money that he feels I stole from him.

His frenzy to find it is clear in the destruction.

It slowly dawns on me, too, that there is something else missing. Something I didn't see outside.

My bike.

I am disgusted with myself that I thought of the laptop before my bike. What does that say about me? I am suddenly grateful that the laptop is gone, that it's been taken away so I have an excuse to stay away, that I have an excuse to keep from helping him again.

But my bike. I cannot live without that bike. It is my livelihood. He knows this. And even though I can easily buy a new bike, it is symbolic of what he has tried to do here.

I am a little surprised that he thought of that.

I stumble back outside and circle the little house, but the bike truly is gone.

I pull the door shut behind me and lock it, the keys nestled in my pocket. I start the walk down the hill, down the road toward the llama farm. As I pass them, they snort at me, and I make a face at them and resist the urge the scream. It is not their fault. I keep walking. Soon I am at the Town Dock. A ferry has just come in, and people are streaming off it with their bags and their bikes and their cars.

'Nicole!'

I hear my name, and I turn instinctively. Steve is waving at me as he leans casually against his SUV, his smile warm.

In an instant, I am crying. The tears stream down my face, and I drop to the ground, hugging my arms around my knees.

'Nicole.' His whisper is urgent in my ear, and I feel his hands under my arms, lifting me up. 'Nicole, what happened?'

Steve's expression is full of worry. I have to tell him it's nothing, that he should go back to his SUV and find a paying customer and leave me here on the ground. But I can't. I cannot stop crying.

He lifts me up as easily as I lifted that laptop and carries me to his Explorer, gently placing me in the passenger seat, closing the door. As I wait for him to come around to the driver's side, I stare vacantly toward the National Hotel, the shops that abut it. People are on the sidewalk – not as many as during the season, but enough, because the ferry has just come in.

One catches my eye. A tall man, salt-and-pepper hair, all angles to his face, overdressed in an overcoat and black trousers. I stiffen. It can't be. But then I realize it can. And even though it has been a long time, there is no forgetting that face.

He had said he was only the first one here. Now I know for sure he was not lying.

As I watch, Carmine Loffredo pushes the door open to Veronica's gallery.

The driver's door opens, and Steve climbs in, starting up the SUV.

'You OK?' he asks softly.

I have stopped crying, but my anxiety is no longer just about my house. Carmine Loffredo is here. On the island. This is whom he was waiting for. This is whom he'd warned me about. And Carmine has found at least one of my friends. It won't be hard for him to find Jeanine. Steve. And finally, me.

While I want to rush to the gallery, warn Veronica, I do know Carmine won't hurt her. He will merely use her and her penchant for conversation to get one step closer to me.

Steve still has no idea why I am upset, and within minutes we are past the harbor and the hotels and restaurants and up the hills and into the heart of the island. He finally pulls over next to a stonewall that snakes its way up and down and out of sight.

'Tell me what's happened,' he said.

There is a stone in my throat, one that's keeping me from talking. I shake my head until I feel his hands on my cheeks and he is forcing me to look at him.

'What happened, Nicole?' Steve's voice is firm. He is not going to let me get away with not telling him.

I try to concentrate on why I ran to him in the first place. 'My house,' I manage to whisper, and then it comes out – everything I found when I got home from the beach. Steve is not touching me anymore. He is leaning back against his door, his usually bright eyes dark. 'You left it like that?'

'Yeah,' I say, wiping my nose with the back of my hand, leaving a long streak of tears and snot.

Steve is nodding, and I can see he is thinking hard about

something. Finally, he turns and puts the car into gear. We head back down toward town.

'Where are we going?' I ask, but I don't really have to. I knew the moment I told him that he would take me to the police station. So when he pulls into the parking lot, I am not surprised. I don't really want to do this; I can't have the police probing into my life. But unless I tell Steve everything, I cannot say no.

I am still not ready to tell any more than I already have. So I go with Steve into the building and he demands to see the police chief, who happens to be having a coffee and doing something on the computer when we are brought into his office.

It's not as though I don't know Frank Cooper. We have had drinks together at Club Soda and we've played darts. You cannot live on an island this small and not know mostly everyone. But Frank Cooper, for the first time, will know that I have a past. That I have a past with a man who carries a gun. A man I've described as being FBI. Because that is going to come up. It's inevitable.

'Nicole's place was trashed, and her bike was stolen,' Steve tells Frank, his voice husky with anger.

Frank immediately stands up; his face clouds over with concern. 'What happened?'

I tell him what I told Steve. How I came home from the beach and what I found.

Frank puts his hands on his hips. 'It's that guy, isn't it? The one staying at the Blue Dory?'

For a second, I am thrown off. I don't think I told anyone where he was staying, except maybe Steve. But it's possible Veronica knew, since he'd commissioned the painting. I nod, despite my new suspicions. I cannot mention Carmine.

'Zeke Chapman, is it?' Frank says, going around the back of his desk and dropping down in to his chair, reaching for the phone.

I want to stop him, but I am unable to.

Steve squeezes my hand as Frank calls the Blue Dory and finds out that Zeke Chapman has not yet checked out.

'Don't mention this to him, Alice, OK? I'm going to be stopping by in a few, but I don't want him to know.' Frank thanks her, says goodbye and hangs up, standing up again and facing me. 'I'm going over there. You stay here with Steve until I get back.' He starts for the door.

'Frank?' Steve holds his hand up. 'One thing: he's FBI and he's carrying a gun.'

Frank stops and looks from Steve to me, nothing in his expression giving away what's going through his head. And then he finally speaks.

'No, he's not, Steve.' He gives me an apologetic smile. 'Nicole, I'm sorry I did this without talking to you first, but Veronica bugged me to check this guy out for you. You have to keep in mind that she was only looking out for you.'

I know what's coming now. I pull my hand out of Steve's and hold my hands in front of me tight so as to keep them from shaking.

'I'm afraid Zeke Chapman isn't who he told you he is. I don't know who he is, but Zeke Chapman, the real FBI agent, died fifteen years ago.'

FIFTEEN

S teve is staring at me, and I am unable to look him in the eye.
'Stay put,' Frank says again as he leaves the office.
It is quiet for a few seconds before Steve says, 'Nicole?
What's this all about?' Steve is the only one I've told about
having a relationship with him all those years ago. He is also
smart enough to put two and two together: that I have been here
for fifteen years and that when I knew him, it must have been
before the real Zeke died.

'Nicole? Who is Zeke Chapman?' Steve asks when I don't answer.

Again I have the urge to tell him everything, to get it all out
there, but I cannot do it here. I cannot do it while in the police
chief's office. It would be far too easy to be overheard and thrown
in jail, something I have been avoiding successfully all this time.

I sink down in one of the straight-backed chairs behind me,
my head in my hands. I have to think – and think fast.

Steve misunderstands and sits next to me, his hand on my
back, gently massaging it.

'Was he impersonating this FBI agent even back then, when
you knew him?' he asks.

This question makes it easier. I look up and smile sadly. 'It
appears so.'

'Oh, I'm so sorry.' He truly is, too, and I feel guilty about
deceiving him. We had both taken other names back then. It's how
we got to Paris, those fake passports easier to get through Tracker's
contacts than they would be now, after 9/11 and Homeland Security.

As I am remembering, the old irritation surfaces. He used me
in so many ways. I was the one with the computer skills and the
one with the contacts. I was such a little fool.

I am still a fool now, to get caught up with him again.

He was so good at that, though, making me believe in him.
And the attraction had been there from the start, was still there
– enough to make me, a grown woman with a real life now, forget
about all of it and let him seduce me. Seduce me with a laptop.

I am thinking all of this to keep myself from remembering what happened at the end, why I had to leave.

It would've been better if he'd been caught. If he'd been thrown in prison.

If I'd never sent that postcard.

This was all my fault, the mess I found myself in now.

'I need to go home and clean it all up,' I say.

'The police will go over there first,' Steve warns me. 'They'll need to take evidence.'

Fingerprints. A panic rushes through me. They will find my fingerprints, too. I cannot let that happen.

The tears begin again, but this time I have conjured them. 'I have to be there. I don't want to know that they've gone through my things, too.'

Steve nods, as though he understands. 'I'll take you over there, but you have to come home with me. I can't let you stay there by yourself.' His words are said matter-of-factly. He has settled it without my OK. But as long as I can get there, I might still be able to do something.

'I want to go now.'

'We have to wait for Frank.'

'I don't want to. I want to go home.' I sound like a petulant child. 'Do you think Frank sent someone over there already?'

Steve opens the door and disappears. I begin to pace, my hands shoved in my pockets, every muscle tense. This is not happening.

Steve comes back with Reggie McCallum. I know Reggie from Club Soda; he's a good dart player.

'Nicole, I need to get your prints,' Reggie says. 'We need to take prints from your house, but we need to eliminate yours first.'

They can just match my prints up with those in the house. I actually have no idea if my fingerprints are in a federal database. It's possible that they were taken from a glass or something else I touched at my house. Do they have his prints? He said they didn't catch him, but they did know where we'd been.

My whole life is unraveling, yet I cannot let anyone know. I force a smile at Reggie and say, 'What do I need to do?'

He takes Steve and me to a counter in a small room, where he has laid out the equipment: an ink blotter and a small card with spaces for each of my prints. Reggie apologizes as he smears ink on my fingers and rubs them from right to left on the card. When I am done, he hands me a paper towel. The ink smudges on the rough surface, and a shadow of ink lingers on my fingers.

As we leave the room, Frank Cooper is coming toward us, a frown on his face.

'He's not there,' he says.

'Where did he go?' Steve asks. I cannot speak. It feels as though a cotton ball is stuck in my throat. 'Did he get the ferry?'

'I don't know. His things are there, but he isn't. I've got a car out looking for him and one at the docks and another at the airport, just in case he's just dumping his stuff and leaving it here. But as far as I know right now, he's still on the island somewhere.'

'He's probably long gone,' Steve says, and it makes sense to him. But I am not so sure.

'I'd like to go back to my house,' I tell Frank. 'I want to be there when you take your evidence.'

'You can't get in the way,' he warns, but with sympathy in his eyes. He knows how violated I feel.

I agree, and the three of us leave his office. Steve and I drive together in silence, following Frank in his police cruiser. I stare out the window, the familiar landmarks passing but I barely see them. I can't keep them from doing what they're going to do. I should have stayed in the house. I should never have gone out. I should have never gotten into the car with Steve, told him anything. I could have kept all this quiet, just cleaned up and pretended it never happened. Waited for him to come back.

But then I think again about Carmine. How his presence changes everything.

Steve parks behind Frank, and we climb out of the Explorer. Another police officer has already arrived. Frank waits for me to unlock the door and I let them in, standing back so they can pass through. I feel Steve's hand at the base of my back.

'You OK?' he asks.

I shake my head. Of course I am not OK, but I cannot open my mouth to say the words.

I hear muffled voices from within as Frank and the other officer, his name is Bob, take in the destruction. Suddenly, Frank's head pops around the door.

'Is anything missing, Nicole?'

'My bike,' I whisper. 'It was outside.'

'Anything else?' It is as if he knows. As if the spot in the pantry underneath the potatoes has told him that something was there and now it's gone.

'My laptop computer,' I say, more loudly this time. 'It's new. I just got it.' I remember that I'm supposed to be in the chat room with Tracker tomorrow morning. How am I going to do that now? It will be like before. I won't be there, and he will suspect the worst and won't hear from me for another fifteen years.

Somehow I have to be there.

'Nicole?' Frank is talking to me.

I give him a small, sad smile. 'I'm sorry.'

'Why do you think he would take your computer and bike and nothing else?' Frank asks.

'Maybe he needed a way around the island?' I try, ignoring the part about the computer.

Frank grins. 'OK, maybe. But what about the computer?'

I cannot tell Frank that it was a present. That he gave it to me. That would open me up to too many questions I won't answer. I have also told Steve that I ordered it myself. I have to keep my lies consistent.

'It was new,' I say again. 'Who wouldn't want a new laptop?'

'Was there anything on it? I mean, could he steal your identity or anything with what's on it?' Frank is serious, yet his words make me want to laugh out loud.

I shake my head. 'No. I barely had time to get it booted up. There's nothing on there.'

'No passwords saved or anything?'

Again I remind myself that they have no idea who I am. That wiping out my tracks on a computer is second nature, and no one will be able to see where I've been because I am so thorough.

'No,' I said flatly.

Frank flashes a relieved grin. 'Good. That's good to know. You wouldn't want anyone to get any of your information. It takes years to clear up identity theft.'

Again, I resist the urge to laugh.

*   *   *

It takes an hour. Steve and I sit in the wicker chairs outside my house, not saying anything. He seems to know that I don't want to talk, and I am grateful for that. Finally, Frank and Bob come out of the house, Bob carrying some sort of kit that I assume has whatever evidence they feel they could collect.

Frank approaches me as Bob goes to his cruiser. I have never seen so many police on this island as I have today.

'Nicole, I'm sorry about the mess.'

Steve stands up. 'I'll help her clean up, Frank.'

'That's not the only thing,' Frank says, and I can see he's trying to choose his words carefully. 'Nicole, you shouldn't stay here. He might come back. You can't be here alone.'

'He's probably off the island by now,' I try.

'You don't know that.'

'She's going to stay with me,' Steve tells Frank. 'I'll take care of her.'

I am no longer in control of my own person, but I cannot argue. 'That's right, Frank. I'll stay with Steve.'

Frank looks from me to Steve and back to me again. 'I'll send a cruiser past every now and then, just to make sure everything's OK. I'll send someone by here, too, in case he comes back. I checked with the ferry company, and the last two captains have not seen anyone fitting Zeke Chapman's description on board. And he wasn't on either of the flights that went out today. No one's seen him at the marinas, but that doesn't necessarily mean anything, since we can't keep tabs on all the boats out there and who's on them. Unless we find out different, though, you should assume he's still on the island, and you are not safe.'

I have never been safe. I know that now.

'I'll be with Steve,' I say again.

Frank shakes Steve's hand, leans in and gives me a little peck on the cheek. 'You'll be OK, as long as you're aware of your surroundings.'

I will not be OK, but to appease him, I say, 'Thanks, Frank.'

We watch him drive away, and then Steve and I step into my house. He has not seen it before, and he gasps loudly. 'Oh, Nicole, this is awful.'

I cannot argue, going to the utility closet and pulling out cleaning supplies. No time to waste.

SIXTEEN

would rather go to the Yellow Kittens for a drink, but settle instead for a cognac with Steve at his house. I don't want to be out in public. He is somewhere on the island, and Carmine is here, too. It wouldn't take much to find me here at Steve's. But I don't quite know how to get out of staying here without telling Steve everything, so I settle into the folds of his big sofa in his den, trying to look relaxed, but I am about as relaxed as a cat perched under a bird feeder. Steve sits across from me, nursing his own glass. When we left my house, it was spotless, the bags of trash outside in the bins for pickup.

'I'll help you get that couch to the dump on the weekend,' Steve promises, 'and then you can find another one.'

How can I tell him that there may never be another one? That while picking pieces of glass jars out of my tub, I realized that my time here may be close to over?

But because I am not completely ready to accept that, I tell Steve that I will look in the local paper to see if anyone is selling furniture. I also have to call my landlord, let him know what's happened. Why there will be new furniture in the house.

As I'm talking, I notice his computer on the desk in the corner of the den. Immediately I admonish myself for what I am thinking, what I had thought about earlier: that I can sneak onto his computer when he is asleep and contact Tracker.

'I think you're not telling me everything, Nicole,' Steve says softly.

His words startle me. Not just because I was so engrossed in my own thoughts that I almost thought I was alone, but because he is challenging me. That is not the way our relationship works.

'It's been a long day, Steve.' It seems like forever since I was painting on the beach.

He leans forward in his chair, his elbows on his knees, and stares at me. 'Zeke Chapman isn't his real name. And he seems to think that your name is Tina. Is your name Tina, Nicole? Is that your real name?'

The panic bubbles up inside me. I feel it in my throat, which is closing up. I cannot speak.

'I'm sorry I have to ask, but you've been acting strangely ever since he came to town.'

He's right. But I can't tell him. I can't tell him any more than he already knows.

It's no longer because of me, though. It's because of him. Because I can't put him in danger.

When I was in the house, I found something. Something that Frank and Bob missed, because why would they pay any attention to a postcard of the North Light? It was stuck to the refrigerator with a magnet.

If they'd taken it down and turned it over, they would've seen it was addressed to Daniel Adler at the federal penitentiary outside Raleigh, North Carolina. There was no note written.

He hadn't indicated that he still had the postcard. Or even if he ever did. He had just said he'd seen it.

The destruction at my house wasn't his style, at least not the man I used to know. But it *was* Carmine Loffredo's style.

A chill rushes up my spine. Carmine probably has not been charged with just finding me. We both stole that money from Carmine's boss. I wonder where he is hiding, because I know he must be if he knows Carmine is here. He doesn't know the island like I do, though, and he doesn't know the best places to go.

Steve is watching me. I have to give him something.

'You're right,' I say. 'I have been acting a little different. It's just that I never thought I'd see Zeke again.' Saying the name is difficult for me, and I choke it out, then take a sip of my cognac, as if it can wash it away. 'It's been a bit of a shock. And now, with him breaking into my house and trashing it, well, I am just so embarrassed that I got caught up with him again.'

I have no idea if I sound contrite. I am doing the best I can, but I don't know how much longer I can keep this up. Especially when Steve asks me again: 'What's your real name?'

He knows. Am I strong enough to admit it?

I chew on my lip for a few seconds, then say, 'It's Tina.'

His face crumbles. 'Why?'

I know what he's asking. 'I came here to get away from my life,' I say. 'You did the same thing with Dotty.'

'But I didn't change my name. I didn't lie about it.'

'I needed a fresh start,' I whisper as a tear slips down my cheek. I never wanted to hurt him.

'What's your last name?'

If I tell him, he'll be able to find me online in one of those news stories. He'll know everything. But do I have a choice? Is it time to tell?

'I'm not that person anymore,' I try.

'You can't escape your past, Nicole.'

I feel myself smile in spite of myself. 'Yes, yes, you can.'

But he is shaking his head. 'No. See what's happened? This man, Zeke, or whatever his name is, has come here because of what happened in the past. If you know who he really is, you should tell me. You should tell Frank.'

'I can't tell Frank,' I say before thinking. '*You* can't tell Frank. Please.'

Steve scratches his beard. 'Can you tell me?' He knows that there is more.

I can't even look at him. My eyes settle on the computer on the desk again.

'Nicole?' His voice is stern, touching a memory of my father, and I look back at him. 'Isn't it time for you to come clean?'

I want to. I really do.

I shake my head and give a short chuckle. 'It's not nearly as sordid as you might think.' That might be the biggest lie of them all.

Steve surprises me then. He stands up. 'I'll make us some supper. I've got some fresh cod I picked up earlier. How does that sound?'

Relief rushes through me, and I grin. 'That sounds wonderful. What can I do?'

He shakes his head. 'You can stay here and finish your drink.' He goes to the kitchen and I hear the sounds of dinner being fixed. I know now that it's not going to be that easy. If things were normal, I would be in there with him, peeling potatoes, cracking jokes with him.

I get up and move toward the desk, the computer drawing me with its invisible lure. I casually move the mouse and it springs alive, the wallpaper a snapshot of the Bluffs.

I glance toward the kitchen, and while I cannot see him, I can hear him. He is humming. Steve always hums when he's cooking, but it is an absent humming, something he doesn't even realize he does until I point it out to him.

I am not going to point it out now.

I sit and log into my VPN, immediately doing a search. I need to know what someone will find if they search for Zeke Chapman.

The first thing that comes up is an obituary from the *Miami Herald*. I click on it and scan it. It is an obituary from fifteen years ago, telling me that Zeke Chapman was a special agent with the FBI and had been killed on the job. It doesn't mention what he'd been investigating, only lists his wife, Lauren, as his survivor and asks that all donations be made to the Policeman's Fund. A memorial service was scheduled, but no burial is mentioned

I still hear Steve humming. Something is sizzling. The fish. The refrigerator door opens and closes.

I stare at the obituary, reading it over and over. I don't need to see stories about how Zeke Chapman was killed and where and why. I'm pretty sure Frank Cooper already knows, and if Steve mentions that my real name is Tina, lines will be drawn and conclusions made.

'What are you doing?'

Steve has come up behind me, and I tense.

'Just looking for something.' I am surprised my voice sounds normal, considering he has startled me.

He looks over my shoulder. 'How was he killed?'

'He was shot.' I close my eyes for a second and I can hear the report of the gun. Who would believe that I didn't even know he'd had a gun?

'Where did you get it?' I'd asked him.

'Get what?'

'The gun, asshole. Where did you get it?'

He grinned, putting his hand up to my cheek. 'Don't worry about that. No one can trace it back to us.'

'Us? You mean you.'

'I'm not the one with the connection to him, Tina. Even his wife knew about you.'

That had been a mistake. But I'd only wanted to find out if he would be jealous, if the only reason he wanted me was because of what I could do for him. He didn't believe that I was only messing around with Zeke and wasn't really serious about him.

Problem was, Zeke thought I was serious. He wasn't in Paris to bring us back home. He was in Paris for me. Until he discovered I didn't want to be found.

'What's going on, Nicole?'

I blink and am pulled out of my memory. 'Nothing. It's just been a really long day.' I log off the VPN and move away from the computer.

'What were you doing there?' It has not gotten past Steve that I've taken an extra step on the computer.

I shrug. 'Nothing, I guess.'

'What site were you on?'

'It's a VPN. It's—'

'I know what a VPN is. Why do you need one here?' He is daring me to answer.

'It was just reflex.'

'Reflex?'

How is he to know that the computer is an extension of me? He has no idea who I am or what I am capable of. I think carefully how to answer him.

'I used to be pretty good with computers,' I finally say, getting up. 'Can I set the table?'

I don't wait for an answer, but go into the kitchen and start taking plates from the cupboard. I carry them to the table and place them across from each other. Steve says nothing as he goes back to the stove and tends to the fish. The microwave buzzes, and he takes out two baked potatoes, which he puts on a plate and hands to me. I notice, too, that there are carrots cooking.

Soon we are sitting at the table, eating in silence. This is the first time I have ever been with Steve and not known what to say. It is awkward, even more awkward than after his declaration that we should get married. So I just keep eating and hope that this will pass.

'How good?'

The question comes out of the blue, and my hand freezes, the fork just inches from my mouth. I put it down and ask, 'What?'

'How good were you with computers?'

I shrug.

'Is that why you never had one before? Did you do something illegal with it before?'

He is so close to the truth it literally hurts not to tell.

I shrug again.

'You can't keep not answering me, Nicole.'

'You don't want to know.'

'Yes, I do.' Steve sits back and folds his arms over his chest. 'You're my friend, Nicole, but I feel like I don't even know you right now.'

I am quiet.

'Please tell me who you are,' he whispers.

I swallow hard, blinking against the tears that have sprung into my eyes. I have no more strength left. I cannot fight it anymore. He is my friend, possibly the only true friend I have ever had.

SEVENTEEN

'**M**y name is Tina Adler.'

I know the moment I tell him my real name that I am laying myself open. He can now do his own Internet search and find out everything. But if I tell him first, maybe he won't be jaded by what he reads. Maybe he will see that Tina Adler is not Nicole Jones, or vice versa. Maybe he will see that Nicole Jones is a decent person who regrets everything and had to make her life over and not a person who has been lying to him for fifteen years.

'I grew up in Miami. My father was Daniel Adler.' There it is, put on the table next to our plates of fish.

Steve's eyebrows rise slightly. He knows the name. Who wouldn't?

Before he can ask anything, I say, 'Yes, that Daniel Adler.' Financial advisor or, rather, con man. The man who'd bilked millions out of the rich and famous. The man who'd died in federal prison because of what he'd done.

I was fifteen when he went away the first time. Went to prison for insider trading.

'Clients tell me things.' I still can practically feel the tickle of his breath as he whispered to me. It was his way of justifying it, as though having clients tell him things meant that it was OK to use that information any way he could.

I had already hacked into his business accounts, but the real hacking didn't start until he was gone. I didn't do it to steal anything. I did it just to prove that I could get past the firewalls, through portals, replace source codes and end up in places I shouldn't be. I did it for kicks. My mother slept until noon, her cocktail glass on the table beside her, the knife she used to cut herself in the drawer. She didn't know, didn't care what I did, as long as I left her alone.

Even though my father had done everything he thought he could to keep me out – every software program available to keep people like me out – I always found a way back in. I did it for years before I had to go away, so I knew what he was up to from the beginning. I saw the transactions, the wire transfers. If I'd been around when they caught him at his final game, when his clients had stopped talking to him because they'd lost everything and they discovered he'd taken it all, I could've given them even more than they had. It didn't matter, though. They had enough, and he was locked up for life. They must have been so angry when he died after only ten years.

Steve is waiting for more. Now that I have started, he believes I will continue, but I'm not sure I can. He really doesn't need me to confess anything else. He can find everything he might want to know online.

Steve clears his throat, realizing that I am not going to say more.

'When did you meet him?'

I know whom he's referring to.

'I was twenty-two.'

'Where did you meet him?' It is as if we are now at a cocktail party, asking those first questions you ask of someone you don't know.

I close my eyes and see him walk through the door at the Rathskeller, his hair tousled, his eyes bright, moving around, looking for somewhere to land. He was the most beautiful man I'd ever laid eyes on. Tall, with broad shoulders, a face perfectly sculpted. But his back was too straight, his movements stiff. He was trying too hard. Trying too hard to look rich. I knew rich boys. They had a casual elegance about them, the way they carried themselves.

He almost walked past me, but I sidled around a couple of people so I was in front of him. He noticed me, smiled, and I felt as though the world had disappeared and it was only the two of us.

'Hi,' I said.

'Hi, yourself,' he said. 'I haven't seen you around here before.'

'It's my first semester.' I held out my free hand. 'Tina Adler.'

A long, slow smile spread across his face as he took my hand, caressing it. 'Ian Cartwright.'

We spent the whole evening together; he never left my side.

He wasn't like the others, I thought when he kissed me. He didn't know who I was, who my father was, so he wasn't just interested in my father's money.

When I realized I'd been wrong about that, that he had planned to meet me, I was so in love with him that I didn't care.

I had been so stupid.

'Nicole?'

I feel drained, as though I have had a three-hour therapy session. I have been remembering what happened after, but what happened before was just as important.

I give Steve a shy smile. 'I'm sorry. I thought I'd left it all behind me. Miami. I met him at the university.'

'University of Miami? You went there?'

'One semester. Wasn't a good fit.' Steve didn't need to know about how I'd hacked into the school's computers, stolen final exams and sold them. That was one story that wasn't reported. The university did a good job in covering it up and quietly expelling me.

'Your father just died.' Steve says it matter-of-factly. Of course he would have heard. It was in all the papers. On the TV. You don't steal millions from celebrities without becoming a media sensation yourself, and if you die in prison it's an even bigger story.

'Yes.'

'Is that somehow connected to this man's visit here?'

Steve is too smart. For a long time, I was the smartest person in the room. A little of that feeling has stayed with me, regardless of my new identity. I chose friends like Veronica and Jeanine, whom I have always felt would never find out about me because they just didn't have the curiosity or the smarts to do it. Steve, well, I thought I was safe with Steve, too, because our relationship has always been the same. I never thought he'd start challenging me.

Like he's doing right now.

'No one knew where I was,' I say softly.

'So how did he find you?'

I sigh. 'I sent a postcard. To my father, when he got sick. He saw it.' Again, I wonder how did he see it, exactly? I'd sent it to the prison. It's possible that someone intercepted it there. Carmine's boss, Tony DeMarco, probably had connections there, so that could have been how they'd seen it. But Ian, I wasn't so sure.

Steve does not notice that I have been sidetracked. 'And he came here when he saw it.'

'I didn't write anything on the card. No return address. It was just a postcard. From here.' And as I say this, I realize I have been underestimating everyone's intelligence and overestimating mine. Because of that postcard, I risked everything and it looks as though I will lose everything.

Steve's expression tells me he is thinking the same thing.

'So he wouldn't have found you without it?'

I don't have to say anything. He knows the answer to that. I am not going to admit out loud how stupid I was.

'Why have you been hiding from him?'

The questions just keep coming. I don't know how long I can take it.

'He thinks I owe him money.' I sigh. 'I owe him money.'

'How much?'

I wonder if he'd believe me if I told him exactly how much. Sometimes the number shocks even me. And I'd been in control of it.

When he realizes I am not going to answer, he changes tacks. 'Did you steal the money, Nicole? From him?'

He believes my silence confirms the answer.

I get up and start clearing the plates from the table. Steve helps me, but I can see he is thinking hard about the little bit I have given him. Together we clean up the kitchen, put away the food that we haven't eaten. I crave another drink, but I can't risk it. I will end up telling him more, and I'm not ready yet.

There is one thing I do say, though, when we are done.

'I have to use your computer in the morning.' I am not asking him. I am telling him, and it doesn't get past him.

'Why?'

'I can't tell you.'

'You can't use it unless you tell me, Nicole.'

'It's nothing illegal.' Not yet.

'Tell me.' He leans against the counter, his arms folded across his chest. He is not my friend right now. He is a man who is angry that I have betrayed him all these years.

I can't blame him. So I say, 'I have to meet someone in a chat room.'

He mulls this over for a few seconds, then says, 'You're really good with computers.' It's stated as fact.

I nod.

'A hacker?'

I nod again.

'You can use the computer, but you can't do anything illegal.'

'I won't. I just have to meet up with someone. He's a friend.' He might be my only friend after all this. But he is as much a ghost as I am.

'What's his name?' Steve doesn't trust me about anyone now.

'Tracker.'

'That's not a real name.'

'No.'

'What's his real name?'

I am tired of this. I can't do it anymore. 'I don't know, Steve. I never knew. And he doesn't know my name, either.' Although as I say it, I realize he must know now. He wasn't stupid, could figure out that my disappearance coincided with what he'd helped me with, connected the dots.

'How can you live your life like that?' he admonishes me.

'I haven't. Not for fifteen years.'

We stare each other down for a few minutes.

Finally, he says, 'This Zeke Chapman or whatever his name is, he wants you to steal money, doesn't he? He wants you to hack into somewhere and steal it and give it to him?'

'He never exactly told me what he wanted me to do,' I say. 'But I think that's probably right.'

'You're not going to do it, are you?' He says it like it's a dare.

I shake my head. 'No. I left him there, at the Blue Dory, to show him I wouldn't do it. And then later, well, when I got home . . .' My voice trails off.

'So why do you need to talk to this Tracker person?'

'So I can make sure I can go back to my life and not be bothered again.'

Steve frowns, understandably confused. 'How can you do that?'

'It has nothing to do with you.'

'But you're going to use my computer.'

'Just tomorrow morning. Then I'll go home and leave you out of it.'

'You can't go home. He's waiting for you. He'll hurt you.'

'He won't hurt me, Steve.' Although as I say it, I am not entirely sure.

'What was done to your place – that was a violent act. He won't stop until he gets what he thinks is owed to him.' Steve unfolds his arms, and his expression changes slightly. 'You're not going home.'

'But—' I stop myself before I mention Carmine.

'If I'm going to help you, you really need to tell me everything. Because I have to know what I'm getting myself into.'

EIGHTEEN

Steve is going to help me. I let that sink in for a few seconds. 'Why?' I finally ask. 'Why are you going to help me?'

'Because you're my friend. Because you have kept me sane since Dotty died. Because without you, my life will be empty. Do I need to go on?'

I feel a rush of emotion, and the tears spill down my cheeks. He does not move toward me, just lets me cry. I put my hands over my face. Finally, I feel his hand on my shoulder, and I sink into him, my head against his chest, his beard tickling my forehead.

After a few minutes, I finally stop crying and pull away. I wipe my eyes with the back of my hand.

'You don't have to do this,' I say.

'I know that.'

He is waiting for something, for more of my story, but I am too spent. 'Can we pick this up in the morning? It's been a long day.'

Steve stares at me for a few seconds, and it dawns on me that he thinks I might leave in the night. I might disappear and he would never see me again.

And for the first time, I realize that I could. I could slip out of the house in the dark, wait for the first ferry in the morning and take it, back to the mainland. But I can't do that just yet; I need to figure things out first. I need to know exactly what's going on before I go out there unarmed. And, most of all, I need to be prepared.

'The guest bedroom is all set up,' he says finally.

'Thanks,' I say and follow him into a room with pink flowered wallpaper and a four-poster bed covered with a white bedspread.

Steve leaves me alone, then returns, carrying a T-shirt and a pair of sweat pants. 'You can wear these.' All of my clothes have been cut up, so what I am wearing is all I have. 'I've left an extra toothbrush on the sink in the bathroom.' My toothbrush had been dropped in the toilet bowl at my house.

I take the clothes and thank him. He gives me a sidelong

glance as he steps out of the room, shutting the door behind him. I hear his footsteps go down the hall to his room and then another door shutting.

The room is bathed in the glow of a lamp on the bedside table. The window shows my reflection. Suddenly I shiver and turn the light off, the room cast in darkness. It takes a few seconds for my eyes to adjust, and then, with the help of the light of the moon outside, I see shadows around me. I quickly undress and put on the clothes Steve has brought me. I step into the little bathroom adjacent to the room and find the toothbrush. I brush my teeth in the dark and rinse my mouth out using my hands as a cup. When I go back into the bedroom, I creep over to the window and peer outside. I see nothing but the road and a few trees. I reach up and pull down the shade before anyone can jump out and say 'boo!'

I cannot stay here past tonight. I probably shouldn't be here now, but Frank Cooper said he would keep an eye out, so I am counting on that.

In one fluid move, I slide into bed, pull the covers up under my chin and stare at the ceiling, hoping that I will be able to sleep.

I force myself to stay in bed until six thirty. I have been awake for hours, tossing and turning, catching only snippets of sleep that are interrupted by dreams of strangers destroying my house. Finally, when I smell the coffee brewing, I allow myself to get up and venture to the kitchen, where Steve hands me a cup and I settle at the table. He sits next to me.

'You need to meet this Tracker at seven, right?' he asks, as though our conversation from the night before has not been imprinted in his memory, like it is in mine.

'That's right.' I take a long drink of coffee. It is too hot, but I ignore how it scorches my tongue.

'What's the plan?' He leans forward, closer to me.

I have been mulling this over all night. Should I tell Steve about Carmine? I still want to keep him in the dark as much as possible, but I don't think it will be easy to get rid of him. He seems determined.

'It might not be safe for you to know,' I say softly.

'Oh, the whole, if I tell you I'll have to kill you thing?' He laughs, but I can hear the strain behind it. He wants me to trust him, but he has no idea what he is asking or what risk he is taking.

'It's something like that.'

'I'm a big boy. I can take care of myself.'

I shake my head. 'These people, well, they play for keeps,' I say.

'These people? You mean, Zeke?'

I put my cup down. 'His real name is Ian. And he's not the only one who knows where I am.'

Confusion crosses Steve's face. 'What do you mean?'

'I don't know for sure that he is the one who trashed my house.' I let that sink in for a second, then add, 'He told me that he just got here first.'

'What did you do, Nicole?' His expression is stern, and while I know he is not my father, he is acting more like my father than my father ever did. Daniel Adler didn't care what I did, as long as I stayed out of his business. When he caught me at his computer that first time, my fingers on the keyboard, his files open, he sent me to France two months early to visit my grandmother for the summer.

She had a computer.

A year later, Daniel Adler was in prison.

The memories are all coming back now, fresh and vivid in my head. Memories I'd pushed away so far I thought they were gone for good.

I look into Steve's eyes. They are searching mine, searching for the truth. Searching for who I really am. I want to scream that I am Nicole, that Tina doesn't exist anymore, but she has been emerging ever since I saw Ian in his car at Club Soda that night.

In his car.

I sit up straight. 'He had a car here,' I say. 'Remember, we saw it that night at Club Soda? A black BMW, I think it was.'

Steve looks uncomfortable.

'What is it?' I ask.

'I talked to Frank this morning. I called him before you got up, just to see if there was any news. They found the car. Last night.' He pauses. 'It was at the airport.'

'But I thought they said he wasn't on the flights that went out yesterday. Or was he?' And then I have another thought. Is that how Carmine ended up here? The ferry wasn't the only way people got onto the island.

'Frank thinks you should stay here, inside, not go out, until they find him.' Steve has answered my question in a roundabout way. Frank Cooper does not think Ian was on any of the flights if he thinks I should stay with Steve.

'But what if they don't find him?' My imagination starts to go a little crazy. I think again about Carmine.

Ian had not come up with the plan on his own. While I had been under his spell, I wasn't so far gone to know that he wasn't all that savvy. He had been greedy and desperate, which made him dangerous and careless.

When he first came to me with his idea, acting so innocent ('You could do this, couldn't you? I mean, with your skills, you could hack into anywhere, right?') I'd suspected that something else was going on, but once the plan had taken hold of me, I couldn't shake it. It was a challenge, something that could put me on the map. And it did, but with all the wrong people.

Steve smirks. 'What do you think – that he's swimming with the fishes?' He chuckles, but the sound dies in his throat when he realizes I am not laughing with him. 'Nicole, you don't think someone—'

'I don't know what to think,' I say. 'There were some very bad people involved. People I didn't know about until after.'

'After what?'

I take a deep breath. It's time. 'I hacked into a bank and transferred money to accounts in other places.'

There, it is out. And I see from his expression that he has not looked me up on the Internet, that he has waited for me to tell him. That he trusted me enough to tell him myself.

'How many accounts?'

He doesn't need me to tell him. Just from the little I've told him, he knows there were a lot.

I hadn't thought about right or wrong, only how I was going to do it.

It wasn't anything dramatic, either. It wasn't very different from anything else I'd done. Ian had given me the list of account numbers, but first I had to get into the bank's system and find them – and find the portal that would allow me to move the money out without alerting anyone right away.

I liked the sneaking around. My ability to be invisible behind the firewall, changing the source codes so I could access the passwords and, with just a few clicks, transfer millions across the oceans, thousands of miles away. Something intangible became tangible, although it never felt like stealing. I didn't make that connection right away. It was merely a puzzle to be solved. I wasn't slipping a bracelet into my pocket at the department store.

When I saw the transfers go through, I felt the thrill ripple through my body. I suppose I should have wanted Ian with me, but I didn't. I wanted to feel my success by myself, because even if I'd tried to explain to him how I'd done it, he would never have understood the technicalities.

The only person I yearned for at that moment was Tracker. He understood me like no one else. He knew what I was capable of and encouraged me. He was the only one I ever truly trusted.

'How many accounts?' Steve is persistent.

As he repeats the question, pulling me out of my memory, my thoughts begin to race. Ian gave me one username and password when we were at the Blue Dory. Just one. Not multiple accounts. One.

'A lot,' I say. 'There were a lot of accounts.' I glance at the clock. It is five to seven. I get up, my coffee cup in my hand. 'I have to use the computer,' I say, ignoring the look of disbelief and shock on his face.

Steve starts to get up, too, but I put up my hand. 'I have to do this myself. We can pick everything up from here when I'm done.' I see his expression change; he isn't happy about this. 'Please, Steve.'

Maybe it's something in my tone, but he backs off. He starts clearing the breakfast dishes without a word, leaving me to head into the den. The computer sits on the desk, and I turn it on. I've seen this computer here a hundred times and never touched it, never had the urge to touch it, before yesterday. Well, maybe that's a little bit of a lie. Sometimes when Steve wasn't looking, I'd run my hand across the keyboard as I passed by, just to get a little thrill. Knowing what I could do, but choosing not to. I'd been proud of myself for that, feeling that I'd changed.

What a fool I am.

I log into the URL that Angel has given me for the chat, and I get into the room easily. No one else is there, and I hope this isn't some sort of trap. And then . . .

Est le soleil? Is the sun shining?

I feel my heart quicken, my fingers moving quickly.

Non, le ciel est nuageux. No, it's cloudy.

Tiny. So you're alive.

You, too. Tracker is here, using the French phrases that we'd devised to make sure that both of us were who we said we were.

Angel said you need help.

I've been offline since then. I don't know my way around anymore.

Like riding a bike.

It's what Ian had said.

Can you help navigate? I type.

You know I will. You've got your safeguards in place?

Yes.

Good girl. See, it's not so hard.

Easy for you to say.

So what are we doing?

I just need some information right now. I'll decide later what I'm going to do with it. I need as much information as I can get on Ian Cartwright and Paul Michaels. Addresses in New York and Miami.

I'm not a private investigation service. I can almost hear the tension behind his words. This is not what Tracker had thought I'd ask. Before I can respond, he writes, You can find out all that yourself. Google it.

I already did that, and there's nothing. I didn't think there would be. Where I need to get the information from, I have to get behind a pretty serious firewall, probably more than one. It's a system that might not have any open portals.

Where exactly are we hacking into?

The FBI.

NINETEEN

Even if the police found Ian's fingerprints in my house, I'd be surprised if he'd ever used his real name again, considering. When I left him, he'd been using the name Paul Michaels, the name on the passport I arranged. I have no idea if he's still using that name – he might not be. But it's the only one I know. The fact that he has been calling himself Zeke Chapman here on the island makes me wonder if he truly has taken on that persona, but he had to realize that it would muddy the waters, since Zeke is dead.

Every time someone mentions his name, I cringe inside.

I am the reason Zeke died that day.

The FBI? Tracker's message pulls me out of my thoughts.

I need any information relating to those two names in connection with those accounts fifteen years ago. You know the ones. I pause. I also need the names that went along with all those accounts. Names and pertinent information – employment, places of residence, that sort of thing. Ian had told me that the job was 'just like before.' I wonder if this new plan is targeting one of the victims.

I had seen the stories in the paper about the theft. It was too huge for anyone to keep it under wraps. Ten million. But there had been no mention of the victims, just the amount stolen and the search for the hackers who did it. When the real Zeke, the FBI agent, showed up at my father's house, more interested in me than my father, I began to question everything. I never had names. I had anonymous usernames and passwords. Nothing was personal. At least, not for me.

It was only then that Ian told me about my father and Tony DeMarco.

You can do some of that yourself, Tracker is pointing out.

I didn't keep a list of the accounts. I had been safeguarding myself. I really only need the information on the accounts on our original list. The list I had been given, culled from some unknown person – unknown at least to me. Ian had been very tightlipped, said I didn't need to know and it was better that I didn't. I was fine with that. The papers said it must have been an inside job, someone inside the bank, but I never knew who it was.

I'll post them here within the hour. I knew Tracker would have it. I'm going to need some time for the other. I don't know exactly how long. I'll leave you a message, so check back.

And then he was gone.

I stare at the screen, wondering what I can do myself. He is right that I can get some of the information on my own. At least, I used to be able to. But I am afraid that if I try to get in myself, I will leave a trail. I'm too rusty. I hate relying on Tracker, putting him in this position, but I need to find out about Ian.

Steve finds me sitting in front of the dark computer screen, my head in my hands.

'Did everything go OK?' he asks tentatively.

I look up at him. 'I know you want to help, but this might be bigger than I thought. I can't put you in danger. I'm going to have to leave.' I stand up, realizing that I have no clothes except the ones I wore yesterday. Maybe I can borrow some from Jeanine or Veronica. I am sure they'll have heard by now about my house and the state it was in when the police arrived, and they will want to help. But can I afford to lean on any more friends?

'Who is after you, Nicole? Just answer that, OK? And let me be the judge of how much danger I'm in.'

I can't help myself. I give him a small smile. 'The FBI. Ian. The people he was working for.' I don't mention my father or Tony DeMarco.

His eyebrows are clear up into his forehead. 'You're kidding.'

'I wish I wasn't.'

He sees now that I am dead serious. 'Can't the FBI help you?' he asks innocently.

I chuckle. 'The FBI wants to put me in prison, Steve. For a very long time.'

Steve shakes his head slowly. 'This is beginning to sound like one of those bestselling novels. The FBI and computer hackers.'

And murder. But I can't tell him that. He will find out. Just not now. I have already been diminished in his eyes. I am not ready for more.

'I'm going to need a new laptop,' I tell him.

Steve eyes me warily, and then says, 'Mike Burns lives over near the Great Salt Pond. He refurbishes machines in his house. It's not really a business officially, but it is. It's just not something he tells the IRS about.'

I don't like the idea of a refurbished computer, but it will have to do. And if Mike Burns is running a business without really running a business, I can count on his discretion.

'I'll take you over there,' Steve offers. 'After you get dressed.'

I shake my head. 'I'll find my way.' And then I remember. My bike. He is one step ahead of me.

'I'll take you down to the Town Dock. Maybe you can rent a bike.'

I hate the idea of renting a bike that isn't mine. But I have no choice. 'Thanks, Steve.' I pause. 'For everything.'

When Steve drops me at the dock, he gives me a little worried wave. But I see a ferry coming in, packed with tourists. It's starting, and I am comforted by the fact that Steve will be busy for at least the next couple of hours. Busy enough to leave me alone and let me do what I have to. He has given me Mike Burns's address and has called ahead, telling him to expect me.

I find my way to the bike rental shop where I do my business. The bikes are lined up in a row, like soldiers, but I balk at their ordinariness. I need something more powerful, something with more speed.

Like the mopeds that are lined up next to them.

I have no driver's license, though, nothing that would allow me to rent one. For the first time, I decide to use my relationship with Pete in a way that's not altogether honest.

I put on my best smile and walk into the shop. It is a big garage with bikes hanging on walls, helmets filling shelves, baskets tucked inside each other in the corner. It is a mess, and it smells like rubber and gasoline. I drink in the scent.

'Hey, Pete,' I say to his back.

Pete Marley and I struck up our partnership just a week after

I arrived on the island. He is overweight, but his fingers are nimble and he can fix anything that's wrong with a bike.

'Nicole. I heard. Are you OK?' His voice is laced with concern. I am not surprised he knows. The island is small.

'Yeah, I'm OK.' But I see there is something else.

'A guy was here, asking a lot of questions about you.' He pauses. 'Not *that* guy,' he adds, and I know whom he means.

I feel a flutter in the middle of my chest. Carmine has been busy visiting my friends. 'What sort of things is he asking about?'

'Like, when do you do your tours, that sort of thing. He wanted your phone number. Something funny about him, though. Didn't feel right. I had him leave his info for you.' Pete reaches under his counter and pulls out a book, flips through it and turns it around so I can see.

Tony M is all it says. And a phone number. With a Miami exchange. 'Thanks, Pete. You did the right thing. I appreciate it.'

'You familiar with him?'

'Yeah. I am.' I say nothing more, and in true Yankee tradition, Pete merely nods.

'OK, then.' He seems to know that I am not going to take down the number for myself. He slips the book back under the counter.

'I need some transportation,' I say as calmly as I can. It is not as though I have not expected Carmine to start tracking me all over the island. It just makes me feel as though I have to move more quickly, although to what end, I am still not quite sure. Again I think of Ian and wonder where he is. Despite the way we'd left things, I am worried about him.

Pete waves his arm across his body. 'Any bike of mine is a bike of yours.'

'Until I can replace mine,' I assure him. 'But I was wondering if I could take a moped. Just for a couple hours.'

His eyebrows rise slightly. 'Never took you for a biker chick,' he teases.

I remember my chat handle and then push it aside. 'Just for a couple hours,' I say again, then wait for him to give me the contract and ask me for my license.

But instead, Pete reaches around to the board behind him and plucks a set of keys off it. He doesn't ask for a driver's license. He may not even know that I don't have one, which makes it easier.

'Number four. It's out front. The number's on the gas tank.' He pauses. 'You've driven one before?'

I remember the wind in my hair as I sped down the Rickenbacker Causeway. It had been Zeke's bike, the real Zeke, and he was behind me, his arms wrapped around me as he whispered instructions in my ear.

'Absolutely,' I assure Pete, taking the keys. He doesn't have to know it was so long ago.

But somehow he does know, and he follows me outside to the line of mopeds. Despite his girth, he slips between them and pulls one out. It is nondescript, a dull midnight blue. He climbs over the seat and twists the handle as he pushes down on the pedal. The engine roars to life, and he climbs off it, handing it to me. I straddle it, but then he holds up his hand to tell me to wait, runs back inside and comes out again with a helmet, which he fits over my head. It is bigger than a bike helmet, and perhaps it will disguise me a little more. No one will think to point me out on a moped to a stranger.

'Be careful,' he says loudly as I teeter on the moped, but I soon have my wits about me and remember how it's done.

It's different riding a machine than a bicycle. It's more clumsy between my legs, and I begin to think that I could have gone just as fast on a bike. My bike. But the damage is done, and I'm here, now, making my way toward Great Salt Pond and Mike Burns and his refurbished computers.

I am trying to be aware of my surroundings, possible strangers – or not – but instead I am remembering Zeke; the moped is bringing it all back.

Every once in a while, FBI agents would show up at the house in Miami and puff up their chests and let my father know they were watching him. By the time it was Zeke's turn, my father had been out of prison for eight years and I had stolen millions and transferred the money to accounts all over the world.

My father wasn't home that day. But I was.

It was too coincidental, me meeting Zeke. He knew I was the hacker, and it was me he was there to see, not my father.

He didn't have the proof yet – they were still trying to follow my tracks – but I didn't know any of that then.

It wasn't all lightning and thunderbolts when he walked around the pool, casting his shadow over me as I quickly closed my laptop and shoved it underneath the chaise lounge. I squinted up through the sunlight, covering my eyes with my hand, but I couldn't make out his features.

'What can I do for you?' I asked the shadow.

He flashed a badge. 'I'm Special Agent Zeke Chapman. I understand your father isn't home.'

I shifted up onto my elbow to get a better look, but didn't expect much. They'd all paraded through here, these agents on their babysitting missions, usually washed up and at the end of their careers.

I was surprised to see he was good looking. And young. Maybe only a little older than me. The way he wore his suit jacket told me he worked out. I sat up.

'I'm Tina Adler,' I said, holding out my hand.

He hesitated, then took it. His hand was large and calloused, not like that of a man who worked behind a desk all day. I swung my legs over the lounge and offered him a drink. I was wearing a pair of running shorts and a tank top, and as I stood, I toed my laptop even further underneath the lounge.

'I hope I'm not interrupting anything,' he said, staring at my feet, and I realized I hadn't pulled anything over on him. Maybe that's when he knew for sure, or maybe I just wanted him to be that smart.

I shrugged. 'Not much.' I stared into his eyes then, straight on, daring him to challenge me. He blinked a few times, and I realized he was trying not to smile.

'Do you know where your father is?' he asked, his voice a little more rough, forcing himself to be all business.

'I'm not his keeper,' I said. 'He might be at his club.'

'He's not there.'

'Well, then, I don't know where he is. Sorry.'

Zeke turned and looked out over the pool at the beach and the deep blue ocean beyond. 'Nice place.'

'It's OK.'

If my nonchalance threw him, he didn't show it.

'Is this what you do with your days, Miss Adler?' He hadn't turned back around and was talking to the ocean. 'Sit by the pool and watch the ocean?'

'It could be worse,' I said flippantly, although he had just watered that small seed of guilt that ran through me occasionally. I hadn't done anything with my life. Nothing legitimate, anyway. I didn't need a job. I had my father's money – and the money that was sitting in those accounts in the Caymans in the Caribbean and the Channel Islands across the Atlantic. But every once in a while, I wondered if this was all there was and I thought about a real job – something that didn't mean I'd be lurking around the Internet, trying to see what I could get into without getting caught.

Irritated that his question had stirred up those feelings, I got up. 'I'll walk you out,' I offered.

He turned back then, his hands pulling his jacket tighter around him, and I saw the wedding ring glint in the sun.

'How long have you been married?' I asked as we walked through the French doors.

'Three years.' His expression changed slightly, and I wasn't sure it was a happy marriage.

When I kissed him three days later, I knew for sure.

TWENTY

M ike Burns lives in a small cottage, not unlike mine. It is nicely kept, a pale yellow with blue shutters and bright pink azaleas flanking the front steps. Just as I cut the engine of the moped and set it up on its stand, the door opens.

'Nicole Jones?'

He is larger than I thought he would be, both in height and weight. He has to be six three or four, maybe three hundred pounds – bigger than Pete, even. A blue bandanna is wrapped around his head, which I suspect is bald because there are no tufts of hair seeping out anywhere. His cheeks are ruddy, as though he has just worked out, or maybe it is just the walk from inside to out. But his eyes are a bright blue, matching the shutters, and his smile is warm.

I nod, holding out my hand. He takes it gently, his smile widening.

'I've seen you at the Kittens.'

I don't generally go to the Yellow Kittens for drinks, preferring Club Soda, but occasionally Steve and I decide we need a change of scenery. I am surprised that he doesn't stand out in my memory, since his appearance seems unforgettable. But maybe that is his secret: he has learned to stay under the radar because of his unrecorded business and somehow, physically, he is able to do that as well.

He leads me inside, and I see that it's not only the outside that's well kept. The sleek wood floors shine, as though he has just had them done, and the furniture is modern and color coordinated. I wonder if there is a Mrs Burns who's responsible for this but feel it would be uncouth to ask.

Mike leads me down a hallway, but before we reach the end of it, he turns into a room to our left. I see immediately that this is his office space. Laptops, desktops, tablets and smartphones litter the myriad shelving lined up against every wall. A desk sits in the middle. Three laptops are open and powering up on its surface.

He doesn't stop but settles into an office chair that looks particularly ergonomic and capable of handling his girth. He reaches around one of the laptops on the desk and pulls out one that looks exactly like the one Ian gave me.

'I'll be honest with you,' he says, his tone extremely business-like now, 'this little baby had coffee spilled on the keyboard. But I've replaced the whole motherboard, and it's just fine now.'

I am leery. I need something that will be reliable. It cannot fail.

'Do you have one that's maybe just a little old? I don't really want one that's had to be completely rebuilt because of a cup of coffee.'

Mike narrows his eyes at me, seeing me for the first time as someone who perhaps knows more than he originally thought. 'I get it,' he says, getting up and circling the room, touching the machines on the shelves gently, as though his fingertips will tell him which one is the best one for me.

Finally he stops, runs his hand along the top of a laptop that again looks like the one I'd had. He picks it up and brings it over to the desk, opens it and boots it up.

'Someone brought this one in a couple of weeks back. Said it was outdated and they were getting a new one. I bought it off him for a lot less than he'd paid for it, but he was happy and I was happy, because all it needed was an update to the new oper- ating system. Works like a dream now.' He gestures for me to come closer to take a look.

If he hadn't told me that it came in a couple weeks ago, I would think that it is actually the laptop I'd had. But whoever had taken that one wouldn't bring it to Mike's clandestine busi- ness, because that person was looking for something. Clues that he wouldn't find. That didn't mean, however, he wasn't looking closely.

I want to check it out, to make sure it works OK, and Mike senses that. He runs me through the systems folder, showing me how much power it has. He points out that it has the most updated word processing program, PowerPoint, Excel and all of those business software programs that I have no use for. But I pretend to be interested in his demonstrations of how each works and works fast, proving that the update has been successful. He then shows me how fast the Internet connection is, even though that would vary with whatever type of connection you'd have.

'I think this one is fine,' I say. 'You've done a great job.'

He gets up, a big smile on his face, pleased that he has pleased me, and rummages around on the bottom shelf behind him. He produces a laptop backpack. 'I'll throw this one in for nothing,' he says, putting the laptop and its power cord inside.

I realize now that I have no money for him, but he interrupts my panic by saying, 'Steve told me he's going to drop by later with the cash. It's all taken care of.'

I am more indebted to Steve than I should be. Again I worry that he is getting in too deep, that if he keeps on sticking with me, he is going to get hurt. But I need his help; I can't do this alone right now. I push away my thoughts as I take the bag.

'Thanks, Mike. I really appreciate it.'

'Thank Steve.'

'I certainly will.'

'I heard about what happened to your place. Sucks.'

'Yeah, it does.'

'So do they think it's that FBI guy?'

Word has not gotten out that Ian is not really FBI, and I am happy that Frank Cooper is keeping that under wraps, although I am wondering just how he's getting along with his investigation. Was the BMW impounded from the airport lot, or is it still there? How soon will he find out who I really am?

A sudden urgency hits me. I thank Mike again and try not to show that I am eager to get out of there. He walks me out to the moped. There is a basket on the front, so I tuck the backpack with the laptop inside it.

'You've got one of Pete's,' Mike says matter-of-factly.

'That's right.'

'Good guy, Pete.'

'Yes, he is.' I am surprised my voice is not giving me away. I climb on the moped and start it up easily, as though I have been riding one of these and not a bicycle for fifteen years. I give Mike a short wave as I go down the driveway and out into the street.

The airport is in the middle of the island. I head up Old Town Road, feeling almost safe in my helmet since I am unrecognizable in it. I think about the route I would take on my bike, turning onto Center Road and then down Cooneymus toward Rodman's Hollow. It feels like years since I've been there, rather than merely days.

I know as I approach the airport that I am avoiding even trying to do the job I gave Tracker, but I need to satisfy this itch before I can settle in with the new laptop.

The BMW is parked outside Bethany's Airport Diner. I spot it immediately, next to a blue pickup that I recognize belongs to Will, the short order cook. There are a few other cars in the lot, but none that I can identify. I pull up next to the BMW. I commit the plate number to memory as I climb off the moped and circle the black car.

I glance around to see if anyone is noticing me lurking here, but I see no one. I skirt around to the driver's side and peer inside. It is immaculate, not even a slip of paper on the dash or between the seats. I straighten up as I hear the door to the diner open and a middle-aged man emerges. He doesn't even look my way as he goes over to a Toyota, climbs in and pulls out.

I tug off the helmet and loop the strap around my arm, grabbing the backpack out of the basket as I pass the moped and go inside. The scent of coffee hits my nose, and I slide onto a stool at the counter.

Will turns around and grins. 'What can I get for you, Nicole?'

'Just a coffee. To go.' I put the helmet and pack on the seat next to me. There are six other people in here: a young couple staring into each other's eyes over plates of pancakes, a man wearing coveralls and two women about my age with coffee and Danish.

'Heard what happened. You OK?' Will asks as he puts the cup down in front of me and pours.

'I'm OK. Where's Mary today?'

'Morning off. She'll be here for lunch. Not too many folks here yet, so I figured I could handle it.'

'I figured you might have more of a crowd here, what with the cops and all.'

Will's eyes drift over to the window. 'Yeah, they were here.

Searched that car outside – the Beemer. Asked if I saw the guy who drove it.' He paused. 'Is it that guy? The one who trashed your place?'

I nod and take a sip of the coffee. It's too strong, as usual, but I need the jolt. 'You didn't see him, then?' I ask, trying to act casual.

'Oh, I did see him. Tall, good-looking guy, right?' He doesn't wait for me to answer. 'He was here yesterday. Had a bowl of chowder. But this was before I knew anything, otherwise I would've called Frank Cooper.' He is concerned that I'm going to blame him for what happened.

'Don't worry about it, Will. You couldn't know.'

He seems relieved and smiles.

'So he didn't leave in the car.' I am thinking out loud.

But Will thinks I am asking him a question. He shakes his head. 'I got busy, so I didn't notice where he went when he left. But obviously he didn't leave in the Beemer. It was here all night.'

'You never saw him again?'

Will narrows his eyes at me. 'I told Frank Cooper all this.'

I shrug, pretending nonchalance. 'Frank hasn't told me much. But I really would like to find this guy.'

'I bet you do.' He hesitates, and I can see that he wants to tell me something more. I wait only a few seconds. 'There is something else. Frank knows already, so it's probably OK if I tell you.'

His tone is slow, methodical, and I want to pull it out of him, but I continue to wait, my heartbeat pounding inside my chest with impatience.

'You know Chip Parsons?'

It takes me a second, and then I remember. He's the guy from the Yellow Kittens who Steve says has a crush on me.

Will clears his throat. 'Saw Chip last night at the Kittens. He told me the guy chartered one of his boats. Paid upfront and all. He was supposed to come by yesterday afternoon, but he never showed.'

TWENTY-ONE

Why would Ian charter a fishing boat?

'When did this happen?' I ask, my mouth so dry it feels like the words are being formed around cotton balls. 'I mean, when did he talk to Chip about the boat?'

'Two days ago.'

'So he was going fishing?'

Will shrugs. 'Don't think so. He chartered Chip's motorboat.'

I am trying to wrap my head around this. 'Was Chip going to take him out?'

'No, guess he was going alone.'

My throat becomes constricted, and I cannot speak. He chartered the boat two days ago. Did he think that I would have already done the job for him and he could escape the island without me knowing? Of course he did. He was going to leave me here for Carmine and whoever else might be coming after me. I shouldn't be surprised.

I find my voice. 'Does Chip trust people that much, to let them take his boat out by themselves?'

Will chuckles. 'Frank made him feel like a real horse's ass for agreeing to it, but the guy paid him extra. A lot extra. In cash.' He starts wiping down the counter, and I know I'm being dismissed. I have gotten as much out of him that I'm going to get.

'I really appreciate this, Will,' I say, and he gives me a short nod. I take the coffee cup, find a crumpled dollar bill in my pocket and toss it on the counter, wishing I could leave more, but I don't have any more.

I head outside and give the Beemer a glance, but it's not going to tell me anything. Frank Cooper is doing his job, and now I have mine to do.

I realize I have nowhere to put the coffee, so I take a sip before tossing it in the trashcan next to the door. I climb onto the moped and start it up. I have nowhere to go, though. I can't go back to my house, and I don't want to risk Steve's anymore. I am hoping that this helmet is disguising me enough, although I'm not a hundred percent sure.

I take off down the road and soon I'm heading to Old Harbor. I follow the road past the dock, the National Hotel and around the corner. Without realizing it, I find myself in front of the Sunswept Spa. I stop the moped in front, trying to figure out my next move, but I linger too long. The door swings open and Jeanine comes out, scurrying toward me. I can't leave now.

She pulls me into a long hug, and for a moment I allow myself to sink into her, the strawberry scent of her shampoo familiar and comforting. But then I pull away.

'Are you OK?' Jeanine asks, the concern lacing her tone. She reaches over and holds my upper arm, as if knowing I need the touch of a friend.

I manage a small smile. 'I've been better.'

'I saw you from the window.' She frowns at the moped. 'I've never seen you on one of these before.'

I give her a sheepish look. 'My bike's gone. I needed something to get around on, and Pete let me use it.'

She eyes the backpack in the basket. The laptop is peeking out from the corner where I have not zipped it shut.

'I stopped over at Mike Burns's earlier.'

I don't have to explain further. It's clear from her expression that she knows about Mike's unofficial business, which tells me that it's the worst-kept secret on the island.

I glance at the spa building and it gives me an idea. 'You wouldn't have a place I could hang out in for a little while, would you? Do you have wireless?'

She gives me a funny look, but it is gone quickly. 'Sure, I guess so. I've got a room in the back.'

She indicates I should follow her, her long skirt swishing as we walk. As I step through the doorway, she cups her hand under my elbow, as though I need the support.

Perhaps I do.

Jeanine leads me down a dark hallway into a room that has an extra massage bed on one side and a washer and dryer on the other. Shelves next to the dryer are filled with white, fluffy towels, bathrobes and white sheets used on the massage tables. A tall shelving unit filled with a massive number of bottles is against the third wall. I peer closely at the bottles, thinking of my smashed jars, and see they are massage oils.

Jeanine chuckles. 'I'm a little bit of an oil hoarder.' She clears off a small table that seems to be used for folding the towels and sheets and pulls over a step stool that's high enough to use as a chair. 'I hope this is OK,' she says apologetically.

'It's fine. Really.' She has no idea that once I begin my work, I will not even notice my surroundings. 'Jeanine, has anyone been around asking about me? I mean, a stranger?'

She frowns, and I see the answer in her face before she says anything. 'No. Who would be asking about you?'

While it would be easy for Carmine to go into a gallery or to ask about my bike tours, it would be more difficult for him to come to a spa and start asking questions. But there is no guarantee that he is not watching the spa, waiting for Jeanine to leave for the day and follow her.

'You haven't seen anyone hanging around outside, have you? A tall man, salt-and-pepper hair, in an overcoat?'

'No.' She is puzzled by my questions. 'Who is he?'

'Just someone who's been asking about me. If you see him, tell me, and then go tell Frank Cooper.'

She chews on her lip for a few seconds. 'So we're not talking about Zeke Chapman?'

I shake my head, unable to look her in the eye.

'Nicole, I'm worried about you.'

'I'll be OK.'

'What is it you need? Can I be any help?'

Her kindness brings a tear to my eye. I blink it away quickly. 'No, this is help enough. But please don't tell anyone I'm here, OK?'

I am struck with an overwhelming urge to tell her everything, as I have told Steve, but I can't put her at risk, too. It is bad enough Steve knows. She comes over to me and gives me a hug before heading back out, but before she leaves the room, she gives me a look that tells me she is not going to give up on finding out what this secret is that I'm not telling her.

'I'll come back in an hour, when I'm done with my client, OK?' she says at the door. 'Maybe then I can work some hot stone magic on you. You're really out of sync.'

No kidding. The door closes, and I am alone.

Except that I'm not. Not really. I open the laptop and hope that Mike has sold me something that works the way it should. I am still leery of refurbished computers, because even though he has told me he's only updated this, he could be lying.

I do a quick check of the system. The history has been wiped clean, as have any bookmarks or any signs that anyone else has ever used this computer. But with a few keystrokes, I could find out everything about it and about who owned it before.

I don't feel like I have the time or the curiosity, though, right now. I type in the VPN URL and navigate my way through it and into the chat room, where Tracker has left me the message he promised. There they are. The list of account numbers. I sit and stare at them, knowing that they are the reason I am holed up in this room, hiding from everyone. The reason why I have been holed up on an island for fifteen years.

But maybe now they can set me free.

I study the numbers, looking at each one carefully, trying to see if there is any sort of pattern. Trying to see if one stands out as different from the others. But I see nothing; they are random in their purest form. It will only be after I find out to whom they belong that the lines might be drawn.

My fingers hover over the keyboard. They are trembling. Part of me is scared, but there is another part of me, that part of me that came back when I saw Ian, that is eager to get started, to prove to myself again that I can do this.

I know the bank that housed these accounts, and suddenly I am transported back. It is as though no time has passed at all, and I am on autopilot. I hunch over the laptop, my fingers flying. The bank probably closed the accounts we'd stolen from, but new ones would have been created, as long as the account owners wanted to stay with the bank. I'm sure the bank made it worth their while, to keep the business. These accounts, while no longer active, would still be in the system, however. Nothing is ever really lost in a computer. What's challenging is finding out where everything might be.

The portal I used before is closed. I sit back and think, trying to remember how I would circumvent the system and find another portal. An open one. I try to think like Tracker. Soon

I am navigating the code, searching for a portal I can slip behind and get inside.

I hear a knock on the door, and it opens slightly. 'Nicole? Can I come in?' Jeanine doesn't wait for an answer, slips in and puts a cup of chai tea on the table next to me. The moment I heard the knock, I closed the laptop cover, and she is staring at it. 'What are you doing? You've been in here two hours already.'

I haven't paid attention, but I'm not surprised that it's been so long. I glance at my watch. I want to see if Tracker has left another message in the chat room. Why didn't I get two laptops from Mike? I don't want to stop what I've already done.

I have no choice.

'Jeanine, do you have a laptop I can borrow?'

She frowns, clearly confused.

'I need two. I've got some stuff I need to do, and it's hard with just one.' I'd had four, back in the day. A couple of desktops and a couple of laptops. Some girls bought shoes; I bought computers.

'What sort of stuff?' Jeanine is suspicious. Her mouth has puckered into a thin line.

'Don't worry. I'm just trying to get some information.'

'Is it illegal?'

'No.' The lie slips off my tongue easily, as have all the other lies I have told her through the years.

While she has never suspected my other lies, this one she does not believe. But she disappears through the door and, after a few minutes, comes back with a laptop that is a lot older than the one I'm using.

'Will this do?' she asks, an edge in her voice.

I nod, taking it from her, putting it next to the other and booting it up. 'Thanks.'

'I don't want to get in trouble,' she warns.

'You won't. I promise.' I can keep this promise. No one will know what's been done on this computer when I'm finished with it.

'Do you want a sandwich?'

'I'm not hungry. But thanks.' My fingers are twitching. I have to get back to this. She notices and to her credit leaves and closes the door behind her. I don't have much time. I can't stay here much longer. I have already stayed too long.

I use Jeanine's laptop to get into the chat room. I am not completely surprised to find Tracker is here. I tell him I am having trouble finding an open portal to get the account information.

Don't worry about it, he writes. I didn't have trouble. On either front.

My ego is crushed. I wanted so much to get in myself. I remind myself that he has not taken fifteen years off.

I'm sending you the list of account owners and their Socials. You might be interested to know that one of those names you wanted me to check is on that list.

I do a double take. Which one?

Paul Michaels. And I only found him on the FBI site in connection with the theft as a victim. Nothing else.

I sit back, trying to wrap my head around this information. He was a victim? How can that be?

Tiny?

Tracker thinks I have left.

I'm still here.

The other name? Ian Cartwright? He's dead.

TWENTY-TWO

D ead? But that's not right. He was in my house. In my bed. He is using a dead man's name, that's all. He, himself, is not dead. When I close my eyes, I can still see him over me, whispering to me.

How? I manage to write, my hands trembling as they touch the keys.

Suicide. Paris. Fifteen years ago.

A date?

June the eleventh.

A day after I left him there.

I am not sure what all of this means.

How did you find out? I ask. Was it online?

It was in the FBI file. Newspapers don't report suicides in private places.

How did he do it?

Blew his head off on a houseboat on the Seine. Police found his passport. Couple who lived on the houseboat next to his identified the body, but it sounds like it was more a generalization.

I can read between the lines. No facial identification. His face was gone.

So they didn't check fingerprints or anything?

Sounds like they relied on the ID given and the passport. FBI made a note in the file from the theft. Story ends there.

But it doesn't. The story begins again here, on Block Island.

I guess it's easy for a dead man to take a dead man's name. Who's going to know? But did he just take Zeke's name here, for my benefit? What name – or names – has he been using all these years?

And then something Tracker has told me hits me hard. I begin typing. The FBI made a note about Ian's death in the file about the bank theft?

That's right.

I sit and stare at the screen for a few minutes, trying to digest all of the information Tracker has given me. But then I have another thought, something so simple that I scare myself.

Ian was identified with his passport. The only passport he had, at least that I knew about, was the passport with the name Paul Michaels. What was he doing with a passport with his real name on it?

And why would the FBI have this in their files?

Because one of their own was killed on the same houseboat the day before.

Zeke knew who Ian was. Zeke had told me himself. He told me he could protect me as long I testified against Ian. But I was scared and not sure I could believe him. He was pushing me to tell him who Ian's source was at the bank, but I could honestly say I knew nothing about that. Zeke didn't believe me.

What if after Zeke was killed and I left Ian in Paris, Ian decided to get even with me? What if he went to the FBI and told them he'd help them find me, told them it was all me? What if they gave *him* protection, and his 'death' was staged?

I mentally slap myself. I am paranoid. But what if I'm right?

Still, it has taken him fifteen years to find me. Would the FBI wait that long? I don't know enough about how witness protection works to even guess.

I see the file that Tracker has left me, and I download it. The list of names springs up on the screen, momentarily distracting me. I immediately find Paul Michaels.

My memory slips back to that day when Ian and I were in bed, brainstorming names we would get on our fake passports.

'Are you sure you can get them?' he asked, his arm slung around me as he nuzzled my neck.

I leaned in toward him. 'I can do anything,' I promised, and he smiled.

'I've always wanted to be a Paul,' he said. 'Would you love me as a Paul?'

'I would love you as anything.' It was before Zeke, before the job. We knew we would need fake IDs if it all fell apart. We were getting our ducks in a row; we wanted to be prepared for anything.

'Will they be authentic?'

I rolled away from him and pretended to pout. 'You have no faith in my abilities.'

'I know what I have faith in,' he said, grabbing me and pulling me toward him. Three days later, we had the passports and the money. But we didn't use the passports for another month.

I look back at the list of names, which takes up two screens. I wonder about the alias. I find it again and stare at it, as if it will start telling me something if I wait long enough.

Tracker is still here. I put my hands on the keys, my head racing, and begin to type.

I want current account information for Paul Michaels. Also addresses and any information we can get. I know I can do a Google search, but I need more than Google can give me. I already have a Social, but I need everything to find out who Paul Michaels is, if he is, in fact, a real person. There's a FAQ form on the website.

Before I can say more, Tracker's message appears. Source code.

I am a step ahead of him for the first time, pulling up the source code for the web page on Jeanine's computer. I scan it. Just as I suspected. A file name for the template of the form. I find what I'm looking for and substitute another code, which brings up the password file for the server.

Be careful of shadows, Tracker has typed. He knows what I am doing. He may likely be doing the same thing.

But I don't see any sign of shadows, which is when a system is spying on itself to make sure someone isn't getting into areas they're not supposed to.

Problem is I now merely have a list of passwords. I need the one for the firewall. I have to get behind it, add a port that I can use to get in easily to start my search.

I'm running a search, Tracker writes, verifying that he's gotten the same list. It's almost as if we are one person doing this. It could take a while.

I don't have 'a while,' but some things can't be rushed. This could take an hour or three days. Or longer.

I create a new tab on my laptop and, just for my own peace of mind, do a Google search on Paul Michaels.

It seems to be a popular name, and I scan the sites, but nothing pops out at me. And then I have another thought. I type in 'Amelie Renaud.' That was the name on my passport, the one I used to get to Paris.

I can barely see the search results because my head begins to spin. I switch to the file that Tracker sent me. The one with the list of account owners we'd stolen from.

I scan through the list until I find it.

Amelie Renaud.

I frantically try to remember how I came up with that name, pulling memories out of my head like socks out of a drawer. Ian, after our discussion about whether I'd love him as a Paul, telling me that I remind him of an Amelie, a childhood friend. He said I should have a French last name. Renaud was good, he'd said.

I take note of the Social Security number for Amelie Renaud. It isn't mine. Whose is it? Is there really an Amelie Renaud? Is it just a coincidence?

I toss that thought aside. There is nothing coincidental about any of this.

A light tap on the door startles me, and before I can close the laptops, Jeanine comes in. She wears a frown, her arms crossed over her chest.

'Nicole? It's been hours.'

I glance at the clock on the screen and see that it has – it's supper time. I can't log off the search, though, it has to keep running. 'Is it OK if I stay here tonight?' I ask. I glance over at the massage table in the corner. 'I can sleep there. It's fine.' I am not going to sleep.

Jeanine comes closer, not trying to see what's on the computer screen, but staring at my face as if she's never seen me before.

I'm not sure she has. This person sitting in front of two computer screens in the dark, this person is me. The real me. I have left Nicole Jones behind, with her bike and her paintings and her cozy little house.

'Can I bring you something to eat?' she asks.

'Sure,' I say, although I'm not really hungry. But it will give her something to do, something that will keep her away for a little while longer.

'Steve called, looking for you. I told him you were here.' She hugs herself tighter. 'He's coming by.'

I pretend that this is not an inconvenience. 'OK.'

'He said something about talking to Frank Cooper.'

I stop breathing for a second. Has Frank finally discovered who I really am? I try to keep my tone light. 'Did he talk to him? Is there some news?'

Jeanine shakes her head. 'I don't know. You'll have to ask him when he gets here. I'll get you some food.' She disappears out the door, leaving me alone.

I flip up the laptop cover to see a message from Tracker.

Got it.

I know he means the password for the firewall. I am crushed; the old competitiveness is back.

You've been away a long time, he writes, and again I am struck by how much our minds meld. We were like this back in the day; it has been so easy to fall into our old rhythm.

What do you have? I ask.

Current credit card number and an address. He has gone even further than the firewall. He has gotten all the way in. I am kicking myself for giving it all up, for not being able to hold my own anymore.

I have done a complete one-eighty. Just a couple of weeks ago, I was content with my life, the life I'd created for myself.

Within seconds, the information Tracker has discovered appears on my screen. I scan it. Paul Michaels lives in Los Angeles.

But this isn't all I need anymore. **I've got another name. Amelie Renaud.**

Give me a few minutes.

I want to beat him to this one, but I don't have time to do anything because the door opens and Jeanine comes in with a plate. It's full of sprouts and sliced tomatoes and cucumbers and chick peas. I pick up the scent of raspberries. She has given me some of her homemade vinaigrette. A crispy flatbread sits next to the salad.

'I hope this is OK,' she says apologetically, her eyes veering toward the laptop screens. I have not closed them. 'What are you doing?' The question is pointed; she expects an answer.

'I'm trying to find out information about the man who's on the island,' I explain.

She puts the plate down next to me, and I pick up the fork and spear a tomato. It is sweet and juicy, and I realize I'm hungrier than I thought.

'The man you've been sleeping with?' she asks, her eyebrows rising into her forehead.

'The one and the same,' I say.

'I thought you said his name was Zeke.' She notices that I am looking at information on Paul Michaels.

'No. It's not.' I don't know how much more I can say without telling her everything.

'So what is his name?'

Just then, a message pops up on the screen, distracting her.

'Who's Tracker?'

But I am not thinking about how to explain it to her. I am seeing that Tracker has found Amelie. She is in Paris.

I am not quite sure how to process this. Amelie Renaud is a real person, not just a figment of my imagination. Not just a name on a passport that I have used.

The passport.

I used it when I came back. It was in my backpack as I crossed over to the island on the ferry.

I never got rid of it. I didn't expect to stay here, so I kept it close by for another quick escape. But as the years passed, I almost forgot that it existed. When I close my eyes, I can see its hiding place.

Its expiration date is long past. But I need to go get it. Before the police find it.

TWENTY-THREE

'Who is Tracker?' Jeanine is still asking. She has pulled up a stool and is staring at my screens. 'What's that?' She points at the code.

'I just needed to find out some information,' I say.

'From where?' Her tone is casual, but I can see the determination in her eyes. She does not want to be left out. 'Who is Tracker?' she repeats, not willing to give it up.

'An old friend. He's helping me.'

'Helping you do what?'

I stall by taking a big forkful of salad. In the meantime, the door creaks open and Steve sticks his head in. He looks from me to Jeanine and then at the computers in front of me.

'So have you told her, then?' he asks, coming in and shutting the door behind him.

'She has told me very little,' Jeanine says, with a bit of an attitude. 'I've brought her food and a laptop, but she won't say much. She's got some friend named Tracker.'

'Oh, yes, Tracker,' Steve says, as though he and Tracker go way back. I am still eating, hoping to stall as long as possible.

'So you know who this Tracker person is?' Jeanine demands, her hands on her hips as she confronts him.

Steve gives her a smile. 'Yes.' And he turns to me. 'Nicole, are you going to tell her?'

If I tell Jeanine, that's one more person who knows. One more person whom I will probably be putting in danger. She can get the *Reader's Digest* version. I swallow, then say, 'Zeke isn't Zeke. He's an old boyfriend named Ian, and he's been looking for me because I left him without even leaving a note.'

'That's all?' she asks, knowing it isn't.

I nod. 'That's all.' I shoot Steve a look that tells him if he spills any more of the story, he's going to regret it. He seems to get it, because he doesn't push it. Instead, he says something I'm not expecting.

'Frank Cooper is looking for you.' His expression is neutral. I can't tell if Frank Cooper looking for me is good or bad.

'Did he say why?' My mouth has gone dry; it is all I can do to get the words out.

'He said he needs to see you as soon as possible. He said it would be best if you came to him.' He lets that lie between us a few seconds, then adds, 'I told him I didn't know where you were, but if I found you, I'd let you know.'

Steve has covered his bases. And I also notice that he is not pushing me out the door. Does he have the same ominous feeling about this that I do?

'He chartered one of Chip Parsons's boats,' I say. 'Ian, I mean. Not Frank. But he didn't show.'

'How do you know that?'

'Talked to Will at Bethany's. He saw Chip at the Kittens last night.'

Steve's eyebrows rise into his forehead. 'Why were you out at the airport? Was it because the car is there?'

And then I remember the license plate.

I feel a sudden surge of adrenaline. This is something I can do, something I can find out. Granted, Frank Cooper probably already knows, but he won't tell me, I feel pretty sure of that.

I don't answer Steve, but turn my back on him and Jeanine and find the website I need. It doesn't matter anymore; Steve knows, and Jeanine suspects, so I let them watch me at work.

It is surprisingly easy to find an open portal on this site. I make a mental note that after all this I need to contact them about that. I used to do that, sometimes, back then: hack in somewhere just to see if I could and if so, I would anonymously let the system's owners know, so they could add security and keep people like me out. I know there are hackers who do that on a regular basis; some companies specifically hire hackers to find security holes in their systems.

Maybe if I survive all this, I can start a new business.

I enter the BMW's license plate number and wait. Steve and Jeanine are ominously quiet behind me, but I can feel their eyes on me, on the computers, on what I am doing.

When the information pops up on the screen, I can barely believe my eyes.

The BMW is registered to Tony DeMarco.

Why is Ian driving a car registered to *him*?

My head is spinning, and I barely hear Steve's voice, until he puts his hand on my shoulder and asks, 'What does this mean, Nicole?'

I shake my head.

'Who is Anthony DeMarco?' Jeanine asks.

If I had known what the search would bring up, I would not have brazenly done it in front of her. Because now I really do need to give her an answer.

'He was one of my father's business associates,' I say flatly, unable to look at her for all the lies I have told her over the years.

'Your father?' In all these years, Jeanine has not known me to have any family, and now I have a father.

I nod, but I am distracted. Why is Ian driving Tony's car?

The question keeps circulating in my head until it lands on something that makes my heart pound. I have been worried for Ian with Carmine here, but he did tell me that he was only the first one here. Maybe he was sent ahead, and now that Carmine has arrived, that's why he's disappeared. Maybe that's why he chartered Chip Parsons's boat. Because his job was done.

But that was wrong. The job wasn't done. I hadn't done what he'd asked. I'd run away from him.

I look from Steve to Jeanine. 'I can't tell you any more. I think that it could be really risky.'

'Risky, how?' Jeanine demands, her brow knitted into a frown.

'There are some scary people after me.'

The money wasn't all going to Ian and me. It was going to the person who'd set the whole plan in motion from the start. Who'd known that I could do the job but would never do it if he were the one to ask. He had to find someone who I would do it for: a poor boy who was desperate and wanted to be rich.

For a moment, I feel sorry for Ian, sorry that my father used him like that. My father was a pathological con man, a greedy man who used both of us for his own purposes. The millions that I transferred went to his accounts set up specifically for my transaction.

My father wasn't the only one who was going to benefit from

my skills. Some of the money was going to Tony DeMarco. Tony was one of my father's most important business associates. He sent my father his first client, and then more and more. My father gave Tony kickbacks, or, as they say in the financial industry, 'finder's fees.' He thought he was going to make a lot of money off my transactions.

Until he found out that one of the accounts we broke into was one of his, and his money vanished. I had rerouted it into the account I'd set up to pay Tracker that I hadn't told anyone about. It was the only account that wasn't frozen because the Feds couldn't find it. I didn't know Tony was the account holder. All I had were numbers. But if I had known, I don't know whether it would have made a difference. After all, none of it was personal.

Tony DeMarco thought my father and I planned it together. So he went to the Feds and in exchange for his testimony about my father's business and, by extension, me, he got a pass. It took a couple of years, but my father went to prison for life. I had disappeared, and no one could find me.

I didn't know any of this until the accounts of my father's arrest and trial came to light in the papers and on TV. They'd found an old picture of me, cropped it into an unattractive mug shot. If anyone here had seen the photo, no one had ever made the connection. I was only a small part of the story anyway, even with my mysterious disappearance, because my father stealing from celebrities and billionaires was too juicy and far more interesting to the journalists than trying to decipher how I managed my crime.

Ian must have told Tony it was all me, otherwise he wouldn't have survived Tony's wrath. A bubble of anger rises in my chest. Any empathy I might have had for Ian dissipates as I think about how it seems he is now working for Tony DeMarco, how he has no problem using me.

'You're a computer hacker.' Jeanine states the obvious, but her eyes are wide with the revelation. I am glad, however, with the distraction. I can see from the look on Steve's face that he has done his homework. That he has been busy on Google and he knows all about me, about what I did.

'I haven't done this for a long time,' I tell Jeanine, unwilling to look at Steve.

'So why now? This old boyfriend – Ian, right? – was he a hacker, too?'

'No.'

'So why was he here, really? What's going on?'

'I owe him some money.' I wish it were that simple.

'Is that why he broke into your house? Did he think you had it there?'

'I don't really know,' I say, still unwilling to tell them about Carmine. 'I think it's more of a control thing.'

She studies my face, and I allow myself to look her in the eye for the first time. 'I loved him,' I say.

She gives me a sad smile and reaches over, brushing a curl off my forehead. 'I know.'

'Nicole, what does this mean?' Steve interrupts, indicating the computer screens. I know what he is asking.

I turn the question over and over in my head, not willing to face the answer. Because I know what it has to be.

'It means I have to leave.'

TWENTY-FOUR

'Leave?' Jeanine frowns. 'Leave, where?'

'Leave the island.' As I say the words, my heart sinks. I think about flying along the familiar roads on my bike, the majestic Bluffs, Rodman's Hollow, Friday nights at Club Soda with Steve, yoga and hot stones with Jeanine. Painting on the beach, pinks and reds mixing with purples and blues, the puffy white clouds winking on the horizon over the ferry that brings the tourists who have helped me survive all these years.

It is though I am dying and my entire life passes before my eyes.

'I can take you over,' Steve says simply.

Jeanine turns on him, her eyes dark with anger. 'What is wrong with you? You'll take her? Take her off the island? This is her home.' She swings around to face me again. 'You're going to let him win? You're going to let him run you off?'

She does not even realize that she knows when I say I have to leave, that I mean I have to leave for good. I am not merely going to go to the mainland to shop for a big screen TV or go to a Red Sox game. I am going to take the ferry and disappear into the landscape, never coming back. I can never come back. Because, as I suspect, Frank Cooper knows now who I am, too, and I have no hope.

My life is slipping away with every second.

I glance at the laptops on the table. They were always my home, but I found a way without them. Yet I am back where I started. The last fifteen years don't matter. I will always be on the run. I have just been fooling myself.

I think again about the passport. And those other things I've kept hidden.

'I need to go my house,' I say.

Jeanine gives me a triumphant smile. She thinks that I am going to stay. I let her think that.

I look at the computer screens. They are still searching for the password that Tracker has found. Something tickles the back of my brain. 'Can I keep this going here?' I ask Jeanine. This is yet another clue that maybe I'm not leaving, and she nods enthusiastically.

'Is there anything I need to do?'

I shake my head. 'No. Just leave it be.' I close down the other laptop and stuff it into the backpack. 'I'll just take this one for now.'

'Do you need a ride?' Steve has his keys out, he's flipping them around and around. It is the only annoying habit he has.

'No. I've got one of Pete's mopeds. I'm good.' I lean over and give Jeanine a quick hug. 'See you later.'

Her arms wrap around me, and I feel her warmth. A sadness rushes through me. I pull away before I begin to cry.

'I'll follow you,' Steve says, and I don't even try to talk him out of it. He is determined. I can see it in his face.

It is starting to get dark outside. My stomach growls. Jeanine's salad was not enough. I am tempted to ask Steve if he wants to go to Club Soda for a hamburger and onion rings, but I push the craving aside and climb onto the moped.

'You know, Frank does want to see you,' Steve says as I put on the helmet. I notice that although he has promised Frank that he'll tell him when he's found me, he isn't exactly running over to the police station. I am grateful for that.

'After,' I say simply and start up the engine. I am already down the road before Steve gets into his SUV.

I know I can't outrun him on this machine; he is soon right behind me. I glance around at the familiar sights: the National Hotel, the art gallery where I see Veronica adjusting a painting in the window. I wave, and she lifts her hand in response, but she is confused. She doesn't recognize me. I don't stop to explain.

I pass the farm and smell the llamas. It's been so long since I've noticed their scent; it's almost as though I'm here for the first time again.

My house is just up the hill, and as I approach, I see a police car sitting in front. That's right. Frank said he'd be watching the house. But it is most likely much more than that now. I need to get into my house without him seeing me. I glance back at Steve in the SUV, and suddenly he is waving me away, pointing up

the street. I am not exactly sure what he is saying, but I keep
going past my house without even a second look from the cop
in the car. In the little side-view mirror on the moped handle, I
see Steve pull in next to the cruiser. He gets out, and the cop
gets out and they shake hands. I recognize Reggie McCallum
from the station.

I almost run off the road, so I tear my eyes away from the
mirror and pay attention to my driving. I don't know what
Steve is up to, and I need to know, so I turn around and start
back the way I came, now looking at my house from the top of
the hill. I stop by the side of the road and watch Steve as he
chats up Reggie, who is leaning against his cruiser, laughing.

And from this vantage point, I see an opportunity.

I park the moped as though I am a tourist and I stand, looking
out over the water. For a moment I am mesmerized by the sight:
the bright pinks and oranges and purples of the sunset crashing
across the sky, illuminating the water below. Something passes
through me, a calmness, that sense that I felt when I first landed
on the island that this was my home. A feeling I never even had
in Paris, even those days when we were our happiest.

We *were* happy there. We left Miami with our fake passports
in those days before 9/11 with little scrutiny. He was Paul and
I was Amelie, and we slept and watched movies as we flew across
an ocean to our new home. We were so young that we didn't
feel a sense of urgency, merely a sense of adventure. We were
rich and we were in love. We were fugitives.

But that happiness didn't last. There was no way it could.

I turn away from the sunset, away from my sense of safety,
and look back at my house. Steve is still sweet-talking Reggie,
but I know that Reggie will soon wonder why he is there.

I cross the road and the property line between my house and
the house next door. The ground is soft under my sneakers. I
speed up and skirt around the side of the house. I cannot see
Steve or Reggie from here.

My bedroom is back here, and once before when I locked
myself out of the house, I realized that the window closest to
my dresser doesn't lock properly. A few jimmies, and it slides
up easily. I am happy that I had taken out the storm window the
week before, to let in the cool spring air for better sleeping,

because the screen is easy to maneuver, and soon it slides up as well.

I push my backpack through and hear it land. I follow it, shimmying through and land on the floor of my bedroom.

This should only take a few minutes.

I pick up the backpack, go over to the closet and open the door slowly. I never got around to oiling the hinges, and it squeaks. I almost jump with the sound, and freeze for a moment. But when it's obvious no one has heard it but me, I go into the closet and stoop down. There is the shoe rack, neat as the proverbial pin as I had straightened it after the destruction. I push aside the rack, the shoes shimmying on the little metal rods. I close my eyes and touch the raised edge of the floorboard. I know everything is here, since I already checked, but I am still anxious that someone else has been there and I will find my hiding place empty.

I dig my fingernails into the crack and pull up the board. I reach inside. Relief rushes through me as I open the backpack, shoving aside the laptop before I begin stuffing the piles of money next to it.

TWENTY-FIVE

When I have filled the backpack, I feel around inside the floorboard until I find it. The small plastic bag. I yank it out and let the board drop back down, concealing the cash that won't fit. Unless I find a way to get back in here and get the rest, it will have to stay. Maybe the next tenant or the police will discover it – or maybe not.

I crawl out of the closet, the backpack heavy. I am holding the plastic bag. Everything is still there. The passport, the driver's license, the Social Security card. I take out the passport and open it in the little light that's cast through the open window and see that face. The face of Tina Adler using the name Amelie Renaud to escape. The picture and name on the license match the passport. It was risky using the passport to come back, but I'd had no choice. I'd already said goodbye to Tracker and I had not set up any connections in Paris to get new documents quickly. I didn't think I'd need to leave.

I thought about what Tracker told me about Ian. That he was found with his head blown off on our houseboat. Who was that dead man?

I shake off the thought. I have to get out of here.

I put the things back in the plastic bag and stuff it into the backpack. I go over to the window and drop the backpack to the ground, following it in one fluid movement. I carefully pull down the screen and then the window, shrug the backpack over my shoulders and make the climb back up to the moped, which is still parked where I left it.

I have no idea how much time has passed; it seems like hours but is probably only ten minutes, give or take.

As I put the helmet on and climb onto the moped, I see Steve is still talking to Reggie, but Reggie is backing away now. Clearly Steve has outstayed his welcome. I can almost hear him say, 'I thought she was meeting me here. Really.'

I decide not to take my chances and drive past them, but go

back up the hill and around the turn. I am still wearing the
backpack and the weight of it vibrates against my back. I have
no idea how much money I've managed to salvage. I can only
hope it's going to be enough.

I find myself coming up on the Bluffs. I slow down and pull
in near the wooden staircase. I have such an urge to go down
there, to sit on the rocks, feel the wind in my hair, against my
face and watch the water. To hear it rush through the stones.

I get a catch in my throat when I think of the stones I'd so
carefully collected through the years.

I shut down the engine, climb off and put the helmet in the basket.
I push the moped to the side, hiding it amid the brush. I don't have
a lock, and I don't want to run the risk of anyone stealing it.

With the backpack secure against my body, I begin the descent.
With each step, I feel freer; I take deep breaths, tasting the salt
in the air. The backpack becomes heavier, a burden I'm forced
to carry, but a necessary one. I need this money. I cannot start
a new life without it.

The tears spill down my cheeks as I finally reach the bottom.
I don't even bother to wipe them away. I make my way along
the rocky beach to the sand until I find the spot where I can look
up and see the majestic Bluffs hovering over me, their beauty
overwhelming. Because it is twilight, they are dark shadows
against the sky. I drop down onto the beach and cross my legs,
settling in as the sky darkens further and the edge of the Bluffs
disappears into the night. The wind whips around me as if in a
frenzy; it fills my ears with a white noise.

I think about the driver's license and passport. Neither of them
would be particularly useful, because their expiration dates are
long past. But I might be able to get the license past a rental car
employee, especially if they are distracted by something. I was
always good at distraction.

I know I'll need a credit card to rent a car or catch a plane.
But I'm lucky. Amelie Renaud is a real person with a real credit
card, and the credit card number is just a few keystrokes away.
I don't look much like Amelie, not anymore, but if I take off
my glasses and straighten my hair, I can say that I've cut it and
that's why my face looks a little fuller in the picture. A haircut
can change everything.

While before my actions were frivolous, I need to do this now to survive. I do not want to get caught. I have lasted this long, and I would like to live the rest of my life being free. I don't like thinking what this means. That I will disappear off this island as I once disappeared from Miami, leaving people behind who I love.

Zeke should never have followed me.

I don't know how long I've been sitting here, my fingers touching the soft stones at my feet. I scoop a couple up and stick them in the front pocket of the backpack. Wherever I am going, they will go in a jar so I can remember.

Finally, the sky is black, the only light from the bright moon that's risen over the horizon. Stars speckle the sky, winking at me, telling me it's time to go.

I stand up and wobble a little. My feet have fallen asleep. I shake them out and make my way tentatively back to the stairs. My eyes are adjusted to the dark, so I can make out shadows, which is how I see an odd-looking shape beyond the stairs on the other side. It does not look like an animal, but something else. Something familiar, but my brain isn't registering it as anything in particular.

Until I get up close and I almost trip over it.

It is a bicycle.

The frame is bent and broken, as though it has been tossed from the stairs. I look up, half expecting to see the person who has done such a thing, but there is no one there. I lean down and touch the metal, then pull my hand back as though it is on fire. It may be dark, but I know this bike.

It's mine.

I cannot grasp why someone would do this. Why steal the bike and then destroy it? They had already destroyed my belongings. Why not just damage it at my house and leave it there for me to find? Granted, someone was bound to find the bike here. This is a highlight of the island; everyone comes here, tourists and residents alike. The police would be alerted, and I would eventually find out – yet another way to hurt me.

I lift up the broken frame and carry it over to the stairs, where I lean it up against the railing. It is mangled beyond repair. A sob catches in my throat as I step around it to go back up, but before the tears can come the moon moves out from behind a cloud and illuminates the beach in front of me.

The bike is not the only thing left abandoned here.

I am afraid to move toward the body that lies just beyond the path I took to come back.

I wait for it to move, but it doesn't. It just lies there. The moon slips behind a cloud again, and it's darker.

I take a step. And then another. By the time I reach it, the moon is peeking out again and I can see his face.

I take a gulp of air, unaware that I'd been holding my breath.

Carmine Loffredo looks peaceful. His eyes are open, as if he is admiring the stars above him. He does not move his head. He does not see me. He is clearly dead, although how, I'm not entirely sure. It's too dark, even with the moon shining, to tell. And I am not about to poke around the body to find out.

It surprises me a little that I am not panicking, but I chalk that up to the fact that I know what kind of man he was and that this was probably the only way he would meet his end. I am merely relieved that he is gone and is no longer a threat to me or my friends.

Somehow I know that Ian is responsible for this, but he is still among the missing. Like me.

I can't stay here any longer. I have to put as much distance between me and Carmine Loffredo as I can. I take the steps two at a time – not even the heaviness of the backpack can slow me down. I have never left the Bluffs so quickly before.

The moped is where I have left it, still hidden and untouched. I slip on the helmet, tightening it around my chin before climbing on and starting the engine. I take one last look down toward the water, the bike, Carmine, and while my first instinct is to go to Steve's, I begin to worry that it's not a good idea. Carmine might be out of the picture, but there is no guarantee that he is the only one here with an agenda. And I cannot forget that Frank Cooper is looking for me.

The only place I can think of to go is Pete's. No one would think of looking for me there after hours. I can return the moped and call Steve from there. Pete will be home now, but I have a key. Pete gave it to me when I started my early morning tours.

Even though I feel as though I am hidden enough by the helmet and the darkness, I am still on alert, but I see no police cars on my way. A few people are out taking walks, enjoying a brisk May evening. I might be doing the same under other circumstances.

When I arrive at the bike and moped shop, I am careful to pull around the back. I let myself in, not taking off the helmet until I am safely inside. My eyes adjust to the darkness; it is a different dark than outside. I take in the scent of gasoline and rubber and make my way to the counter, where I find Pete's small lamp and turn it on. A yellow glow casts itself across the room, and I keep it on only long enough to dial Steve's number on the old rotary phone.

'Where have you been?' Steve asks irritably when I identify myself.

'I went to the Bluffs. I didn't mean to stay so long.' I am not lying. 'I found my bike.'

'Where?'

'At the bottom of the steps at the Bluffs. It's all mangled. Like someone threw it over the side.' I think about the impact against the stones, and I'm glad I couldn't see the full damage in the darkness.

'But why?'

'Beats me.' I pause. 'It's not the only thing I found. There's a body.'

I hear Steve take a short intake of breath. 'What? Who?'

I know he is thinking about Ian, so I quickly say, 'It's a guy named Carmine Loffredo. He works for Tony DeMarco. He was here to find me. I think he's the one who broke into my house and trashed it.'

'Why would he want your place trashed?'

'We stole money from Tony DeMarco. His was one of the accounts we stole from. He wants his money back. He wants to get even.'

Steve is silent for a few seconds, then he asks, 'Do you have it, Nicole? Is that what you needed to get at your house?'

'It's my money. Money from the bike tours. Pete pays me in cash.' I realize he has never known how I have managed financially. 'I don't have a bank account,' I explain. 'When I have to pay bills, I go to the bank and get a bank check, like when I'm paying rent or for my phone.'

'You don't have a driver's license, either,' he says, 'do you?'

'No. Not really.'

'What do you mean, not really?'

'I have a license, but it's expired. It's got a different name on it. I didn't want to risk using it for anything when I got back. I didn't want to use the same name. That's why I became Nicole.' I pause. 'It was in the house, too. I had to go back and get it, because if they found it, they might be able to trace it back. You know, to what I did.'

'Why keep it in the first place?'

'A quick escape. Just in case.'

'Why couldn't you just get another one?'

'Because I only knew one way to get another one, and I couldn't run the risk of anyone finding out where I was.'

'So you've been hiding here on the island. In plain sight.'

'Until Ian found me.'

The words sit between us for a few seconds, then he asks, 'Where is he?'

'I have no idea.'

'Do you think he's responsible for that man's death at the Bluffs?'

'Maybe. Probably.'

'So when you got there, you didn't see the body? Or your bike?'

A small chill begins at the base of my spine and moves slowly to my neck. 'No.' We both know what that means. That the bike and Carmine happened while I was on the beach.

'You didn't hear anything?' Steve asks.

'It was windy. You know how the wind is over there. You can't even hear yourself think.' I hope it is a good enough excuse, so I am not also accused of more than stealing.

'Where are you, anyway? You know, Frank Cooper came by a little while ago. I told him I'd have you call him when I saw you.'

'Then it's a good thing I called you, because you haven't seen me.' I pause, knowing that Steve is aware I have not answered his question. 'He knows, doesn't he?' I ask. Steve knows what I mean. Whether Frank knows that I am Tina Adler.

'Yes, I think he does.'

It is as I suspected. 'So is he camped out on your doorstep waiting for me?'

'No.'

'Why not?'

'I think he wants me to do the right thing. He wants *you* to do the right thing,' Steve says. 'He also knows that you can't leave the island without anyone seeing you.'

I think about how he must have people watching at the ferry and the airport and the marinas. 'I have to figure out how to get past him,' I say. 'I don't want to leave any more than you want me to, but I guess I was stupid to think that I could stay here forever and no one would ever find me.'

'I asked you something not long ago,' Steve says, his voice cracking a little. He clears his throat and continues. 'Marry me.'

'Oh, Steve,' is all I can think to say.

'I'm serious. You've told me everything, I think, and a husband can't testify against a wife. If we get married, I can protect you.'

He doesn't know that I cannot be protected. Not at all. Not anymore.

'Jeanine saw what I was doing earlier,' I say.

'She doesn't really know, though. She didn't understand what was going on.'

I feel bad about that, but it's the best way. I remember the computer running the password scan. I wonder if it has finished, if the password to get through the firewall has been uncovered. Tracker had already found it, but I need it. One last time. For something I don't want him involved in.

'You didn't tell me where you are,' Steve says.

'You can't know.'

'I won't tell Frank.'

I know that he would rather die than give me up, but I can't risk it.

'Are you OK?' he asks.

I look around the bike shop. 'I'm fine.'

'Call me in the morning. We can meet somewhere. I need to know you're OK.'

'I'm fine,' I say again. But then I promise to call. I hang up the phone. I realize I am exhausted and I need to sit down, lay down for a little while and think about what I'm going to do next.

Pete has a couch and a small refrigerator in the back room.

This room has no windows, so I turn on the lamp next to the couch and find a six-pack of beer and some crackers in the fridge. I want a shower in the worst way; I've been wearing the same jeans and T-shirt for two days now. I go into the bathroom, which is the size of a closet with just a toilet and a sink, and I rinse my face with cold water, blotting it dry with the hard paper towels from the dispenser.

I go back out to the couch and take a beer and some crackers. What I would give for a burger and onion rings at Club Soda.

I weigh my options, now that Frank Cooper knows.

I could call in an anonymous report about Carmine's body and my bike at the Bluffs, and while the island's law enforcement is distracted by that, I could go to the dock and hop on the next ferry to the mainland and disappear. It would be easier over there. More people, more cars, more ways to blend in. But I would need more there, too. I'd need a current driver's license, a bank account, a credit card. Amelie Renaud won't take me very far. I was foolish to think I could use her. That had been a desperate thought, and there is nothing more dangerous than desperation.

I run my fingers through my hair. I think about Steve's offer. The one to marry me. For a brief second, I consider it. It would be easy, too, to do it. Not just so he couldn't testify, but because then I would have a legitimate identity. I could get all of those things I need. But then I would have to leave him behind, breaking his heart in a way that would be even worse than when Dotty died.

No, I cannot do that to him.

I need Tracker. He is my connection to the outside world. Even though I know Steve will do anything for me, Tracker is still the only one I can turn to.

I feel as though I am too slow on the uptake. It's not only my computer skills that are rusty, all of me is rusty. I thought I'd planned for this day, but it's been so long that I forgot my plan included a fifteen-year-old driver's license and passport. The more settled I got here the more complacent I became. I should have always been at the ready for survival off the island.

I can only hope that I have enough time.

TWENTY-SIX

I am so aware that I need to leave here before the sun comes up that I only manage a couple of hours of sleep. My head is spinning with what I need to do.

I need to get in touch with Tracker. I need a new driver's license, a credit card, a passport. And I need that password.

I have my laptop, but there is no Wi-Fi here. I have to go back to the spa. I am not sure how I'm going to get in without Jeanine. I am sure that Frank Cooper is watching her as well, but maybe not right now. He knows I can't leave the island in the middle of the night, so it doesn't really matter where I am until morning.

I creep out to the counter and dial the familiar number.

'W-who is it?' I have awoken Jeanine from a deep sleep.

'Jeanine,' I whisper loudly. 'It's Nicole. Wake up.'

'Nicole?' She is still half asleep.

'Yes, it's Nicole. I need you.'

'Nicole?' Her voice is more alert now.

'Yes. I need your help.'

'What do you need? You know, Frank Cooper is looking for you.'

'I know. Can you meet me at the spa?'

'Now?'

It is four a.m.

'Yes. I wouldn't ask if it wasn't important.'

'It has to do with that laptop, right?'

'That's right. I just need to see what's going on with it, and then I'll leave you alone.'

'Right now?'

'Please, Jeanine.'

'OK, OK. I'll be there as soon as I can.' I hear the irritation in her voice, but I know she will come.

It will take her about ten minutes once she gets in the car. I am just a couple of blocks away, but I don't have the patience to wait here. I pick up my backpack and go out the back door into the night.

There is no sound except the shuffle of my feet on the pavement.

I cut through the little alley that runs between the spa and a house that has a string of brightly colored buoys hanging on the small white picket fence. Jeanine has always wanted to buy this house, to live in it herself, rather than on the other side of the island.

I touch the fence, just for an instant, as though the buoys can give me some sort of strength. I then turn toward the back door of the spa, the one that will lead into that little room where the laptop sits.

I tense when I hear the footsteps approach. It's too early for Jeanine. I brace myself.

Ian steps out from the other side of the building. 'I need your help, Tina.'

My heart starts to pound, but I ignore it, glaring at him. 'What are you doing here?' My whisper is louder than it should be, and it carries on the still air.

'Shush,' he says, putting a finger to his lips. He isn't as put together as he usually is; his hair is tousled and his clothes are dirty. He looks as though he has slept on the beach. He probably has. He does not have keys to a bike shop or friends who can let him into spas.

'Where have you been?' I hiss.

He shakes his head. 'I wish you hadn't talk to the cops. You could've just cleaned that shit up at your house and kept your mouth shut.'

I feel the same way, but I don't want him to know that. 'It was the right thing to do, Ian.'

He sneers at me. 'And you're all about doing the right thing, aren't you, *Nicole*?' He spits out my name.

I ignore him. 'So did you shoot Carmine, Ian? With the gun you let Veronica see?' It is a stab in the dark, but I see in his expression that I am right in my suspicion that he is not innocent in this.

'It was either him or me. I didn't want it to be me.'

'Whose idea was it to steal from Tony, Ian? Was it my father's or was it yours?' It is the first time I have confronted him about this.

'He told me Tony couldn't say anything because his money was dirty,' Ian said. He snorts. 'Guess he didn't figure the Feds would be all over his shit because stealing from a bunch of rich assholes was worse than stealing from a scumbag mobster.'

'Was the whole job just a cover-up for stealing from Tony?'

'It wasn't *that* personal. Except maybe—' He stops.

'Maybe what?'

'He wanted to see what you could do. It was personal like that.'

My father wanted to see if it was in my genes. The stealing. I didn't disappoint him.

'You gave me the list of account numbers,' I say. 'You knew exactly who we were stealing from. Where did you get those numbers anyway?'

'It doesn't matter.'

'I think it does.'

'I think if it did, then you would've asked me back then, isn't that right? It doesn't really matter now. That's not our problem.'

He is right on one hand, but on the other, I do think it's our problem. But I can also tell from the tightness of his jaw and tone of voice that I am not going to get it out of him. Not right now, anyway.

'Tony's looking for both of us now,' Ian is saying. 'Carmine's dead, but he'll send someone else. He wants his money. Just tell me where it is, and I'll get it to him and we'll leave you alone.'

'I don't have it. I told you.' I pause. 'Why does it matter anymore, anyway? I mean, Tony's got money. However much we stole from him fifteen years ago, well, it's probably just a drop in the bucket, right?'

He shakes his head. 'It's the principle, Tina. He got shown up. And then your father ripped him off. He got your father back, but now he wants you, too.'

I sigh. 'I still don't see—'

His eyes get darker with his anger. 'You may think that this is some sort of game, Tina, but it's for real. I'm asking real nice. I know you've been online, I know you've probably hidden it, but you have to tell me where it is, for both our sakes.' I see now that his anger is laced with fear.

'I know this isn't a game. I have been online, that's true, but I haven't done anything with any money, because there isn't any. Not anymore. I told you that. I've been trying to figure out what's been going on while I've been here.' I pause, then say, 'I understand that you're dead. That they found your body on the houseboat. You killed yourself.'

He gives a short snort. 'I had to get away somehow. You can't blame me, since you pulled your own disappearing act.' He pauses. 'You've been right here. All along. And no one has ever known?'

I think about Steve and Jeanine, worry about how it's going to be for them when Frank Cooper finds out that they've been helping me. He will wonder if they have known all along, and it might be difficult for them to prove that they haven't.

'So what is the job you wanted me to do? It's for Tony, isn't it? So we can pay back what we owe him. But what I want to know is your connection with him now. I know the car you were driving is registered to him. Are you working for him?'

'I didn't think you were interested. Will you really help me?' He is talking about the job, ignoring my question about Tony.

'Maybe. Maybe I'd like to put it all behind me, too, and really get a fresh start somewhere.' I don't think Tony is going to go away all that easily, though, even if we pay him back.

I see the headlights of a car approaching. Jeanine. It has to be Jeanine.

'You have to leave,' I say. 'Can we meet later? Say, in a couple of hours?'

He hesitates, curious, and then he says, 'Where? You know this place.'

I say the first thing that comes to mind. 'The Painted Rock.'
'The what?'

'It's a rock. It's painted. You can't miss it.' I begin to tell him where it is, when he touches my lips with his finger.

'I'll find it.' His eyes search mine, and I see a familiar longing in them. He takes his finger away, leans over and brushes his lips against mine, and to my dismay, I feel the familiar stirring. I am disgusted with myself. I pull away, but he is already gone.

I am standing there when I hear the car door slam. I scurry around to the front.

Jeanine is wearing a pair of flannel pajama pants and a North Face jacket with a scarf wrapped around her neck. Her hair is tousled, pulled high on her head with two chopsticks sticking out of it. She gives me a nod and lets us into the spa, closing the door behind us.

'So what's so urgent?' she asks. 'You look like hell.'

I smile despite myself. 'So do you. I just need to check that laptop.'

She doesn't say anything, and I smell the rosemary incense as we go down the hall. She lets me go first into the room where I find my laptop undisturbed. It isn't off, but merely sleeping, and with one touch it springs to life, my search complete.

With just a few keystrokes, I find Amelie Renaud. I have to use her, at least at first. I rummage around a small desk in the corner and come up with a scrap of paper and a pencil. I scribble Amelie's information: her Social Security number, her current address, and, most important, her credit card information, including the security code on the back of the card. I know I can't get an airline ticket; the security at airports is too strong these days. I've heard enough grumbling among my friends who've flown to know that my expired driver's license will be caught immediately. But trains? No one checks identification on a train.

I will have to get to Boston. Providence is closer, but more risky. I will buy a couple of train tickets – one to New York, one to Washington. There is only one train line that runs between Boston and Washington, and I can get off anywhere in between if things look dicey. I'm not sure how quickly Amelie will discover someone has used her credit card, but if she's like everyone else, she'll report it immediately and the card will be deactivated. The train ticket, though, will already be in my hand.

I might only have the chance to use the credit card number once. But I don't know that I really need to use it more than that. Tracker has connections in New York, connections that can get me a whole new identity.

I glance at the clock on the laptop. I don't have much time if I'm going to meet Ian. I haven't really decided whether I will, though, and I'm too distracted by thoughts of how I can survive at the moment.

I go to the chat room and don't see Tracker there. I leave him a message: I need you. Meet me here at seven o'clock.

But I'm not sure I can wait that long, so I go to the other room and find Angel, the hacker who led me back to him. I ask that we meet in a private chat room.

I thought you had everything you needed, Angel writes when he comes into the room.

Can you tell Tracker to meet me where we were before? I type.

He's not available.

What do you mean?

He's on a job for someone else right now. I can help you.

I don't like the sound of this. I am rusty, but not that rusty. Thanks anyway, I say and log out quickly, just in case someone else is watching. The plan that has been circulating in my head dissipates as I wonder what's going on.

I may still be able to find Tracker's connection in Miami, the one who'd taken care of our documents the last time. But Miami is too far away. I'm not sure how I'll be able to get there without some trouble. And even if I get there, I have no idea if the connection still exists.

It has been such a long time.

I sit back in my chair and take a few deep breaths. I will manage somehow. I will be able to escape. I have to.

I see the edges of the bills in my backpack. I think about Ian waiting for me, and suddenly my thoughts turn to Zeke.

I don't like to think about Zeke, what happened that day, because it was all my fault.

After that first time Zeke came to the house to check up on my father, I didn't give him another thought. But a couple of weeks later, he showed up again.

'Miss Adler?'

Again, I was by the pool, and he startled me. I hadn't heard him approach, the soles of his shoes moving across the tiles silently, stealthily. I shut the laptop cover and squinted up at him from the chaise lounge.

'Zeke Chapman? FBI?' He was disappointed I didn't immediately recognize him.

I flashed him a smile. 'Sorry, but you all march through here and
I'm bad with names.'

He gave me a small smile and sat down on the edge of the
chaise lounge next to mine. He cocked his head toward the laptop.
'Working on something?'

'Just playing around.'

He ran a hand through his hair and the sun again caught the
glint of his gold wedding band.

'Is your wife FBI, too?'

He laughed. 'Oh, no. She's a teacher. Elementary school.'

'So she likes kids. You got kids?'

'No.' The answer was short, clipped, and I wondered how long
they'd been trying.

'I suppose you're looking for my father.'

He leaned toward me and smiled. 'No. I was looking for you.'
It was the intensity of his stare that unnerved me, that made me
tingle all over, a feeling I'd only ever had before with Ian.

'Why?' I whispered.

'Because you're prettier than your father and seeing you doesn't
feel like work.'

'So this really is work?'

Zeke sighed and sat back again. 'I'm afraid so.'

'You're keeping an eye on me to find out if I know anything
about my father's business.'

'Give the girl a gold star.'

'I don't know anything.'

'I figured you'd say that.' He spotted my drink on the glass
top table next to me. 'You got any more of that?'

I raised my eyebrows. 'It's Scotch. You drink on duty?'

He made a show of looking at his watch. 'Oh, look at that,
my shift is over.' When he looked back up at me, his eyes were
twinkling and his smile was infectious.

'Sure.' I swung my legs over the side of the lounge and went
over to the bar, where I poured him a short one, then thought
twice and added a little more. I brought it over to him.

He'd gotten up and was staring across the pool at the ocean
beyond it. The water was a mix of turquoise and cobalt blue, the

blue sky dipping into it and casting a bright shimmer across the horizon.

'You live in paradise,' he said.

I handed him the drink. 'I suppose.'

'Why, it's not paradise?'

'Sometimes a house can be a prison, you know what I mean?'

His Adam's apple twitched; his lips pursed into a straight line. He lifted the glass to his lips and took a long swallow. When he was done, he turned to me and said, 'Yeah. I know exactly what you mean.'

There was a longing in his eyes that caught me off guard. I didn't mean to do it, or maybe I did, but I kissed him. For a second, I thought he was going to move away from me, but then his hands were in my hair, and his lips opened. They were softer than I'd imagined, and when I took him up to my room and we undressed each other, there was an intensity, a need in him that made me breathless. Ian had never *needed* me like that.

I didn't realize he suspected me for three weeks.

TWENTY-SEVEN

The sun is coming up, and the streaks of pink and orange dance across the sky. I sent Jeanine home when I started my search for Amelie Renaud, but not before I asked her if I could borrow her bike, the one that doesn't have any gears. I teased her when she bought it, how she wouldn't be able to get up the hills on the island, and what was the point in a bike if you can't even get around properly.

So when I asked to use it, she raised one eyebrow. 'Really? I thought you have one of Pete's mopeds.'

'I took it back.'

She rolled her eyes and sighed dramatically. 'OK, fine. It's out front in the bike rack. How long will you be?'

I knew she was trying to figure out where I was going. 'I'll be back in a couple hours. Maybe sooner. Don't worry, I won't run off with the bike.'

'That's not what I'm worried about,' she said, a hint of sadness in her tone.

I pulled her into a hug, which was unexpected, since she is the hugger. I felt her arms go around me, and she held me tight for a few seconds.

'I'll be fine,' I said when we pulled apart. But she still had that look in her eyes, the same one Steve has now, the one that thinks every time they see me will be the last time.

One of these times, it will be. But not now.

I shrug on my backpack and climb onto her bike. She left it unlocked for me.

Her bike is uncomfortable between my legs. The seat is too big, the handlebars too high. I keep reaching for the speeds, but then I realize they're not there and I pump the pedals hard to keep my momentum up. I take Old Town Road and turn onto Center, which runs around the perimeter of the airport. I think about the BMW. Is it still there, or has Frank Cooper impounded it? Do they even have a place for abandoned cars on the island, or do they send them over to the mainland on the ferry? I am wondering about that as I approach the intersection with Cooneymus. Rodman's Hollow is there, not too far. I could ditch the bike and hike the trail down to the beach. Hide for the day.

Instead, I move onto Lakeside, past Fresh Pond until I get to the intersection with Snake Hole Road and Mohegan Trail.

There it is: the Painted Rock. Someone has painted it as if it is a ladybug, red with black dots on its back. Clever.

I painted it once, a beach scene with twilight streaks of pink and purple. It was painted over the next day, bright yellow with 'Happy B-day Mary' in bright blue. The Painted Rock is an island oddity, painted first in the 1960s as a Halloween prank and then frequently, sometimes every day, since.

As a landmark, it is a good one, and as a place to meet someone, perfect. But as I stand, straddling the bike, I glance around in all directions and see no sign of Ian, or anyone else for that matter. My first reaction is relief. I don't have to do this; I don't have to face him. But then a small panic begins to rise in my chest.

I am alone out here. Standing next to a ladybug rock. I am a sitting duck, a good target for anyone who might want to get rid of me, the way Ian got rid of Carmine.

I glance down Snake Hollow. I push the bike into a thicket of brush, hoping it won't be seen. I hide next to it, watching the road, aware of the trail behind me, the one that leads to Vail Beach. Anyone who does not know the island might not even recognize the trail for what it is, it is so overgrown.

I hear a car coming, but it speeds past. I glance at my watch. Ian is late. If he is coming at all.

Another car approaches, slows down and stops in front of the Painted Rock. It is not Ian in the driver's seat, but a stranger. As I try to make out his features, I see movement in the passenger seat. Someone else. Another man.

The passenger door opens, and the man steps out of the car. He looks at the rock, then out over the roof of the car. I shrink back further against the brush.

'She's not here,' he says, his voice carrying on the breeze so I can hear him clearly.

The man behind the wheel opens his door and steps out. He

is blond, husky and stiff in a suit, as though he's not used to wearing one. The Hispanic man who gets out of the passenger side is not as formally dressed. He is wearing jeans and a white shirt and a navy windbreaker.

'Let's spread out, see if she's here somewhere, hiding,' the driver says. It is clearly not a suggestion, but an order. He is in charge. The Hispanic man steps away from the car, closing the door.

They both look back up Lakeside Drive, and right at that moment they have their backs to me, so I take the chance and turn and flee down the trail toward the beach.

The trail is barely that. It is overgrown and tough to navigate, rocks and roots and overgrowth protecting this path to one of the most secluded and yet beautiful beaches on the island. I had been here a year before I discovered it. No one had mentioned it, because so few actually venture here. There are no services, no way to bring beach paraphernalia while trying to sidestep the obstacles. The beaches on the eastern side of the island are familiar, beaches as you'd expect beaches to be, with soft sand and gentle waves. This beach, Vail Beach, is rough and difficult, with an undertow and surf that crashes onto the rocky shore with a violence that only some can appreciate.

I do not stop to see if they are after me, and finally I reach the point where the green growth parts and I can see the cobalt water ahead of me. I hear nothing behind me, so I continue down the path to the water. Once on the beach, I turn to see the rocky cliffs, but no one is coming down the trail.

The beauty takes my breath away. I have always known why I stayed, and why I am now resisting leaving. But I am not here to admire the scenery. It's possible that they have now found the bike, abandoned in the brush. So I turn to the right and begin to run along the rocky beach, stumbling here and there when my foot hits a stone the wrong way.

These men are not from here, I can tell. They will not know that anyone can walk the beach all around the island, that you can get to any beach from any beach. I am heading toward Black Rock Beach. From there, I can get up into Rodman's Hollow.

I don't dare look back, but I can't help myself. No. I see no one. The backpack is heavy against my body, and I wish I could dump it, but the laptop is in there. I wish I had a cell phone. I'd thought about a prepaid one at one point, but I've never really needed one, since my whole world is within walking or biking distance. I have my phone at the house, included in my rent, and anyone who needs me calls on the landline. I pay for long-distance calls, but since I don't call long distance, that has never been an issue.

Thinking about mundane things keeps me from thinking about what I am actually doing. If Ian had showed up, I would have talked to him. But the strangers' arrival in his place makes me both angry and scared. Ian clearly told them where I was going to be. I remember his threat about anonymous tips. But since I had told him I would do the job, why would he want me caught?

I skid slightly on the rocky beach as I try to figure out what Ian is up to. I start to run again. I feel the sweat on my back, running down my cleavage, around my hairline. I push up my glasses, which are slipping down my slick nose. My calf muscles are taut, tight, unused to running and the way it makes my body work. I long for the familiar feel of the bike.

I don't know how far I've gone until I realize I'm here. I'm at Black Rock Beach. The trail that goes up the Bluffs is just ahead. I make a beeline for it. It is still so early in the morning that no one is on the beach to see the crazy woman running for no reason.

It doesn't take me long to reach Black Rock Road. From here, I find the trail that goes into Rodman's Hollow. It is a three-mile hike to traverse the Hollow on the trails. I slow down to a jog and then finally to a walk. I feel fairly certain that they have not followed me, or if they have, they will not be able to find their way through the Hollow easily. I think about going to Fresh Pond, just to regroup, but it's time to get out of here, to get back and see if Tracker has come back to the chat room. I make it to the wooden gate and turnstile, where my hike would normally have started. No one starts on the beach; it's the place they end up.

My detour has landed me on Cooneymus Road. I am starting to wonder about whether this was a good idea. My goal is to get to Steve's, but he lives up near the Great Salt Pond. I'm afraid it's too long a walk, and anyway, Frank Cooper and anyone else who's looking for me is watching his house.

But Jeanine's place is just down the road. I look at my watch again. It is eight o'clock in the morning. My run from Vail Beach and through the Hollow has taken longer than I thought. The spa opens at seven, with an early-morning yoga class. Jeanine might be there, or she might be home catching up on the sleep I stole from her. I know I am an imposition and am pushing the boundaries of friendship, but I have no choice.

I start to run again, the backpack slapping against my wet back, my feet happier on pavement than sand. I see her house ahead, a two-story gray clapboard house with a wide front porch. Her car is not in the driveway. I walk around to the back door and cup my hands around my eyes, peering through the window. The kitchen is dark, but I see a coffee cup perched on the counter next to the sink.

I know where she keeps her spare key, and I find it under a pot on the back deck. I let myself in and breathe in the familiar scent: potpourri and sea salt and morning coffee, familiar, comforting smells that help me relax.

I find a water glass and fill it, drinking it down in one gulp then filling it again and drinking again. Although I'm breathing normally again, now I'm a little chilled as my sweat dries.

I put my backpack on the floor next to the stool at the kitchen island. The coffee pot still has at least one cup left in it, and as I pour it, I can tell Jeanine has not left too long ago as it is still warm. I put the cup in the microwave to heat it a little more. I reach into the fridge to get the milk, and when I finally take a sip, it is smooth and rich and warms me. My stomach growls, though, reminding me that coffee is not breakfast. I am not sure when I'll have another chance to eat, so I make myself a couple of eggs and toast. While I eat, I take my laptop out of the backpack and set it in front of me. Jeanine has wireless. I end up in the chat room. It's still empty. No sign of Tracker. No note, no nothing.

A small bit of panic rises in my chest, and I think again about those men. The man in the suit could be a fed, but the other one, I'm not so sure. I've seen my share of agents, and that one just didn't have the look about him. His clothes, for instance. He could be undercover. I try to remember if he looks familiar. If he's been on the island and I have noticed him, yet not noticed

him. But I am coming up blank. Neither man was familiar, not
in the way Ian was when I saw him outside Club Soda that night
I was with Steve. The night it all started to unravel.

And as I am thinking, it pops up. On the computer screen.
What I have been waiting for.

Are you there, Tiny?

Tracker is back.

TWENTY-EIGHT

was worried, I write. I thought you'd left. Angel said you were unavailable.

He told me. He was wrong. I'm sorry. What's going on?

I need something, like before. You know, you hooked me up.

It takes a few seconds longer for him to respond this time, and again I panic. But then: Everything like before?

Yes. And a credit card.

Where?

I know he is asking where I'll pick the documents up.

New York.

Again, I wait a few minutes. I tap my fingers on the granite, take a drink of coffee, nibble a piece of toast.

That's going to take a couple days.

When?

Friday.

Three days. I have enough money to hold me over. Anyway, I have to get to Boston, get the train.

Same name? he is asking.

No. I think. Elizabeth. Elizabeth McKnight.

I need a picture.

That's right. Hold on, I say, switching to a new screen and the camera. I can see myself, what I will look like. I am flushed, still, from my long run. I comb my fingers through my curls, straighten out my glasses, lick my lips and take a basic head shot. I save the image and send it to Tracker in the chat room.

Background, is all he writes after about five minutes.

What?

You're in a house. Can you get rid of the background? In Photoshop?

I may be able to get back into hacking, but I have never used Photoshop. I don't know how, I admit.

OK. I'll take care of it. And then, You look different.

I'm older.

You look better.

I cannot help myself. Maybe you could send me a picture of you.

Sorry, sweetheart, but you know the rules.

I'm at a disadvantage. If we were in the same place, you would know me but I wouldn't know you.

A smiley face pops up on the screen. I tried. I'd tried back then, too. Tracker did know what I looked like. I am as uncomfortable now with that as I'd been before. But I can't dwell on it. This is all about my survival.

So, where on Friday? I write.

Chinatown. There's a tea shop on Mott Street. Go in and ask for their special jasmine tea and they'll take you to the back. You pay them then.

How much?

Twenty.

I glance at my backpack. OK.

Tiny?

Yes?

Nothing else?

I think about everything he's doing for me. Everything he has done. I can't ask for more. No. Thank you.

Be careful. And if you can, let me know how you are. I've missed you.

I've missed you, too. But he is gone before I hit return, so he doesn't see my sentiment.

I log out of the chat room and sit back, staring at the computer screen, where my face stares back at me. The face that will be on my new documents. What does Tracker really think about me? He says that I look better than I used to, but what does that really mean? I find myself fantasizing about him, that he might be the person I meet in Chinatown. He knows when I will be there; he knows what I look like. Maybe he will want to meet me as much as I've wanted to meet him and he will make it happen.

I finish the last of my coffee and push the daydream out of my head. I can't get distracted.

I need twenty thousand dollars. I hop off the stool and stoop down, opening the backpack. Carefully, I take the stacks of bills out and count them. I am just short. I could use Amelie's credit card number to get a cash advance, transfer it to an account.

I have been lying to Ian. There is still an account. At least I think so. But I am afraid to try to use it or even to set another one up. It feels too risky. There is only one other solution.

I have to go back to the house and get what I left behind. There is at least this much left there. I stuff the bills back into the backpack. I know I should just leave.

But I procrastinate. The longer I stay here, alone, without anyone knowing where I am the safer I am. The safer Steve and Jeanine are. I think about those two men. Are they Carmine's replacements? Have they done something to Ian, something that made him tell them where I was?

From Jeanine's front window, I can see the water. I stand, drinking in the scenery, hoping to imprint it so firmly in my memory that I never forget it.

When I turn back, I know it's time.

I call Steve.

'Jeanine?' He knows her number.

'It's not Jeanine. It's me. I'm at her house.'

'Nicole? What are you doing there?'

'I need you do to something. Jeanine's bike is in the brush near the Painted Rock on Snake Hollow. Can you go pick it up and bring it back to the spa?'

'Why are you at Jeanine's and why is her bike there?' Steve's tone is wary.

'I ran into Ian.' I hear him take a breath, but I don't give him time to say anything. 'I was supposed to meet him, but two men came instead. I didn't like the look of them, so I took off down to Vail Beach.'

'How did you end up at Jeanine's?'

'I ran along the beach up to Rodman's Hollow.'

He gives a short snort. 'Of course you did.'

'I didn't know what else to do.'

'OK, fine. You should have called me.' He pauses. 'You know, Frank's got Reggie watching my house.'

'I figured. Do you think he'll follow you?'

'Maybe. But I can figure out a way to ditch him. Can I pick you up and take you somewhere?'

'No, I'm all set. I'll call you later.' I hang up, and before he can call back, I dial another number. This time for a taxi. There are only a couple of drivers I haven't had much contact with over the years, and I make sure that the one I call is one of them.

I wash and dry my dishes and put them away. I go upstairs to Jeanine's room and find a pair of yoga pants, a white T-shirt, a blue cotton sweater and a pair of socks. Things that I will easily fit into. I take them downstairs and squeeze them into the backpack. I sit at the island and wait. It seems like forever until I hear the honk out front, and as I am about to let myself out the back, I see a baseball cap with the Red Sox logo on it hanging on the back of a chair. I slip it over my head and let myself out, locking the door behind me and putting the key back where I found it under the pot. I turn around the corner of the house and climb into the waiting taxi. I tell the driver to take me to Hydrangea House on Corn Neck Road, a small bed and breakfast. He doesn't seem to recognize me, and I am relieved.

I also don't know the owner of Hydrangea House, which is why I have chosen it. Lillian is new to the island and does not bat an eye when I check in for one night. And she does not seem to think it's odd that I am paying with cash. She shows me to a room with big windows, the sun casting a bright light across the wooden floors. The bed is covered with an old-fashioned white bedspread and plump pillows. Clean towels are piled at the end. I tell her I'd like to take a shower, and she directs me to the bathroom down the hall, not seeming curious that I am dragging a heavy backpack with me and no other luggage at eight-thirty in the morning.

The shower feels good as I wash away the rigorous run along the beach. Jeanine's clothes carry a faint scent of strawberry, and for a second I am overwhelmed with sadness, but then I push through it. I have no time for sentiment.

Hydrangea House has free Wi-Fi. I sit cross-legged on the bed and open the laptop. As it boots up, I pick up the phone by the side of the bed and dial the spa. Jeanine comes to the phone immediately.

'Nicole? Where are you? Steve dropped off my bike. Told me

you had to ditch it and run along the beach and you were at my house. He said he went by my house, but you were gone. Where are you?' Her words run together; she does not take a breath until she is done.

I should have known Steve would go to her house, which is why I'm glad I got out of there when I did.

'I'm safe,' I say. 'You can't know where I am right now. I'm worried that you and Steve are being watched. Just do what you normally do and I'll be in touch.'

'All of this has to be a mistake, Nicole. Can I do anything to help?'

Despite what she is learning about me, I am touched that she still feels loyal to our friendship. 'You already did. I borrowed some yoga pants, a T-shirt and a sweater. I hope it's OK.'

'It's fine. You should have taken more. It's not a problem. I just want you to be OK.'

Tears well in my eyes, and I fight to keep them at bay. 'I'm OK, really I am.' Am I? I have to believe I am, or I will fall apart.

'You should call Frank Cooper. You know, about *him*.' She means Ian.

'I will,' I say, crossing my fingers as I speak. 'But can you promise that you won't say anything? I mean, this is something I have to do.'

A slight hesitation, then, 'I won't. But how about if you tell Steve and me where you are, and we'll come to you? We can bring lunch.'

'I need to be alone right now. I have to figure out what's going on. Is that OK?' I ask her out of friendship only. It must be OK, because there is no other way.

'Yes.' But I can tell that she doesn't want it to be.

'I'll call you later. Thanks for everything.' I hang up before she can say anything more, the same way I did with Steve. I have spent years with Jeanine and Steve, treasuring their friendship, and now I am lying even more than before.

I turn back to the laptop and log in to the VPN. There is one thing I need to do before I buy my train tickets. I go to the bank website. It is really too easy, even now, even fifteen years later. I click on 'forgot username' and am taken to a page where I am prompted to put in my credit card number and an email address. On an alternate screen, within minutes I have a free email account. I put that into the prompt. Moments later, I have an email confirming who I am and am directed to a page to set up a new password.

And then I am in. All I needed was the credit card number.

Amelie Renaud has only charged little more than fifty U.S. dollars on her account. Her payments are due on the ninth of the month, which means she is in the middle of the credit card cycle. This is what I was looking for. No one checks his credit card balance until his payment is due. She won't even know what's going on the card right now.

But the bank will. And the bank will know that Amelie Renaud is in France, not the United States, and they could flag her account. I find the page where I can report that I will be leaving the country and the card should not be flagged if foreign charges are made. This takes about five minutes.

From there, I go to the Amtrak website and make my reservations from Boston to Washington, leaving day after tomorrow.

My hands are shaking as I hit the payment button, not because I am using Amelie's credit card but because this is final. I sit for a few minutes, staring at the screen, until it grows dark and the laptop goes to sleep. I take off my glasses and wipe my eyes before I climb off the bed and go downstairs to ask if I can use the printer. It's not a problem, so I print out the train ticket and bring it back upstairs, folding it carefully and putting it in the front pocket of the backpack.

The backpack. I will need a bigger bag. Something sturdier. I have a gym bag in my house, but it's not big enough. I don't own luggage because I don't go anywhere. I know where I can find something suitable. The shop next to Veronica's gallery sells duffel bags. Some say Block Island on them, but others are plain. I will need a plain one.

My head is spinning with everything I am doing and everything I need to do. I lie down on the bed and close my eyes. Just for a few minutes, I tell myself, just to regroup a little.

There is a knock at the door. It startles me awake. I glance at my watch and see that I have been sleeping for four hours and it is after lunch. I push down the irritation with myself as I get up on one elbow.

'Yes?' I call.

'You've got a visitor.' The owner's voice is muffled. It doesn't really sound like her, but it could just be that she's talking through the door.

I get up slowly and cross the room. 'Excuse me?'

'You have a visitor.' Yes, it's her. I recognize her voice now.

I reach for the doorknob and turn. I barely have the door open when he pushes inside.

TWENTY-NINE

'Steve?'

He comes in and shuts the door behind him. He is carrying a big brown bag that smells remarkably like onion rings. He holds it up. 'I brought you something to eat.'

'How did you know where I was?' I am definitely confused.

'I stopped back over at the spa after I did a tour. Jeanine told me you called her. I checked her caller ID when she went out to be with a client. I recognized the number. I know all the B and B numbers on the island.'

I feel stupid. Of course he has to know all the numbers of all the bed and breakfasts, hotels, condos, every tourist accommodation on the island. It is his job.

'Reggie has been following me around like a dog, but he got distracted.' He is over at the little desk in the corner, opening up the bag he's brought.

'Distracted how?'

'They found him. That guy. Carmine.' He takes out napkins and makes little placemats out of them before putting the cheeseburgers and onion rings on them. I see now that he has a second bag, and he takes out a couple of Del's lemonades.

My stomach growls despite myself, and he grins. 'Nice to see that you're still alive and well,' he says. 'Come on, it'll get cold.'

But I am still thinking about what he's told me. 'Who found him?'

'No one we know. Couple of tourists here for the first time. Too bad about that.'

They will always associate Block Island with a dead body now.

There are two chairs in the room, and we pull them over to the desk. I pick up a burger and after I take a big bite, let out a long sigh. 'Thanks for this.'

Steve is watching me as I eat. He is trying not to let on that he is, but his eyes are following my every movement.

'So, I guess all the police on the island are at the Bluffs now,'

I say, mulling this over in my head. This is what I thought of last night, that the body could be reported and I could make my escape.

'That's right.' He knows what I'm thinking. That I could get away now. But I still have something I need to do before I go, and I'm not a hundred percent sure that no one is watching for me, even now.

'Is there an APB or something out on me? I mean, because Reggie's been watching you and they're probably watching the ferries, too.'

Steve takes a deep breath. 'Frank hasn't advertised that they're looking for you. I think he's still hoping you'll turn yourself in.'

I let that lie. 'I'm surprised Jeanine didn't come with you.'

'I didn't tell her I was coming.'

I see a twinkle in his eye. 'You didn't tell her you sneaked a peek at her caller ID.'

'You had a reason not to tell her where you were.'

'I had a reason not to tell you, either.'

Steve wipes his mouth with a napkin, but he still has some crumbs in his beard. I lean over and brush them off, and he reaches up and takes my hand. 'Nicole, I think it's time we talked seriously about what to do.'

His hand is warm and rough, and I carefully pull mine out of his. 'I know what I'm going to do.' I meet his stare, and he knows. He is struggling with it, though, just as I have been these past days.

He suddenly drops his head into his hands and whispers, 'What am I going to do without you?'

I get up and put my arms around him, my face in his neck. We stay that way for a few minutes, until finally I straighten up and go back to my chair. He looks at me then, studying my face as though he wants to imprint it on his brain so he will never forget me. I don't need to do that. He will forever be a part of me.

'I'm a fugitive,' I say, my voice sounding too loud, although it is barely above a whisper.

'But what you did was a long time ago—'

'Steve, I stole millions of dollars. They will throw me in prison.'

'Where will you go?'

I am thrown a little by the change of subject. 'I'm not sure yet.'

'Will you be able to let me know?'

'I have been living here for fifteen years and I never told anyone from my other life where I was.' Until that stupid post-card. I will not make the same mistake.

'But it's me,' he argues.

I want to tell him that I will let him know. I want to tell him that someday we will see each other again. But I can't. It would just be another lie.

'Why can't I go with you?'

'Your life is here.'

'So is yours.'

His words sober me. He is right. Or at least, my life used to be here. It has been slipping away ever since I saw Ian in the parking lot at Club Soda.

'Will you see him again?' Somehow Steve knows I am thinking of Ian.

'No.'

'You ran with him once before.'

'And then I ran away from him.'

Steve's face grows dark, and he looks deep into my eyes. 'What happened with Zeke Chapman? Did you kill him, Nicole? Is that really why you're on the run?'

I first noticed the surveillance car outside the house about two weeks into my affair with Zeke. It followed me to the gym. I could make out a man and a woman inside. They kept a safe distance away, and even though they didn't pull into the gym parking lot, when I drove home later I spotted it again in my rearview mirror.

'We've got a problem,' I told Ian when I called him. We had been careful not to see each other, except in crowded clubs, since we'd done the job. We wanted to make sure a good period of time passed before we were seen together, just in case. We told my father Ian had gone back north, when in fact he was staying in a friend's house in Coral Gables.

'Are you sure?'

'Pretty sure.'

'It's that agent. The one you can't keep your hands off.'

I had told him about Zeke to make him jealous. He had been

distracted the last couple of months, despite the job, and I worried there was another woman. But I didn't tell him the reason for getting involved with Zeke. Instead, I said it was to make sure that the FBI weren't onto us. 'He's OK,' I said.

'I don't think so. Maybe he's with you because he suspects you.'

I'd already had that thought, and I'd tried to push it away, but it wouldn't go. Zeke showed up for the first time right after we did the job, checking up on my father, but what did he know about me? Did he know that I'd hacked into my father's business accounts when I was a teenager? My father had been angry, but then he bragged about me. Said because of me, he knew he needed better security on his computer system. He hired experts who claimed they were the best in the business. He had no idea I still got past their firewalls and safeguards. I knew everything that was going on in my father's business, and I knew where all the money came from and was funneled out to.

If my father had hired Tracker, no one would've been able to get in. Not even me.

Did Zeke hear the story about me? Did he keep an eye on me because of that? I still couldn't believe that he had any idea about what we'd done. How could he be sleeping with me, knowing I might have stolen millions?

I was wary for the next couple of days, watchful for that car. I thought I'd imagined it the first time because I didn't see it again. But then, I realized they were smart. There were different cars on different days, two men, two women, a man and a woman. They were changing it up. But I was definitely being followed.

'I think someone's following me,' I told Zeke one afternoon in bed.

He gave a short chuckle and touched my cheek. 'Paranoid?'

'No. I'm being followed.'

He leaned back. 'Why do you think someone would follow you?' He stared at me in a way that dared me to tell him the truth.

I shrugged. 'I have no idea. My father, maybe?'

'But you have nothing to do with your father's business.' He paused. 'Do you?'

I gave him a sly smile. 'Wouldn't you like to know?'

Later, when I got out of the shower, I peered around the door and saw him with my laptop open on the bed. I didn't let on that

I'd seen him. I gave him a kiss at the door and he said he'd see me the next day. He had a surprise for me. I went back upstairs and opened the laptop. He'd seen nothing; I always made sure I left no tracks. But I had to be sure. I scoured the system, but there were no clues to what I'd done.

Still, I found Tracker and told him I needed the new identities for me and Ian as soon as possible.

The next day, I met Zeke at the door and led him up to my bedroom, as I'd been doing for the last month. But today would be the last time.

'I told you I had a surprise,' he said afterward. He was excited about something. I felt a sense of dread. 'I told my wife. About you.'

I couldn't speak for a few seconds. 'What?' I finally asked. 'Why?'

'Let's run away together.' His eyes were a bright blue, and I could see in them that he meant it. That he wanted to run away with me.

'But—'

'But nothing. I love you.'

All I could think was, we were just sleeping together. It wasn't love. At least not for me. He could see it. He could see it in my face. He pulled away from me, frowning.

'What, Tina? Was I just a good fuck?'

I reached for him, but he swung his legs over the side of the bed and got up.

'No, it's not like that.'

'Then what's it like?' His blue eyes were dark with anger. 'What's it like for you? Because for me, well, I told my wife that I loved someone else. That I was leaving her. For you.'

I didn't feel guilty then, and I still don't. Not about that. But I ponder Steve's question. Did I kill Zeke?

'No. It's nothing like that. It's just the money. That's all it's ever been,' I say, unable to look him in the eye. 'Zeke and I, well, we had a relationship. He was more attached than I was. I guess you can say he got a little possessive.'

'So how did he end up in Paris?' Steve is genuinely curious about this, and I want to tell him, but I'm not ready for that particular story yet. I shake my head.

'I don't want to take that trip down memory lane right now, OK?'

Steve reluctantly nods. 'OK. So what's your plan?'

I smile. 'You know I'm not going to tell you that.'

'It was worth a try, wasn't it?'

'You get a gold star for effort.'

'I think I'd make a pretty good detective,' Steve says. 'I did find you here.'

'You did do that.'

'So tell me what else I can do to help you.'

I look at him warily. 'You want to help me get off the island without being seen?'

'Isn't that what friends do? Help each other?' But I can see the pain etched in his expression. He will help me, but he doesn't truly want to. He wants me to stay, for everything to stay the same, despite everything, despite knowing what I have done. He loves me unconditionally, unlike Ian, unlike Zeke, despite their pronouncements. They both wanted something from me, something they knew I couldn't give them. Steve wants me to stay, but because I must leave, he will help me step out of his life and leave him alone. Because it's what I have to do.

'I need to get on the ferry in the morning. I have to take the first one out.' I had thought I might be able to take the three o'clock, but it's getting too late for that. The jury is still out on whether I can make the five o'clock, which is the last ferry of the day. It depends on whether I can get myself a duffel bag and the money. I could go straight to the ferry from my house. Steve will never have to know.

He is speaking. 'No problem. And I'll go with you.'

'No, Steve, you can't.'

'Yes, I can. And I'll take you wherever you want me to. Where do you need to go?'

I don't want to tell him about the train ticket out from Boston, but I see that he's pretty determined, so I say, 'Providence.'

He nods his head slowly. 'OK. What else do you need?'

'Nothing.'

His eyebrows rise into his forehead and I hold up a hand. 'No, really, Steve, I don't need anything else.' I don't need the ride to the ferry, either, but it is the only way I know to get him to leave now. I have things to do, things that don't concern him. I stand up. 'I have to get some rest. Tomorrow is going to be a long day.' I am anxious for him to leave. I've wasted too much time.

He reluctantly stands, too. 'OK.'

I walk him to the door. 'First ferry is—'

'At eight-fifteen. I'll pick you up at seven-thirty.' He lingers at the door. 'You really have to—'

I put my finger to his lips. 'I really have to.' I can see in his eyes that he thinks if he helps me, maybe I will not disappear forever. I give him a little push out the door. 'I'll see you in the morning.'

I listen to his footsteps go down the stairs before I shut the door. I go over to the window and see his SUV out front. He emerges from the house and looks both ways before he gets into the Explorer. The engine starts. He glances up at the house, and I shrink back into the white lace curtains, hoping he didn't see me. The SUV begins to move slowly down the street, until it goes around the corner and is out of sight.

I clean up the remnants of the lunch Steve brought, putting the trash back into the paper bag it came in and stuffing it in the can next to the desk.

I am stalling, but I need to make sure he is well gone before I venture outside.

I shove the backpack and laptop under the bed. I won't need them for what I'm about to do, and they will be safer here, where no one but Steve knows I've been. If something happens to me, he can lead Frank Cooper here. They will find the train ticket I have printed out, along with all the cash and the passport and driver's license for Amelie Renaud. They will find nothing on the laptop, because I've wiped it clean. Maybe, just maybe, Frank will find someone who can discover my secrets, but it will take a long time to break through.

I take another look around the room before I shrug on the cardigan I've borrowed from Jeanine and pull the baseball cap over my head. I slip through the door, locking it behind me.

THIRTY

I am headed on foot to that store next to Veronica's gallery to get a duffel bag. I hope that the ball cap will keep anyone from recognizing me, at least right away. People here don't really expect to see me walking, anyway. They are more used to seeing me on my bike.

I am feeling antsy because this is only the first part of what I have to do.

I don't know how long it's taken me to get to Old Harbor; I am walking with purpose. Some cars have passed me; I've nodded to people walking dogs, pushing strollers. It's a beautiful day on the island, and everyone is doing normal things. I was normal until last week. What would I be doing if I were home, if I hadn't been discovered? I might be riding my bike up to the North Light or sitting in my rocker on the front porch looking out over the water with a cup of tea. I'd be feeling happy, content with my life. I long for that feeling again.

I walk past Jeanine's spa and then the Blue Dory Inn, where Ian and I met that day I first used my new laptop. It's as though it was a lifetime ago. I circle around and end up at the National Hotel and then the small little strip of storefronts.

I don't see any police cars, and I assume that Steve is right: they are distracted by Carmine's body at the Bluffs, so I boldly walk into the shop as though I am not a fugitive. I spot the bags I'm looking for on a display to my right. I am careful to pick one that does not say 'Block Island.' It is a plain navy canvas with brown leather handles and seems very sturdy.

I bring it up to the cash register, and I recognize Lucille, Veronica's friend. I give her a wide smile as I put the bag on the counter.

'Going somewhere?' she asks me with a wink.

She probably thinks I am going away with Ian for a weekend. Veronica has been spreading news of my love life.

I decide to play along. 'Maybe,' I say. 'How have you been?'

'Oh, same old, same old,' Lucille says lightly. 'You know about the body they found, right, at the Bluffs?'

This is what she's been itching to talk about. She doesn't care about me. She wants to gossip.

'Yeah, I heard. Who is it?'

'No one knows. Frank and his guys have been over there for hours and won't tell anyone anything. Heard he was shot.'

'How do you know that, if Frank won't tell anyone anything?' I have to ask.

Lucille gives me a sly smile. 'My Cathleen is married to Reggie McCallum. He won't even tell *her* anything.' The smile disappears as she thinks about how that's just not fair.

'How much?' I ask.

She looks distracted for a minute, then realizes I'm asking how much the duffel bag costs. 'That's a hundred and fifty plus tax.'

Things are pricey on the island, but I have anticipated it. I took enough cash out of my backpack before coming here, so I give her a few bills and she makes change for me. She begins to put the duffel into another bag, but I put up my hand.

'That's OK, I don't need a bag,' I say with a smile. It is taking all of my effort to act as though everything is normal.

'Oh, OK,' she says, sounding a little put out. But she hands me the duffel over the counter, and I take it.

'Thanks so much,' I say and start to head out. I stop short, though, just before pushing the door open.

A man stands on the sidewalk. He is wearing a windbreaker and a pair of neatly pressed jeans. It is the Hispanic man from the car, the one that showed up at the Painted Rock instead of Ian. He looks casual, his hands in his pockets, as though he is waiting for someone.

Is he waiting for me? Did he see me come in here? Has he been watching my whole transaction with the duffel bag?

I am still uncertain who he is, but I know for certain that I cannot let him see me. I turn and pretend that I have forgotten to look at the fleece jackets, which are strategically behind a rack with several large messenger bags hanging on it.

'Nicole? Did you need something else?' Lucille startles me.

'Oh, yes, I need a new jacket.' I pull out a black one that looks exactly like one I have at home.

Lucille frowns a little, but then puts on her shop-owner smile. 'Of course. I'll take that to the counter. Look around, just in case you see anything else.' She whisks away the jacket, which I am now committed to buying. I glance out the front window. He is still standing there.

I fiddle with a pair of wool socks just beyond the jackets. I am moving closer to the counter, to the back of the store, as though if he looks through the window he will not be able to see me. I grab the socks and put them on the counter next to the jacket.

'It's still a little chilly at night,' I say stupidly, but Lucille is a good shop owner and she merely smiles and rings me out. Fortunately, I've brought enough cash for all of it.

Lucille pulls out a plastic bag but hesitates. 'Do you want to wear the jacket?' she asks.

I hadn't thought of that, but it's not a bad idea. 'Sure.'

Lucille clips off the tags and hands me the jacket, which I shrug on. She is holding the socks and the scissors. 'What about these?'

I chuckle, trying to make light of it. 'I'll just put them in the duffel,' I say. 'No reason to waste a bag on me.' I take the socks and slip them into the duffel. I start to turn away, then turn back as though I've forgotten yet something else. 'Oh, would you mind if I go out the back? I need to get something from Veronica's back room and it's easier from there.'

I wait for an argument but instead she grins and leads me back, opening the door for me. As I step through, she asks, 'Are you OK, Nicole? I mean, I know it's upsetting—'

I hold up my hand to stop her. 'I'm fine. Really.' Although I put on an expression that might tell her otherwise to keep up the ruse.

She leans toward me and whispers loudly, 'Do you think that whoever did that to your place might have killed that man at the Bluffs?'

'I don't know, Lucille. Maybe Cathleen can get something out of Reggie. I'd be interested to know,' I lie.

She purses her lips and nods knowingly. 'I'll let you know,' she promises.

I take a deep breath when she finally goes back into her shop and the door closes.

I take a look at the door to the gallery and wish I could go inside and see Veronica. But I suspect that man is not waiting for just anyone. He is waiting for me to show up. I wonder where the other man is, the one who was with him in the car.

But as I walk past the door, I glance through the window and I see him. I can see all the way to the front of the gallery, and Veronica is talking to him. He is gesticulating with his hands; Veronica has her arms folded over her chest, a serious look on her face.

He motions toward the front, but Veronica does not follow his movement. Instead, she glances around – I can see she is tired of whatever he's been telling her – she looks to the back and she sees me, I can see it in her expression, but then she recovers. She takes him by the elbow and starts steering him out. I duck away from the door and shrink back against the siding, my heart pounding.

In my head I am mapping an escape route, much like when I'm mapping out a tour. I feel myself relaxing a little as I picture the roads in my head, concentrating on the matter at hand.

I won't be able to go out to the road without being seen, but I might be able to cut through some yards and end up on an artery far enough away so I can manage to skirt back to Hydrangea House without drawing attention to myself.

I am about to leave when the door opens, startling me.

'Nicole,' Veronica hisses. 'Get in here.' She grabs my arm, and I have no choice. I am inside, the door shutting off my escape.

We do not go into the front of the gallery, but to the left, behind a wall that hides the stacks of paintings that have not yet been hung. Customers can come back here, go through them and buy them unframed if they like.

'Is he gone?' I whisper.

Veronica frowns. 'I got rid of him.' She leans back and looks toward the front of the gallery. 'But they're outside, talking. Stay back here.' She twirls around, her skirt billowing a little around her calves, adjusts her scarf and puts a hand to her hair to smooth it. Her heels clack against the wood floor. I hear rustling; she is at her small desk, looking through receipts and whatnot, giving a show to the strangers that she is still here and not concerned about anything.

I find an empty space in between paintings against the wall and sink down to the floor, my knees up against my chest, and I take some deep breaths like Jeanine always tells me to do in yoga class. I hate it that I am hiding here.

Finally, I hear Veronica coming back.

'So what's going on?' Her tone is clipped, annoyed.

I scramble to my feet. 'Just tell me: who are they?'

'You don't know?' She seems genuinely surprised.

'No, I really don't. I saw them for the first time early this morning at the Painted Rock. I know they're looking for me, but I don't know who they are.'

'How many people exactly are looking for you?' She is being combative.

I sigh. 'I'm not sure, exactly.'

She rolls her eyes and shakes her head. 'Well, those men are with the FBI. Or maybe they're not. Is it like Zeke Chapman, that they're just saying they're with the FBI but they really aren't?'

Now, that is a good question.

'They say I have to turn you in if I see you,' Veronica is saying. 'You're a fugitive. What's going on, Nicole?'

At least Frank Cooper has been discreet. I couldn't expect as much from the FBI, although I am now wondering how they knew to go to the Painted Rock. Ian had to have told them.

'Nicole?'

I am startled out of my thoughts by her voice.

'Yes, right. I'm sorry, Veronica,' I say softly.

'What did you do?'

'They didn't tell you?'

'Something about computer hacking. I told them that you don't even have a computer, or at least you didn't have one until a few days ago.'

I really wish she hadn't told them that.

'So is it true? Are you a computer hacker?'

I nod. 'But I didn't want to do that anymore. That's why I didn't have a computer.'

'So why did you get one, then?'

It is a perfectly logical question. And for the first time she notices that I have a duffel bag with me.

'What's that?'

'I just bought it.'

'Why?' But even as she asks, I can see she knows. She is putting two and two together.

I don't really have time for this, although as I think that, I wonder why not. I cannot go to my house now. I know they will be watching it, but I would feel safer at Hydrangea House. I need to get back there, and then, when it grows dark, head to my house to get the rest of my money.

I hate it that I need that money. If I didn't, I'd get the next ferry out. If no one's watching it.

I can no longer count on Frank Cooper and his policemen being distracted, since the FBI agents seem to be more interested in finding me than in Carmine Loffredo's body.

I think about the marinas, all those dinghies that could take me out to one of those boats bobbing in the water. Problem is, while I can commit crimes with a computer, stealing a boat isn't something I feel confident about.

Veronica is waiting for an answer. I think carefully about what I'm going to say. She couldn't tell that FBI agent anything when he was here because she didn't know anything. I don't want to give her anything that will lead them to me.

I spot one of my paintings on the floor, leaning against the wall.

'I needed something for my paints and easel to fit into,' I say. 'I don't like carrying everything separately when I go to the beach.'

She narrows her eyes at me. I can tell she doesn't believe me, but she lets it go.

'If you want to hang out here for a little while until the coast is clear, you can,' she offers, her tone softer now. 'I won't tell them anything if they come back.'

'Thanks, Veronica, I appreciate it, but I can't stay.'

'They're outside, you know,' she warns. 'They're watching the ferries, they're watching everything.'

And you can see mostly everything, too, down here, this time of year. If it were July or August, there would be too many people, too much sidewalk and road traffic. But it is still early enough in May for someone to be noticed. Especially a middle-aged woman wearing glasses and a ball cap. For the first time in fifteen years, I wish I still owned contacts and hadn't cut my hair.

We hear the bell on the front door. Veronica peers around the corner, then back at me. 'Someone's coming in.'

She bustles away. I hear the soft mumblings as she talks to whoever has come in, then the front door opens and closes. Where have they gone? I want to check but realize I can make a getaway out the back. I start toward the door, but when I see a shadow cross the glass in the window, I press myself back against the wall. The doorknob jiggles – someone is trying to get in or at least seeing if the door is locked. I didn't even see Veronica lock it after I came in. The face appears in the window. I see half of it, a profile, an eye, a cheekbone, an ear. The Hispanic FBI agent.

I am holding my breath as he puts his palm to the glass and he tries to see into my corner. It is dark here; I am in the shadows. I pull my feet up underneath me, my arms wrapped around my torso, trying to become invisible.

They have seen Veronica go out the front, and for some reason they think I am here.

It hits me then. Lucille. Next door. They have spoken to her, and she told them I was there. She probably told them I bought a duffel bag and a black fleece jacket and a pair of wool socks.

My heart is pounding so hard, I know he can hear it through the window.

Suddenly, his face disappears and I start to let out a breath, but the doorknob begins to jiggle again. This time it is more forceful. Will they break in? Am I worth that? I know Veronica has a good double bolt on the door. She has some valuable paintings in here and does have a good alarm and security system. But they are FBI, and if they have probable cause they might be able to justify breaking in.

I am thinking the way my father used to talk when he got out of prison that first time. I am no better than he is. We are both common thieves. We just went about our crimes in different ways.

The doorknob stops jiggling, and I hear muffled voices on the other side of the door. Deep, determined voices. Will they approach Veronica when she comes back and demand to search the gallery?

I look around frantically. There is no other way out. A small bathroom is to my right. There is nothing on the other side of the opposite wall; the gallery is at the end of the row of storefronts. Even if I could get out, they would be waiting. There are two of them. One could be in the front, the other in the back. My idea about going through yards wouldn't work.

I shimmy around crab-like on the floor, careful to drag the duffel bag with me, and I ease my way into the little bathroom. A stream of light is pooled on the floor, and I look up to see a window above me. I reach over and use my fingers to pull the door closed.

I should have left that night that I saw Ian for the first time at Club Soda. I should have known. I could have bought a duffel bag and brought all my money with me right then and there and disappeared onto a ferry and to the mainland. What had I been thinking? Had I truly thought I could see him and have him see me and my life would not change?

Now I am hiding, huddled in a bathroom. I am pathetic.

I look at my watch. It is well after three. Because they are watching me, I need to wait until darkness falls before I can go back to my house. I need the protection that the night will give me.

But sunset is five hours away.

The way it's looking, I could be here that long, though.

I hear something out front. Voices. Two men, Veronica. She's back. They're arguing. They want to search the whole gallery.

I think about where the back door is, and I know I will not be able to escape unnoticed. I glance up again at the window above me. I am not a large person, and it is just high enough so I will struggle to climb through. But I have to try.

I stand on the toilet and push open the window, which I notice is new and does not make any noise. I give a silent thanks for that as I reach over and grab hold of the screen. With one yank, it's inside, and I lean it against the wall next to the toilet.

The duffel bag has to go first. Even if I wanted to abandon it here, the FBI agents would find it and Veronica would be questioned at length. Maybe even charged with accessory to a crime.

More terminology I learned from my father.

I fold up the duffel as well as I can and drop it out the window. The voices are louder now. I grab hold of the windowsill and pull myself up and through. My legs flounder a little until my feet make purchase with the wall and I am soon halfway out. The ground seems farther away than it should be for an easy fall, but I have no choice. I wiggle through further and then let myself drop down.

I land with a thud on my right shoulder, then roll and get up, grabbing the duffel. I look around quickly to make sure Lucille isn't camped out here, but see no one.

I should get back to Hydrangea House as soon as I can and as discreetly as possible, but I can't waste any more time. I have to go to my house. If those men are here, and Frank Cooper and his minions are at the Bluffs, I have a very small window of opportunity. I say a silent farewell to Veronica as I scramble through a few back yards and zigzag my way on the small streets up to my house.

THIRTY-ONE

I come up to my house the roundabout way, down the hill behind it rather than up the hill in front. I look out toward the water and see the sunlight shimmering across the whitecaps. It's windy, and the sea is rough. I try to imprint the image in my memory. It would be a beautiful painting, bright and blue with a shocking streak of white.

My little house sits alone, with no police car outside. I approach, glancing side to side and behind me as I do, not seeing anyone. I begin to relax a little, breathe a little easier. I hug the side of the house as I circle it, and when I get to the door, it swings open easily.

I stand in the doorway to the mudroom, my heart pounding again. The door should have been locked. But I was not the last one here, so maybe the police neglected to lock it. Would they be so careless?

I listen and hear nothing except the bugs outside. Nothing inside. Still, I wait. I don't know how long I have been standing here when I finally decide that it's time. If someone is this patient, then perhaps he deserves a prize.

I move through my kitchen and then into the living room. I don't want to linger; I can't afford to. The bedroom is only steps away, and I am struck by the bare mattress on the frame. I have not gotten new sheets, a new comforter. I have not gotten anything to replace everything that has been damaged.

The closet door is closed. I push it open and stoop down. It is dark in here, but I don't need any light. I feel around on the floor until I touch the edge of the hiding place. With little effort, I lift up the floorboard and reach inside, the duffel bag ready to be filled.

The overhead light suddenly switches on, and I yank my hand out as if it's on fire. I spin around and see Ian behind me. I stand up quickly and face him.

'That's mine.' He indicates the cash inside the floor.

'No, it's not.'

'Yes, I think it's mine. You lied to me. You had it all along.' He is glaring at me.

'I never lied. I get paid in cash. This is money I've earned. I told you that.'

The concept seems to surprise him, but he recovers quickly. 'No matter. It's still mine.'

I want to argue. I want to scream that I need this money, that without it I cannot get my new identity, I cannot pay for the documents Tracker has arranged. But if I say any of that, Ian will know what I'm doing and I might not be able to get away. I am crazy to even have that thought, though. Will I even be able to get out of my house alive now that he is standing there, greedily looking at my stash? He is wearing a jacket, and I can see the outline of his gun underneath.

'Where are your friends?' I ask, expecting the two men to come out from behind him. After realizing I am not in the gallery, they could easily come up here to check out my house.

'What friends?' Ian has never been very good at lying. His eyes shift around behind me.

'The friends you sent to meet me at the Painted Rock.'

'I don't know what you're talking about.' Again, he cannot meet my eyes.

I glance out the bedroom window. Anyone passing the house could see us standing here.

'The shades aren't pulled down; people can see us,' I say. 'They're looking for both of us, Ian.'

'No, Tina. They're looking for *you*.' His hand is on my cheek, his fingers tickling my ear.

I am wound so tight, every muscle ready to leap, and yet I stay where I am. 'Tell me what you want me to do, and I'll take care of it. Give me till tomorrow morning.'

'I'm not letting you out of my sight again.' His other hand now grips my waist. 'Let's put this money in your bag and go see what you can do with that computer of yours. Where is it, anyway?'

'I've got it in a safe place,' I say. 'So what happens after? Will you kill me?'

He kisses me then, and for the first time I am not aroused. I am ashamed that it took this long, that even Zeke didn't make my passion for him fade. Zeke was a good man, an honest man, who loved me despite who I was, despite everything he believed in. I am sorry that I couldn't love him back the way he wanted me to. And now it's too late.

I let Ian kiss me until he lets go of me. 'So that's the way you're playing it.'

'I'm not playing anything, Ian. I just want my life back.' I am aware that my voice sounds tired, that I am tired.

'Then do what I say, and I'll be out of your way.'

'And your friends?'

'They're not my friends, and this is none of their business. This is between you and me.'

I wonder if I can run, if I can duck past him and out the door and down the hill. I could lose him using my shortcuts; he would never find me at Hydrangea House. But he is one step ahead of me. He reaches into his jacket, and I feel the hard steel against my chest.

'If you try anything, I will not hesitate.' I have never heard this tone from him before. He has never threatened me like this, and I can only trust that he is telling the truth. 'Now fill up that bag.'

I turn and stoop down, unzipping the bag and lifting up the floorboard. I shove the rest of the cash inside and think about the backpack under my bed at Hydrangea House. He doesn't know I have it, but the laptop is next to it. Will I be able to slide it out without him noticing the backpack? I have no choice but to try.

Of course, we may not even make it there, between the FBI agents and Frank Cooper.

I hand him the bag, and he waves the gun around. 'Let's go get that computer.'

He follows me so closely out of the bedroom and into the living room that I can almost hear his heart beating. I take a look around. This is not the way I wanted to say goodbye.

But I am not sure that this is going to be goodbye. At least not yet. I had hoped to come here under the veil of darkness, but since my plans were thwarted, it is still bright outside. The ball cap isn't really going to disguise me, and Ian can't possibly

keep the gun on me as we walk. The quickest and most direct
route to Hydrangea House is through Old Harbor, but we can't
go that way because of the FBI agents. If we take the roundabout
way, we will be going past the Bluffs, and while it's been a few
hours since Carmine's body was found, the police are probably
still there or at least spreading out in the general vicinity, looking
for clues.

'What's going on?' Ian demands.

I tell him my thoughts. 'We can't get there from here. At least
not easily,' I finish. 'It would be better at night. The island is
pretty dark – there aren't a lot of street lights.'

Ian frowns as he glances out the window. 'But it's still a couple
of hours at least until dark.'

I nod.

'So you're proposing holding off until then?'

I cannot think of any other way, and I say so. 'Unless you
don't care.'

But I see in his expression that he does care. That he is no
more willing to get caught than I am, yet he is eager for me to
do the job for him and he will sacrifice a couple of hours for it.

'But we can't stay here, either,' I say.

'Why not?'

'They found Carmine's body. They will think that I did it, or
you did it, and they'll come here looking for me. Put someone
outside, waiting for me. Right now we can get away, but the
longer we stay here the riskier it is.'

'So where do you propose we go?'

I have an idea, and it may be an uncomfortable couple of
hours, but we have no choice. 'Follow me,' I say as I go into
the kitchen and push open the door.

'Where are we going?' he asks. 'I thought we couldn't go
outside.'

But we are not going far. Despite his protests, he follows me,
both of us jogging down the hill. I smell the llamas, see them
in their pen. When we reach it, I unlatch the lock from the outside
and we slip inside and around into the small barn that houses
the llamas.

Ian sneezes.

I put my finger to my lips. 'Shush,' I say, looking around for the best place to hide. There are individual pens in here for each of the llamas; hay is scattered on the floor. I count the pens and realize there are two more than the number of llamas. I tug on Ian's arm and pull him into the furthest pen from the door and we sink into a pile of hay.

'What about the owners?' Ian whispers.

'They've gone to the mainland,' I say. Today is their son's birthday and they've gone to New London for the day. 'They won't be back until after dark, and by then we'll be gone.'

'They leave *those* outside when they leave?' Ian cocks his head toward the llamas.

'They won't hurt us, and they can come inside if they want.' I indicate the pen we're in, with the shut gate. 'They can't get in here with us.' Although I am not sure if they will be upset about our presence. I don't spend a lot of time with the animals.

'It stinks in here.' Ian wrinkles his nose. I am just as bothered by the smell, but there is no choice. I say so.

'Unless you want someone to find us, then you'll never get what you want.'

I have him there. He leans back on the hay, but he still grips the gun.

I am wondering now what I'd seen in him, beyond that day when he sauntered into the Rathskeller and we saw each other for the first time and I felt as though my world had turned upside down. While in bed we were as well matched as we were before, I know he is curious about me, about how I've changed, but at the same time he knows that deep down I have not changed at all. I still opened that laptop. I still ran my fingers across its keys as if it were a sacred thing. I am still telling him that I will help him because I need to show him that I can.

Is that all it is? Or is it just so much a part of who I am that I can never shed it as easily as those skins on the onion rings Steve and I eat every Friday night at Club Soda?

I am afraid of the answer. Afraid that I will always be tempted, that a twelve-step program for computer hackers wouldn't work for me. I lived one day at a time, and as long as I didn't have my own computer, I managed to live like a real person who does not have an addiction. But I still sometimes wake up in the night, source codes and passwords and firewalls taunting me in my head.

I came here to hide, but I realize now there is nowhere for me to hide. I cannot escape it.

Ian sneezes again.

'I didn't know you were allergic to animals,' I taunt him.

He waves the gun at me. 'Don't get all smart with me, bike girl.'

I think about my chat-room nickname and smile to myself, but then I remember. 'What happened to my bike? I mean, it looked like it was thrown down the steps at the Bluffs.'

'How do you know that?' He looks at me warily.

'I found it. And Carmine. Last night. I was there.'

'Where?'

'I was on the beach. I didn't hear anything. The wind is so loud there. It whips through the Bluffs like a freight train. So what happened between you and Carmine?'

Ian's eyes wander around the small barn for a second before he answers. 'I rode the bike out there because I thought maybe that's where you were. I left it at the top, but he was behind me and threw it at me. I deflected it and it got tossed and all fucked up.' He glances at me. 'I've never felt a bike so light.'

'Aerodynamic. So how did Carmine end up dead?'

Again he waves the gun. 'He didn't know I had this. He came after me. He actually fired at me, but I was faster than he was. He got a little fat in his old age. Maybe he thought since he was after you it wouldn't matter so much.' He chuckles. 'He would've been surprised, with you all athletic and everything now. Bet you would've given him a run for his money, too.'

'Who trashed my house, then? You or Carmine?'

'Carmine. I was looking for you, going up to your house and saw him go in there. I hung around a little while, waited till he left and went in, worried that I'd find you there.'

'Worried that you'd find my body, you mean,' I say softly. And then something clicks and it is as though the breath has been knocked out of me. 'What happened while I was gone?'

He shrugs. 'It's been fifteen years, Tina. A lot has happened. To all of us.'

'How did you end up driving Tony DeMarco's car?'

He stares at me. 'How do you know that?'

I chuckle. 'Oh, come on, Ian. The DMV was a piece of cake. So how did you get the car?'

'That's not something you need to worry about.'

'I'm not *worried* about it, Ian. I just want to know. I think you owe it to me to tell me what happened. I mean, how did you see the postcard I sent my father? You couldn't have just walked into my father's hospital room in a federal prison. You're dead, Ian. What would everyone have said?'

'You *have* been busy on that computer, haven't you?'

'You gave it to me. You knew what I could do. Do you really think I'd forgotten? You came here so I could do a job and get you back all that money that you think I'm responsible for taking from you, so you must have figured I was still hacking. But that job was the last one I ever did, and I wish like hell I'd never gone along with it.'

'Don't get a conscience on me here. You didn't have one before.'

'We stole from people we didn't know. Well, not everyone. We knew Tony, and of course, there's Paul Michaels.'

I see panic in his eyes.

'That's right, Ian. You made such a big deal about coming up with your fake name, but you knew Paul Michaels was one of the account owners we were stealing from. Who is he?' I pause, waiting for an answer, but he doesn't say anything, so I continue. 'And what about Amelie Renaud. Who is *she*, Ian?' I ask him in such a way that he knows, knows that I know she's real.

He sighs and sticks the gun in his waistband. I don't think anyone outside of the movies ever does that, but maybe that's where he's gotten the idea. I wait as he mulls over how to answer.

Finally, he tells me.

'She's my wife.'

THIRTY-TWO

H is wife. It throws me off center, mentally and physically, and I slump against the back of the pen. His wife? But I cannot ask the question. I cannot speak. The words are caught in my throat, strangling me. I hear myself make a sound that is merely garble.

'I should have told you,' he says, but not as contritely as I'd expect.

I swallow hard, several times. My head is spinning. Finally, I find my voice.

'How long?' I am thinking back to that day in Miami, the day we fell in love. 'How long have you been married?'

'Fourteen years.'

After. But just.

He does not give me a chance to even formulate another question. 'I didn't know it would be the same. You know, between us.' He takes my silence as permission to continue. 'But when I saw you, that day at the spa, I couldn't stop thinking about you. How I still—'

I put my hand up to stop him from saying anything more. 'You gave me her name. She's on the list. The list of account owners. You knew her, didn't you, before?' I ask. I want to hear him admit it.

'Yes.'

'How?'

'I met her in France. My semester abroad.'

Before we met. Right before we met.

'Did you see her when we were in Paris?'

'You *left* me.' Anger laces his words.

'I'm surprised you could even touch me at all,' I say bitterly. 'You must really want me to do this job. What is so important about it? Is it just because you think I owe you for what happened back then, or is there more to it?' I don't give him a chance to answer, though, because I have another thought. 'What about how you're dead? Who did Amelie Renaud marry? She couldn't marry Ian Cartwright, because he committed suicide in a house-boat in Paris. Who are you these days? Are you Paul Michaels?'

He shakes his head, staring at the hay next to him. I wait. I'm good at waiting. I've been waiting for fifteen years.

'Does she know? Does she know anything?' I ask when it's clear he won't tell me.

Ian looks at me then, with an expression full of hate and anger. 'You think you're so smart. But you didn't find out everything, did you, with that precious computer of yours? You haven't been looking in the right place.'

He is talking in riddles.

'What do you mean?'

'You found Amelie, but you didn't find out everything, did you?'

I am beginning to wonder what I have missed, something so critical that he is smiling so wickedly, as if he has something over me. He does have something over me, but I cannot for the life of me figure out what it is. I decide to drop it. For now.

'Tell me about the FBI agents, Ian. The ones who showed up at the Painted Rock instead of you.'

His smile softens and a tinge of respect comes into his eyes. 'I figured you were there somewhere. They said you weren't. But you know every inch of this goddamned island, don't you? I told them that, but they seem to think they're smarter than you.'

He is not answering my questions. I am ready to scream.

He moves suddenly, grabbing me, his fingers digging into my arms so hard I know I will have bruises. 'You asked me if they caught me.'

'You said they didn't.'

His face is so close to mine I can feel his breath. 'I lied.'

'You cut a deal with the Feds, didn't you?' I ask, my voice louder than it should be because I am angry. I want to hear him admit it.

'You *left* me there,' he says again. 'I took care of it, you know. I took care of *him*. I did that for you.'

I swallow hard, shutting my eyes and then opening them again so I wouldn't see the image imprinted on them.

'So whose body was identified as yours?' I manage to ask.

'It doesn't matter now.'

'Are you in witness protection? Did you tell them it was all me, that you could help them find me? When my father was dying, did they send you to see if you could find out if I'd come out of the woodwork?'

Ian doesn't answer, which makes me think I am right. But he lets go of me, and I shift away from him, out of reach.

I can't stop myself, though. 'The Feds must have thought you had the real inside scoop on where I was if they helped you stage your own death.'

Ian's expression changes slightly, and I begin to question my first instincts. My head is full now with possible scenarios, but I am not sure which one is the right one. He is staring at me, almost daring me to continue. But instead, he begins to talk.

'Tony had the postcard, Tina. I heard him talking about it with Carmine, how he was going to come after you for what you did. I took off, but not fast enough. The Feds nailed me in the Grove later that night. They said they could cut me a deal.'

'So you did sell me out.' I feel as though he has just set a hundred pound weight on my chest.

He shifts a little, won't meet my eyes. 'I couldn't believe you left me like that, with nothing.' He is back to talking about Paris. 'But then, when I couldn't find you, I figured I could get away if I faked my death.' He chuckles nervously. 'It was almost too easy.'

It *was* too easy. No real identification was done, no fingerprints, no nothing. Just the word of a neighbor. I know what happened now. He never really got away. They had been watching him all along, and this was their chance to get both of us.

'And you're wrong about one thing. I didn't sell you out. You sold yourself out. You always told me you hated your father, but you didn't. He challenged you, and you always loved a challenge.'

I hate it that Ian knows me so well.

He stares me straight in the eye. '*You* sent that postcard.'

I don't need the reminder that I'd been stupid, and I am about to say something sarcastic, but he isn't done yet.

'It won't be easy for you, Tina. I told them you killed Zeke. They want you for murder. Not just the money.'

Without thinking, I lunge toward him and take a swing at him, my fist making contact with the side of his face. I am much stronger than I used to be, and the blow surprises him and he stumbles backward, clutching his cheek.

'What the fuck—'

'Right, Ian, what the fuck?' I could kill him, right now, right here, as the rage rushes through me. I remember the gun. Where did he put it?

'I was pissed at you.'

'You were *pissed* at me? I did leave you some money, Ian. It wasn't my fault that they found it before you could get it.' My heart is pounding. The FBI is here on the island, looking for me, because I am wanted for killing one of their own.

I am not going to be able to get away so easily.

I push the anger down, out of the way. I can't think like this. I turn away from him, collapsing into the hay, its smell a mixture of sweet and sour. I feel his hand on my back and I twist around and push it away. He frowns, as if he doesn't understand.

'You're kidding, right?' I ask. 'You sold me out to the Feds. *And* you're married. I don't think so.'

He leans back against the side of the pen and gives me a wistful look. I turn back to stare at the wooden slats between the pen we're in and the next one. It is going to be a long couple of hours, but I still have more questions.

'How is it you're driving Tony DeMarco's car? And that you knew he had the postcard?' I will not look at him, and my questions are muffled by the hay.

He hears me, though, and clears his throat as though he is about to lie.

'I thought he could help me.'

I am so surprised by this truth that I roll over to look at him. He gives me a wan smile. 'I thought he could help me find you.'

I am actually surprised that with the resources Tony has that he couldn't find me until now. I know I left traces. I flew back using the same passport, although I stopped using Amelie's name once I got here. I bought a car in New York with five hundred dollars in cash and headed east, uncertain where I'd end up. I left the car in the ferry parking lot. If they'd just been able to follow the breadcrumbs, they would have found me years ago.

'So he knew that you were considered dead?'

Ian nods. 'I told him everything was your idea. The fact that you left me there with nothing proved it. Having me dead was convenient for him.' A darkness crosses his face, and I know that Ian's desperation had sealed his fate. 'Tony DeMarco doesn't help anyone for nothing. I had to do what he wanted.'

I don't want to know what Tony made him do. The fact that he is carrying a gun says enough.

I don't want to hear any more. I roll over and put my arms over my head, burrowing. I hear the hay rustling and know he is settling in as well. He is done with his confessions, and I don't want to know any more.

THIRTY-THREE

The moonlight streams across the hay in the pen, and I hear footsteps. I sit up quickly to see a shadow looming over me.

'It's just one of the animals,' Ian whispers, startling me further.

I take short, shallow breaths. 'I know,' I finally say. I brush the hay out of my hair and adjust my glasses on my nose. I scramble to my feet. 'OK, time to go.' I have no idea what time it is, but it's dark and we need to move.

As we get outside, a car is coming up the hill toward us, the headlights blinding me for a second. Ian hooks his arm around mine and pulls me away from the side of the road. He leans into me and he is kissing me; this time it's a diversion. The driver will only see a couple kissing in the moonlight.

When the car passes, Ian loosens his hold on me slightly. In the moonlight, for a second, I see a sadness in his face. He knows it's over, too. I wonder whether after I do the job for him he will let me go quietly or call the Feds on me. Or maybe he'll call Tony. The anger is still simmering just beneath the surface, and he is still carrying a gun.

We continue down the road, past Veronica's gallery and the National Hotel, around the curve and the Sunswept Spa.

'Where the hell are we going?' Ian mutters.

'It's a bit of a walk,' I say.

'Where, to Long Island?'

'You mean Rhode Island.'

'Yeah, whatever. Too many islands for me. I'd rather be connected to real land.'

I hear the car turn the corner behind us before the headlights hit us. We move over to the side of the road; Ian's hand curls around mine, his other hand is clutching the duffel bag. I wait for the car to pass us, but it doesn't. It slows down until it is crawling beside us. I look over at it and see Steve has opened the passenger window. If he is surprised to see Ian, he doesn't show it.

'Can I give you a ride?' he asks casually, as though he is merely picking up a fare.

Ian gives his head a quick shake. 'We're fine here.'

But Steve doesn't buy it, and the SUV suddenly jerks forward and across our path. Steve jumps out and comes around the front. Ian's hand tightens around mine.

'What's going on?' he asks, looking from me to Ian and back to me again.

'Just taking a walk,' Ian says.

'Nicole?' Steve is not stupid.

'Ian and I are going back to my room,' I say. I do not want him here. Ian has a gun, and he has used it before when someone got in the way. 'I'm fine. You can go home.'

However, Steve is looking straight at Ian now. 'The police chief is looking for you.'

'Be a pal and don't tell him you saw me, OK?' Ian flashes the smile that used to make me melt and usually charms. Steve is not charmed.

'Why? Why should I do that for you, after what you've done to Nicole?' I have never heard Steve so confrontational. I want to tell him to let it go, that I can handle it from here, but the words get stuck in my throat. Instead, I reach out and touch his arm. He glances down at it, then at my face. 'Why are you doing this? Why are you taking him to your room?' He is genuinely perplexed.

'It's OK,' I say again. 'I'll be OK.'

He doesn't believe me. He turns on Ian again. 'Are you threatening her?'

Ian slings an arm around my shoulder and it is all I can do not to flinch. 'She wants to take me to her room. Last I knew, she was a grown up and could make her own decisions.'

'Nicole?' Steve asks.

A lump forms in my throat, keeping me from speaking. I swallow hard. 'It's OK,' I whisper. 'I'll call you later, all right?'

His anger gone, Steve is deflated. He strokes his beard and studies me for a few seconds before nodding. 'OK. But if I don't hear from you in an hour, I'm going to call Frank.'

He's going to tell Frank Cooper where I am. Where Ian is. He's giving us an hour. Not much time in my world, but I'll have to make it work.

'That's fine,' I say.

Steve gives me one final minute to change my mind, and when I don't say anything, he climbs back into his SUV. The engine roars and he peels away as though he's going to a fire. We watch his taillights go around the corner and disappear.

I shrug off Ian's arm and begin to jog.

'What's the hurry?' I hear him ask from behind. I am moving too fast for him.

'You heard him. He's going to call the police chief in an hour.'

'If you don't call him.'

'He just said that. He's going to call. So let's get this done.'

Ian manages to keep up with me and soon we are approaching Hydrangea House. I open the front door and we go in. Lillian is sitting in the dining room to the left and spots us. She frowns when she sees Ian.

'A friend,' I explain. 'He's just here to pick something up and he'll be gone.'

She doesn't believe me. She's staring at the duffel bag in Ian's hand, and I can see she's weighing whether to charge me for another person in the room.

'Really,' I say quickly. 'He's not staying.' I begin to climb the stairs, Ian behind me. Lillian doesn't say anything, but between her and Steve, my hiding place isn't going to be safe for very long.

We reach the room, and I pull out the key and let us in. Ian puts the duffel bag on the bed and walks around, checking the room out.

'Looks like *Little House on the Prairie* in here,' he says, fingering the lace curtain.

I am pulling the laptop out from under the bed, careful to push the backpack with my money in it further into the darkness beneath. He doesn't notice, and I begin to breathe a little easier. I open the laptop on the desk and boot it up.

'What is it that you need me to do?' I ask.

'It's like before,' he begins, but I hold up my hand.

'No explanations. Just tell me straight out. We don't have much time, and I hope I don't have to get in anywhere that's too difficult or too time consuming. Is it the bank? The same bank?'

'Yes.'

I already know how to get past the firewall, but then I remember. 'I tried to sign in there before and it wouldn't let me in.'

Ian gives me a panicked look. 'What?'

'I remembered the username and password. I tried them, but they didn't work.'

Relief floods his face. 'No, no, those were for the site where you'll transfer the money. You have to find the username and password for this account.'

But before I do anything: 'Whose?'

He hesitates.

'Whose account, Ian?'

He purses his lips, then says, 'Paul Michaels. I'm going after Paul Michaels.'

I am confused. *He* is Paul Michaels. Isn't he?

'Listen, Tina, just do it, OK? Stop asking questions. You said you would do it.'

As if my word still means something. I stare at him for a few seconds, then turn to the laptop. I use the VPN and get to the bank website. 'You haven't made this easy.' I find the portal I got through before. I wish I could get in touch with Tracker, but I can't do that in front of Ian, and I have no idea whether I can even find him quickly.

But as I'm staring at the code on the screen, my head starts spinning and suddenly I'm back in my room in Miami, the palm trees swaying outside my window. I close my eyes and the palm trees disappear and the codes flash in front of my eyes, the ones I was so used to. It has been a long time, but it hasn't. I have changed, but I haven't.

The codes are the same, the language is the same, and my fluency comes back in a rush.

I begin my work. Ian is behind me, watching over my shoulder, but he can't know what it is I'm doing, because I'm not even sure. I'm on autopilot, my memory kicking in, and I remember everything.

The screen begins scrolling itself, the codes turning into usernames until I finally find the one I need. I scribble it on a small pad of paper next to me and begin to look for the passwords. This is easier now that I know what I'm doing, but it still takes me a while to find the right one. I jot that down next to the username, and hold the pad up for Ian to see.

He is on the bed, sleeping. I glance at the clock and see that it has been over an hour – an hour and a half – and I have not called Steve. I reach for the phone and dial his cell number.

'You didn't call Frank yet, did you?' I ask without saying hello.

'What are you up to, Nicole?'

'Nothing. Not really. You didn't call him, did you?'

'You've been up there a long time.'

I realize now that Steve is outside, watching the house, waiting to see if Ian is going to leave.

'You'll see that the lights are on,' I say, getting up and going over to the window. I pull back the curtain and yes, there is Steve's SUV parked by the side of the road. I give him a small wave. 'We are just talking about things. Don't worry about me.'

'Until he leaves, I'm going to worry.'

'I know. He's going to leave soon. Really.'

'I'm staying until he does.'

'OK.' I hang up the phone and go to the bed and shake Ian. He frowns at me as though he doesn't quite know who I am at first, and then recognition enters his eyes.

'Are you done?'

'Almost.' I go back to the laptop and he gets off the bed and scoots the other chair over next to me. By the time he does, I have typed in the password for Paul Michaels's account.

My finger hovers over the key. 'If you are Paul Michaels, why are we hacking into your account?'

'It's my money. I can put it where I want.'

'If it's your money, then why don't you know your own user-name and password? Why did you need me?' The curiosity gets the better of me, and I finally do hit enter.

As I stare at the screen, I am stunned by the two balances I see. 'Why would anyone keep this amount of money in a checking account?' I ask, counting the six figures. 'Especially a debit account, which is easier to compromise than a credit card?'

'Don't worry about that.'

That's exactly what I *am* worried about.

'This isn't really your account, is it? Who is Paul Michaels, Ian? And don't give me any bullshit about how it's you.'

'Just transfer the damn money, Tina.' He reaches behind him and pulls the gun out from his waistband, pointing it at me.

'If you shoot me, you'll never get the money, Steve will hear the shot and call the police, and you'll never get out here alive. We'll both be dead.' I pause. 'Like Zeke.'

He shakes his head slowly, the gun moving closer to my chest. 'You loved him, didn't you?'

'No. I never loved him. And when I knew he knew, I left with *you*. Not with him.'

'But he found us. How did he find us, Tina? You never made mistakes.'

I am astonished he can say it with a straight face, that he can seem so genuinely perplexed as to how Zeke knew where we were. I shake my head slowly. 'I didn't tell him anything, Ian. It wasn't me, and you know it.' And then I tell him what I have known all these years. The reason why I left that night, took all the money I could and never said goodbye.

'It was you.'

THIRTY-FOUR

I knew as soon as Zeke told me he was going to leave his wife that I needed to put our escape plan into action.

'He was looking at my laptop,' I told Ian when I called him from a pay phone on Brickell Avenue.

'Did he see anything?'

'Of course not. But he suspects.'

'Then why did he tell his wife he's leaving her for you?'

'He's going to try to protect me.' As I said it, I knew it was true. Zeke wasn't just willing to leave his wife. He was willing to put his job on the line for me. Even though I had told him I didn't love him, I did care for him. I couldn't let him do that.

'Then let him.'

'I've got the documents and the airline reservations. We leave tomorrow night.'

'Tomorrow?'

'We can't take any chances.'

'It's been a month. Don't you think if he suspected you, he would've already arrested you? I mean, he *is* FBI.'

I couldn't understand why Ian was fighting me like this. We'd talked about having to leave at some point. He was the one who came up with our new names. 'What's the problem?'

'Are we going to be able to get to the money over there?'

'Absolutely. Don't you trust me?' From the hesitation, it was clear that he didn't. 'OK, fine. I'll go by myself. You can stay.'

'You're not going without me.' He really didn't trust me. He thought that if I left, the money would go with me. What had happened to us? Two months ago we were in love, we still couldn't keep our hands off each other, then Zeke showed up and everything changed.

'Then meet me at the airport tomorrow. The flight leaves at eight. We'll be in Paris in time for breakfast.' We'd agreed that Paris was a good choice, since I was fluent in French. I'd also arranged a place for us to live, but Ian didn't know about the houseboat yet. I'd wanted to surprise him, but the way he was acting, I wasn't so sure I should. I shrugged off my doubts. 'OK?'

'OK.' He hung up, and I stared at the phone for a few seconds, wondering if I was doing the right thing. Ironic, since I had already stolen ten million dollars for him.

We were happy, though, those days in Paris – at least, that's what I'd thought. The houseboat rocked gently on the Seine as we sat outside in blue-and-white striped chairs, drinking coffee, flowers in pots surrounding us, the Eiffel Tower towering nearby. In all the time I had spent in France when I was a child with my grandmother, I had rarely come to this city, and we spent our days discovering its treasures and secrets. It was as though the last months had never happened. It was stolen kisses and holding hands as we wandered the cobblestone streets, buying cheese and bread and chocolates. It was Ian again; it had always been Ian.

Until Zeke came out of the shadows as I left the café that night and followed me home.

'You called his office. Zeke's office. You didn't tell him who you were but you told him where I was.' The old familiar anger rises in my chest and I force it back down. I can't afford to let it out. Not yet.

Ian snorts. 'You're crazy.'

'Am I? You set me up.' I give him a sad smile. 'You didn't know how much Zeke loved me. Not really.' I close my eyes for a second and see it all again, then open them quickly so I can push it away.

'You're one to talk,' Ian says, anger curling around each word. 'You're the reason the account was frozen, aren't you? You told him. You told him where the money was.'

So here it is. The showdown.

He was wrong. Zeke knew about everything a month before he showed up day at my house. It was the server raid. That's how he ended up with me, after his people traced my IP address through the maze I'd left behind.

I think about what I am about to do, transferring money out of Paul Michaels's accounts. 'Who is Paul Michaels, Ian?'

Ian takes a deep breath. 'He's no one, Tina. No one at all.'

I still can't figure out, and I'm trying to, when another possibility slams into my head. 'It's Tony DeMarco, isn't it? It's a dummy account set up to launder money, isn't it? You're getting back at him, for everything he's made you do in the last fifteen years.'

'It's not like he'll miss it.' Ian shakes his head. 'I never knew you to do something so stupid, Tina. Why did you do it? Did you think you were finally safe here?'

He is talking about the postcard. I told myself that sending my father a little piece of the peace I'd found would help him die. But it was never about him. It was all about me. I sent that postcard thinking I'd gotten away, and I was going to show everyone up. Instead, it was the beginning of the end of everything.

'Not for nothing, Tina, but I tried to warn you when I first got here. I told you I wasn't the only one. I didn't want you to get hurt.'

'This from the man who's holding a gun on me. A man who wanted me to steal for him before I took off again.'

'You know I wouldn't use the gun on you.'

I stare at him, incredulous. 'How do I know that? It's not as though you haven't used it before. What about Zeke? What about Carmine?'

'Carmine was going to kill me. I had no choice.' He reaches over and touches my cheek.

I flinch and take a step back. He pulls his hand away and looks over at the laptop. I have not transferred the money yet.

'Do it,' he says softly. 'And then I'll leave you alone.'

'How are you going to get away?'

'I can stay underground, just like you.' He pauses. 'Just do it, Tina.'

'What about Amelie?'

Ian grabs the laptop and thrusts it at me. 'Make the fucking transfer, Tina,' he growls.

I tell myself that it's just Tony DeMarco's money, that it's just a number, it's just an account I've hacked into, like I used to hack into my father's business. I took money from him, too, moved it around so he'd have to look for it. I left traces of myself because I'd wanted to get caught. Zeke found me in those traces – that's how he knew what I could do, that's what led him to me by the pool that day. It was another mistake. Trying to show up my father.

I take the laptop and put it on the desk. I pull up the chair and sit down in front of it. My hands are steady, as though I am not being forced to do this. Maybe I'm not. Not really. But I do know that this is the only way I'm going to get rid of him.

I am already in the account, but to transfer I need to go elsewhere.

'You have to tell me where I'm transferring the money.' My voice is calm; I can hardly recognize it as my own.

Ian seems to realize that I am doing what he wants, so he tells me.

'Go sit on the bed. It might take a few more minutes,' I say.

He goes, obedient, happy that I am finally doing what he wants. I can't just transfer the money seamlessly from one account to the other. I have to look for where I make a wire transfer. This is what I did before, and it is not so different. I find the portal I need. I can feel Ian's eyes on my back, but he doesn't know the language, so while I am searching for codes, he gets distracted, picks up one of the magazines by the bed and leafs through it.

I do what I need to do, and it is only a few keystrokes from there, and then I am out, signing out of the VPN, wiping the laptop clean before I close it. Ian swings his legs over the side of the bed.

'Done already?'

I nod and get up. 'I think it's time to leave.'

Ian stands and puts his arms around me, his mouth on mine, and for a brief second I feel it, what we'd had before and what we'd rediscovered. But then it's gone. I step back, away from him, even though his hands are still at my waist and his eyes are smoky with passion.

I shake my head. 'I can't, Ian. It's over. Really over.'

'Tina—'

'Go back to Amelie. Go back to your wife.' I turn my back, wondering if it is the right thing to do with a man I have just spurned and who has a gun.

'Tina.' His tone is soft, and I feel his hand on my shoulder.

I turn, curiosity getting the better of me. I cannot read his expression, but something is going on; he wants to tell me some-thing. I wait.

'We have to leave as soon as we can.'

I can't believe what he's saying. 'What do you mean, *we*?'

'Come with me. We can get away tonight. No one will know.'

I struggle with what he's saying. 'What about your *wife*?'

'New start.' He stares at me, and the rage mixes with a heaviness, a sadness.

'We had that before. Look how it turned out. And how do I know that the FBI isn't waiting outside the door for me? That your plan to get away means they'll take me out of here in handcuffs and you get your freedom?'

'Tina.' He reaches for me, and I let him put his arms around me. I slide my hands around his waist as I lift my face to his and kiss him. He responds, and I feel him grow hard as he rubs against me. For a moment I let him think that maybe I will take him to bed, but then I slip out of his embrace and back up, my arms behind me so he knows it's over.

'I can't. We can't.'

'I'm giving you a way out.'

There is no way out, at least not with him. I shake my head. He sees it now, that I'm telling him the truth. That even if he finds me again, it will never be the same.

He hangs his head, then straightens up, picks up the duffel bag. 'OK, Tina. Good luck.' He starts for the door, his gait slow, as though I am going to stop him.

I don't. He opens the door and I hold my breath, waiting for Frank Cooper or the FBI to come barging in, but no one is there. He turns and smiles at me. 'You've got a head start. They're looking for me, too. For such a small island, there are a lot of places to hide here. I don't blame you for staying here so long. But if you want to save your ass, Tina, you have to leave. Now.'

The door closes and he is gone.

THIRTY-FIVE

I begin to shake, my knees give out and I sink to the floor, hyperventilating. I bring my hand out from behind me and stare at the gun that I have lifted from Ian's waistband.

I don't want to use it, but the familiar heaviness of it, its solidness, feels comfortable in my hand. Despite everything that happened.

In one swift movement, I drop down to the floor and pull the backpack out from under the bed. Cash spills out of it. I need to find a way to make it less conspicuous. I spot the towels Lillian has left for me on the dresser, and I go get them. Carefully and slowly, as if I have all the time in the world, I wrap the cash up in the soft, plush towels. I leave a little out that I put in the front pocket for easy access. I slide the laptop inside as well, tucking the towels around it. The gun lay on the floor next to me. What to do with that? I am wearing yoga pants and a fleece jacket with small pockets. Nowhere to hide it. It has to go in the backpack, too. I tuck it between the towels. It won't be easy to get to if I need it, but I have no choice.

I sit on the floor for a few minutes after the backpack is ready. I look around the room and think about where I was last week, having my weekly Friday dinner with Steve at Club Soda.

I get up and sling the backpack around my shoulder. I have already paid Lillian for the room, but I leave a little more for her on the dresser, just because she's going to make breakfast in the morning but I won't be here to eat it and she will have wasted her time.

I know when I get outside that Steve will be there, waiting for me. I wish that he weren't, but I need him and I am grateful for him. He watches me as I walk around the front of the Explorer and climb into the passenger seat, slamming the door shut behind me. I reach around for the seatbelt before he speaks.

'You OK?'

I nod.

'Where are we going?'

I think about that duffel bag and how much I have lost. 'Did you see him leave?'

He knows whom I am talking about. He cocks his head toward the road in front of us. 'There.'

'Let's see if we can't find him. He's got something I need.'

'The duffel bag?' Steve doesn't wait for an answer, he just starts the SUV and we begin to move forward. I strain my eyes to try to see Ian somewhere ahead of us, but I see nothing but darkness beyond the headlights. Until . . .

I point. 'There.'

'One step ahead of you, Nicole.' Steve cuts out the lights and we are now relying on the moon to guide us. Ian is just ahead, sauntering along the side of the road, the duffel swinging. I lean over and reach inside the backpack, pulling out the gun. I feel the SUV lurch.

'What's that, Nicole?'

'What do you think?' I try not to sound belligerent, but I am not successful. I just want it all to be over.

'You're not really going to use it, are you?' The worry in his voice makes me feel guilty. He had no idea that I was a criminal, and now that I have a gun, I am even worse than he thought. I don't want to keep disappointing him.

'I just want to scare him. I need that duffel.'

'What's in it?'

I can feel his eyes on me, and I turn to stare him down. 'Money. Money that I've earned, not stolen.'

'Why don't you just let it go?'

Why not? I have ways to get more, but I don't want to do it that way anymore. I want the money that I earned by working, giving my tours, money that I made when I was happy. And I need all of it, so I can get the documents I need in Chinatown on Friday. I can't tell him this though, so I just say, 'I can't.'

'Nicole, you could stop this right now. You could go to Frank Cooper and tell him everything. Isn't there some sort of statute of limitations on what you did? Do you have enough money to start paying back what you stole?'

'It's not that easy, Steve. And anyway, Frank isn't the only one here. The FBI is here, too, looking for me, and no one is going to help me. I only have one alternative. I get that duffel and I leave.'

'If what you say is true, how do you think you're going to get on the ferry tomorrow morning?'

'I'm not.'

Steve stops the Explorer and shifts around in his seat so he can look at me.

'Come on, Steve, let's catch up to Ian and get that bag.'

'Not until you tell me what you're going to do.'

'It's better if you don't know.'

'No, it's not.' He watches me for a few seconds and then a broad smile takes over his face. 'You don't know, do you? You don't know how you're getting off the island.'

I shrug.

'I know you better than you know yourself, Nicole.'

That's what he thinks.

'One step at a time, Steve, OK?' I indicate Ian, who is become merely a tiny shadow ahead of us.

'Sure, Nicole.' The Explorer starts moving again, faster and faster until we pull up right next to Ian.

He stops short, sees me and frowns. He reaches around and realizes now that his gun is missing. I wave it in front of the window before I open the door and jump out. 'Looking for this?'

He lunges for me, but Steve is faster than either of us expects. He grabs Ian from behind, locking his arms behind his back. In his surprise, Ian has dropped the duffel.

'Nicole!' Steve indicates the bag and I sweep it up and toss it into the SUV.

'You think you're going to get away?' Ian asks me. 'They're coming for you.'

I feel a twinge of fear at the back of my neck, but I ignore it. 'Come on, Steve,' I say, the gun pointed at Ian.

Steve releases Ian, but in one swift move Ian swings his leg around and catches Steve behind the knees. Steve drops to the ground with a grunt. Ian hovers over him, his fist raised.

'Don't!' I warn.

Ian looks up at me. 'Or you'll shoot me?'

I have shot a gun before, but it is not second nature to me, so when I pull the trigger I feel the report shoot through my arm and I jerk back involuntarily.

'Good try,' Ian says, 'but no cigar.'

My whole body is shaking now. I am barely able to keep my grip on the gun. Ian makes a move toward me, but Steve is on his feet now and he lunges toward him, his shoulders making contact with the backs of Ian's legs, causing him to lurch forward and then down on the ground, face first.

'Come on,' Steve says roughly, and I don't wait. We are both in the SUV; Steve is starting it and the headlights illuminate Ian blinking at us as he struggles to get up. We pass him and the SUV careens down the road.

I am not really aware of where we are going. It feels like Steve has turned around a couple of times, and suddenly I can see the buildings in front of us. A light flashes on, a motion detector, as we move along a gravel driveway. I can see them bobbing in the distance – the boats. Motor boats and sailboats. No fishing boats here. We are at one of the marinas on the west side of the island.

A figure appears in front of us; Steve slams on the brakes so we don't hit him. He is wearing a plaid flannel shirt and a pair of jeans, a baseball cap.

Chip Parsons. The guy Steve says has a crush on me. The one from the Yellow Kittens.

'I knew you wanted to fix me up with him, Steve, but this might not be the time.' I am so nervous, the teasing just comes out without thinking.

Steve's hand closes over mine. 'I called him while I was waiting for you. I figured you'd need some help.'

I appreciate what he's done, but this is one more person who knows where I am and where I might be going. I begin to argue, but Steve says roughly, 'Now, go.' He puts his hand back on the steering wheel.

Something about him, the way his jaw is set, the way he's holding his head is not right.

I see it then, in the light from the building.

The blood on his shoulder.

THIRTY-SIX

My God, I shot Steve. I missed Ian, but I shot my best friend. 'Steve!' I exclaim. 'What did I do?'

He gives me a wan smile, but I can see the pain etched around his eyes. 'Get out of the car, Nicole. Chip can take you to the mainland. He can be trusted.'

'But you're hurt!'

'Don't worry about me. I'll be fine.' He looks anything but fine. 'Just go. Please. You have to leave.'

'What's up?' Chip has come over to the driver's side window, which Steve rolls down. He looks over at me. 'You ready, Nicole?'

'I can't go now,' I say.

'No, we're not going now,' Chip says, misunderstanding. 'But we can leave at first light. I've got a place set up for you to stay until then. You can get a little sleep.'

'But—'

'Chip, can you give us a couple minutes?' Steve asks. He doesn't wait for an answer, but as he rolls the window back up, Chip politely pretends to be interested in something on the horizon. Steve looks back at me. 'Nicole, the bullet just grazed me. It's just a flesh wound. Really.' And to prove it, he shrugs off his shirt so I can see that he is right. There is blood, but it looks more like he's gotten a really bad deep scratch. He winces as he pulls the sleeve back over it. 'Now you can go.'

'Let me clean it up for you at least,' I say. I climb out of the SUV and call over to Chip. 'Is there a washroom in there?' I ask, pointing to the building.

Chip nods, and I go over to the driver's side. Steve gets out, but not as reluctantly as I anticipated. He must be in a lot of pain. Chip sees it now, the blood on Steve's shoulder. 'What happened?'

'Just a little bar fight.' Steve chuckles, but it is not his usual jovial laugh.

'I need to clean it up for him,' I explain.

Chip leads us to the building, and he opens the door to the washroom for us, again discreetly leaving us alone. I close the toilet seat and Steve sits. There are paper towels and I turn the water on, waiting for it to get hot before soaking the towels and pumping some soap into them. Steve has taken off his shirt, and I begin to wipe away the blood and see that the wound is smaller than it looked in the car.

'I wish I had some peroxide,' I say. 'When you get home, you have to put peroxide on it.' I pause. 'Are you OK to drive? Do you want me to go with you?'

Steve puts his hand over mine. 'Nicole, you have to leave. You have everything you need?'

I cannot think about that now, though. 'I shot you,' I whisper. 'I am so, so sorry.' The tears come then, falling down my cheeks, and with his other arm, Steve pulls me close so my head rests on his chest and I can hear his heart beating.

'You've got one more chance,' he says.

'For what?'

'Run away with me.'

I want to. I can't stand the thought of leaving him here. Especially like this. But I can't. My silence gives him the answer. I pull away and give him a sad smile.

'You have to promise to call me. Tell me that you're all right,' he says.

I shake my head. 'It's bad enough that you're helping me leave. They'll question you for hours. Days, maybe.'

'I have nothing else to do with my time. No one to meet at Club Soda.'

'Don't rub it in.'

He is still waiting for me to change my mind. About him going with me, not about me calling. Instead, I help him back on with his shirt. He winces as he moves his shoulder, but tries to cover it up with a grin that turns into more of a grimace. I touch his beard and give him a quick kiss on the cheek. 'I wish I could stay,' I whisper. 'I wish it could all go back the way it used to be.' Scrabble games and burgers and onion rings and walks at the Bluffs. Gossip and clam chowder. My life. The life I have built. The life that has slipped away every minute since Ian showed up.

In the days before I was Nicole, those things wouldn't have meant anything to me. The only things that mattered were Ian and my computers.

I hear something outside, and I realize it's a siren. It's still in the distance. I glance at Steve. 'Who knows we're here?'

He shakes his head. 'Only you and me and Chip.'

Chip. 'I don't think he's as sweet on me as you've always said,' I say. 'I have to get out of here.' I sling the backpack over my shoulder, feel the weight of the money and the laptop inside, and pick up the duffel bag.

'Where are you going?'

'You don't know.'

He struggles to his feet, but he is unsteady. I touch his good shoulder. 'No. Stay.' I brush his white, coarse beard with my lips, lingering for just a moment, breathing in his scent. He smells of the salt that hangs in the air. And before he can say another word, I slip out the door and back into the night. Chip is standing on the gravel road near Steve's SUV, so I go in the opposite direction. He can't hear my footsteps because the sirens are closer now, and by the time he looks around again, I will be on the other side of the building, gone.

I am disappointed that he called Frank Cooper, but not surprised. I have had little contact with Chip Parsons, and maybe he is just a little bit upset that I never expressed any interest in him. But it is probably more that he is from the island and even though I have made a niche for myself here, I am still a newcomer in his eyes.

It will not take Frank Cooper and the FBI long to know that I have gone and in which direction. The island is small, and they will be able to close in on me quickly if I don't find a place to hide. But it can't be too far from the ferry, because that is truly my only way off the island at this point and, even though the odds are against me, I have to try.

I think about how I got away from the FBI agents when I was supposed to meet Ian at the Painted Rock, and Charleston Beach is not far from here. I can go to the beach and make my way around the island that way. It is the long way around but I have all night, and it seems doable, even carrying the two bags.

Soon the sirens are in the distance, and I begin my trek along the perimeter of the island. It is dark and peaceful, the water slapping against the beach, the moon high in the sky, which is dotted with millions of stars. It is the kind of night that calls for some wine and cheese and a blanket on the beach, being thankful for my life. Instead, I am running for my life.

I reach Grace Cove and then Dorry's Cove. I have to make my way around the rocky shore, but it is not daunting. I have done this so many times under better circumstances, as if in preparation for tonight. I don't stop, just keep moving. I try not to think about Steve, about leaving him, about how I shot him.

I can't help but think now about Zeke. About what happened that night in Paris, how Ian has not exactly lied to the FBI.

I am responsible for Zeke's death.

Ian had disappeared somewhere. He did that often, showing back up again a few hours later with wine and cheese or chocolate and we would make love to the sway of the boat in the river. I would turn on the radio and sing softly in French to him. But he wasn't there that day, and instead I was singing along with Edith Piaf when the knock came at the door and Zeke came in.

He looked as though he hadn't slept in days. His suit was mussed and he wasn't wearing a tie. His shirt was unbuttoned at the neck.

I didn't quite know what to say, so I didn't say anything. Zeke stepped toward me, but then stopped when he saw the look on my face.

'Surprised?' he asked.

I nodded. 'How did you find me?'

'You can't hide behind your computer forever, Tina. Sooner or later the computer will give you up.' Zeke smiled. 'All that money. The bank. Did you think you could get away with it?'

I had, but I didn't want to admit it to him.

'You have to know about server raids – how we can trace those paths you think you got rid of. They still exist, Tina, do you know that?'

I was too good leave a trail. But he knew somehow, and he'd known for at least a month before Ian and I left.

'So what happens now?' I asked.

'One of two things.' Zeke shoved his hands in his pockets and shrugged. 'I can take you in. Or you could come with me.'

Wasn't that the same thing? He saw me frown and gave me a tentative smile.

'You and I could go away together. I have nothing left at home. I'll give it all up for you. We can go find an island somewhere, live the rest of our lives in peace. Together.'

I heard something outside, on the dock. Heavy footsteps. Whistling. Ian.

Zeke heard it, too, and he stepped away from the door, closer to me. 'Don't worry. We can get rid of him.'

But I didn't want to get rid of him, and Zeke could see it in my face. His smile faded just as the door swung open. Ian came in, not seeing Zeke at first, but then he did, and he stopped.

'Who's this?' Ian asked me, his eyes not leaving Zeke's face.

'Zeke Chapman,' Zeke said, since I couldn't find my voice.

'Oh, right. The other man.'

Zeke looked stricken, as though he hadn't considered that I was serious about Ian, but then he composed himself. 'Yes, I guess so.'

'Are you here for her?'

'Yes.'

They were talking as though I wasn't even in the room.

Ian rolled his eyes and gave me a funny look. 'Then take her.'

Fury rose through my chest. 'What do you mean, take her? Why do you think I want to go with him?'

'Because he's here, isn't he? You must have called him. No one knows where we are.' His eyes flickered slightly, and that was when I knew. Knew that he had somehow gotten word to Zeke where I was.

'I'm not going with him.'

Zeke stood up a little taller then, straightened out his shoulders. 'Well, then,' he said, his voice suddenly steady and strong, 'I have to take you in.' His hands disappeared for a second and when they emerged again, he was holding handcuffs and a gun.

'What are you doing?'

'Taking you in. Charging you. You stole a lot of money, Tina.' He swung the gun around toward Ian. 'You, too.' It was a challenging move, and if he'd wanted a fight, he was going to get it.

Ian moved closer, but I couldn't stand here and watch this, especially since Zeke had a gun. Without thinking, I lunged toward Zeke, the move surprising him enough so that when my hand made contact with his arm, he dropped the gun. It fell to the floor with a thud. I stared at it a second before I heard a loud click.

Ian was holding a gun on Zeke. Another gun. Where had he gotten it?

'Feels a little different to be on the other end of things, doesn't it?' Ian said, his face dark. 'Tina, get the stuff together.'

Even though I'd been distracted, I knew what he meant, and I grabbed the two carry-ons we'd brought with us and began stuffing our clothes into them.

'We'll just find you again,' Zeke warned.

I'd closed the suitcases and stood waiting for my next instructions.

'Rope.'

I found some in a drawer while Ian shoved Zeke into a chair. All I could think about was how Zeke had found us and I would end up spending my life in prison, or at least the next twenty years, and I was too young for that. I knelt down and began tying Zeke's foot to the chair.

Suddenly his leg swung out, the rope dangling, and he was somehow underneath Ian's arms, the gun flying across the room.

'Grab it, Tina!' I heard Ian shout just before he grunted as Zeke punched him in the stomach.

On autopilot, I saw Zeke's gun on the floor and grabbed it, swinging it around to hand to Ian, but something happened and it went off, the sound echoing against the wood, and Zeke was on the floor. I stood, staring at him, the gun hanging from my hand. I felt Ian take it from me. Zeke stared up at me with a puzzled expression.

'I love you, Tina. It doesn't have to be like this,' he said, his voice almost a whisper.

'Isn't that sweet?' Ian asked. 'Are you sure you don't want to go with him, Tina?' His voice was laced with venom, and for the first time I saw how jealous he really was, but his words faded away as Zeke's face grew white, his blood trickling toward my feet.

I took big gulps of air and yet I still couldn't breathe.

Ian was shaking me. 'Tina, get your shit together.'

I blinked a few times, his features coming into focus, and I glanced back down at Zeke. His eyes were half-closed, his mouth was moving but I couldn't hear what he was saying.

'Where did you get it?' I asked.

'Get what?'

'The gun, asshole. Where did you get it?'

He grinned, putting his hand up to my cheek. 'Don't worry about that. No one can trace it back to us.'

'Us? You mean you.'

'I'm not the one with the connection to him, Tina. Even his wife knew about you.'

I glanced at the suitcases on the bed. Ian was leaning over Zeke, his back to me. I reached up onto the shelf above the bed and grabbed the backpack that I'd prepared the day after arriving here. A glance inside told me Ian had not taken the money or the documents, trusting me. Quickly, I slipped his passport out and dropped it on the bed, slinging the bag over my shoulder and running for the door. I pushed my way outside, the air hitting me in the face like a splash of cold water. It had grown darker, the outlines of the buildings across the river just shadows. The light bled out of the small window of the boat.

I couldn't go back inside. I couldn't see him like that again.

I ran up the dock and I was halfway up the stone steps when I heard the muffle of another shot.

THIRTY-SEVEN

I rest when I reach the Bluffs. I cannot leave this island and not pay homage to this beautiful place. I have never been a religious person, but the Bluffs have been my church. I made my confession here, alone and utterly repentant, the first time I came, the day I began my jars of stones.

I stare up at the shadows and notice now that the sky is brightening. Streaks of light have begun to paint the sky above the dark water. I think about my brushes and canvas and try to imprint this image in my memory, if I ever get a chance to paint again. Veronica would love this painting. She would gesture wildly with her hands as she enthusiastically told a customer about how I saw this scene the night I was escaping the island.

Veronica. And Jeanine. I never had women friends before, not really. There were some girlfriends in school, but they didn't understand me, didn't understand my obsession with the computers. I sequestered myself in the chat rooms, becoming friends with people who hid behind their monikers like me, secretly entering places we shouldn't and bragging to each other about it.

I will miss my friends, and soon they will know the truth about me, so it is probably good that I will be gone before they find out. I don't think I could handle their reactions and disappointment.

I don't allow myself to think about Steve anymore. Despite his protests, he will move on and find someone else to hang out with on Friday nights and play Scrabble with.

I resume my trek. Once or twice I hear sirens, sense the slow-moving cars with their headlights trained along the sides of the roads, hoping to catch me. But so far I see no one as I climb over rocks, clutching my duffel bag. I drop it once and for a second wonder if I could leave it here. I could probably get to New York with just what's in the backpack. But I won't be able to pay for the documents and I don't want to stay in the city. I am too much an island girl now. I crave peace and quiet, and even though it would be easier to hide there, I can't stand the thought of it. I haven't figured on where to go, but I'll know it when I get there.

By the time I reach what I've always thought of as my beach, the beach where I've done my painting just below my house, the sun has started to come up. I still have a little time before the ferry leaves. I have to plan it just right, when I get on the ferry. I can't risk Frank Cooper stopping it. Granted, if he figures out I'm on the ferry, then he can easily have someone waiting on the other side, in Point Judith, to take me into custody. But I have had hours to formulate a plan, and I think it will work.

This beach is a good one because you can't see anyone on the beach from the road. I take a seat on the sand and pull my laptop out of the backpack. I am close enough to houses that have wireless Internet that it's easy to get online. Soon I have logged into my VPN and quickly go to the websites for the different charter airlines that fly out of Block Island. I make a reservation on one of the flights that leaves in an hour and a half. I make the reservation in the name of Tina Adler. I pay for it using Paul Michaels's credit card number.

This might not keep Frank Cooper and the FBI from checking out the ferry, but they will have to go the airport at the same time the first ferry leaves the island, just in case this reservation is real. I can only hope that luck will be on my side, and I can get on the ferry and hide and somehow make it to the mainland without getting caught.

While I am sitting here, I think about what Ian said about Amelie Renaud. How I hadn't done a thorough search on her. I have all of her pertinent information, like an address and credit card number and Social Security number. Things I couldn't find with a simple search. But I have missed something, so that is what I do. A simple search.

And within seconds, I see it. I see what Amelie's role has been in everything.

Amelie's entire career has been with the bank. She rose through the ranks from customer service representative, more than fifteen years ago, and is now the bank's Paris branch manager.

She is the one who gave Ian the account numbers, I am sure

of it. I know all too well how persuasive Ian can be when a girl is in love with him. She gave him the numbers, and then he married her.

I see that her husband is an American named Roger Parker, the name on the account Ian gave me. The account he wanted me to transfer the money to. Ian still doesn't realize how much information I can find online if I'm motivated enough.

In a photograph, Ian stands with his arms around Amelie and their two children; they look happy.

I close down the laptop. It is time to go.

As I approach, I see Old Harbor is a ghost town. There are a couple of cars on the roads, and when I look up the hill toward my house, I see a police car parked outside.

The ferry is sitting at the dock, bobbing up and down. I don't see anyone on it; but that doesn't mean there isn't. Even though I've never taken the ferry to the mainland, when I first came to the island I got into the habit of watching them, just in case a situation like today's arose.

The one thing I am afraid of is that the police are lurking somewhere. It dawns on me that if Ian is working with them he will tell them I have a duffel bag. He does not know I still have the backpack.

I settle down on the sand and wonder how much more cash I can fit into the backpack. I end up taking out some of the towels to make room and manage to get quite a bit inside. Enough for my documents and then some. I look longingly at the cash I have to leave behind, but I have no choice. Some lucky beachcomber will find it and feel that he has struck it rich. It is my good deed of the day.

The backpack really isn't heavier than it was before, since I have shed the towels. I consider using one as a turban, to hide my short locks, but that will draw more attention so I abandon the idea. I do take off my glasses and smooth out my hair as much as I can, cursing my curls for the first time.

There are a couple of cars already lined up to get on the ferry. In the first, an old Honda, the driver is drinking a cup of coffee from a Styrofoam cup and smoking a cigarette, the smoke drifting out the window. The second is a Volvo with a woman at the wheel. She is familiar, and it takes me a few seconds but I finally place her. She has taken my bike tour, but she is not a tourist. She is new to the island, just here this past year, and owns a small shop where she sells jewelry made out of shells. I take a chance and go over to the car, knocking on the window on the passenger side. It whirrs down and I lean in.

'Hi there,' I say, forgetting her name.

'Nicole! So good to see you!' I rub my arms, and she takes the bait. The door unlocks. 'Hop in, it's cold out there.'

I do as asked and slid onto the heated seat. 'Thanks,' I say, closing the door.

'You headed to the mainland?'

I nod.

'I'm going to Boston for a girls' weekend with my friends,' she says. 'It's the last chance I've got before the big tourist push, and my husband can deal with the business for the weekend.' She gives me a wink.

I remember now that her husband commutes to the mainland every day. They moved here after their youngest child graduated college, giving her the chance to start this business that she'd always wanted. I try to figure out a good excuse for me to go to the mainland, but it turns out I don't need to. She chatters on and on about her husband and her business, and giving me all the gossip about the women she's meeting but whom I don't know.

In the sideview mirror, I see a police car slide past us, going up the hill.

I am relieved that it does not stop as the ferry's gangplank begins to come down.

'Do you have your ticket?' the woman whose name I can't remember asks.

'I have to get one,' I say.

'Oh, I have commuter tickets,' she says. 'Want one?'

I insist on paying her for it, discreetly pulling a twenty out of my bag and handing it to her.

'It doesn't cost that much,' she protests.

'Consider it payment for giving me a warm place to wait,' I say with a smile. I am not insincere. Once we are on board, I will miss these heated seats.

A few more cars have lined up behind us now. I constantly

check the mirrors but still have not seen another police car. I can only hope they are at the airport, waiting for me. When they start letting the cars on the ferry, my heart beats harder, and I force myself to continue to smile and nod as the woman babbles on about her weekend plans.

The cars begin to move forward onto the ferry. We hand over our tickets, and once we've parked on board, we get out of the car.

'Cup of coffee?' the woman asks.

'Just going to use the facilities,' I say and make a beeline upstairs. Instead of going into the ladies' room, I slip into the men's room and lock the door. I lean against the wall and take some deep breaths, letting the backpack drop to the floor. I am hardly home free, but I have made it this far, thanks to the good luck of meeting up with what's-her-name. I keep hoping her name will come to me, but I seem to have blocked it completely.

I am in the men's room for about five minutes when someone knocks. 'Taken,' I say, lowering my voice.

Whoever it is walks away.

I have been in here for twenty minutes before I feel the boat begin to move. I still don't feel like I can breathe. Frank Cooper could have someone on board who will grab me when I emerge.

When another knock comes on the door, I know I have to come out. I feel the man's eyes on me when I open the door. 'Sorry,' I mutter. 'Wrong one.' I sidle past him and take inventory of where I am.

A few people sit at tables near the snack bar, holding coffee cups and having a jovial conversation. I go outside, the salty wind slamming into my face, and I shiver in the cardigan. I walk the perimeter of the ferry, expecting at every turn to see Frank Cooper or Ian or one of those FBI agents. But I see no one familiar – no police officers.

I do not see the woman I came on board with, either, though, and I begin to panic. Was she a plant? Someone put there to make me feel comfortable enough to let my guard down?

But suddenly she is standing beside me.

'I thought you jumped ship,' she says with a laugh. 'Coffee?'

She has bought me a cup, and I take it despite wanting to flee. But where would I go? I am now more trapped than I was on the island. I look back toward the place where I have lived for the past fifteen years. It is getting smaller and smaller the further we get away from it. The sky is a bright blue, the water a deep cobalt mixed with turquoise. Seagulls fly overhead, and I spot my little house just up from where the llamas are. I didn't realize you could see it from here.

'You don't have your bike,' the woman says to me.

I shake my head and take a sip of coffee that scorches my tongue.

'Do you need a ride somewhere when we get to Point Judith?'

'I was going to call a cab,' I say.

She rolls her eyes and waves her hand in front of her face. 'Don't be silly! Where are you going?'

'Providence,' I say.

'I can take you. Don't worry about it. I would love the company,' she says, and as I thank her, I remember her name.

Susan. Her name is Susan.

EPILOGUE

I went missing a year ago.

There are a lot of places along the border in Vermont where someone can hike into Canada. No one can see the forest for the trees, and I took advantage of that. So much for Homeland Security.

Even though I had been expecting the police to be waiting for me in Point Judith, there was no one. I read in the paper later that they were all at the airport because of the charter flight reservation. Apparently a local taxi driver, Steve McQueen, who was a close friend of Tina Adler, aka Nicole Smith, told the police that he dropped her off there after he helped her hide for the night while she waited for the flight. I could only hope that he wasn't in too much trouble for that.

I don't know what happened to Ian – there was no mention of him, but I do know that the money from Paul Michaels's account never went anywhere, and Tony DeMarco would find a bonus there, thanks to a wire transfer from Robert Parker's account. The money went the wrong way – at least, that would be the way Ian would see it. So while Ian didn't get the money he thought he was owed, Tony did get his and had no reason to kill him. Not yet.

Susan drove me to the train station in Providence. When she got back to Block Island after her girls' weekend and found out she'd harbored a fugitive, I was already halfway to Vermont after hitching a ride with a couple of elderly women who took pity on me because my husband had abandoned me. I never picked up the documents Tracker arranged for me. I didn't trust anyone anymore, except for Steve, and that 'other job' Tracker supposedly had still worried me. I'd had the idea of going to Canada, but I couldn't officially go through customs. So I bought some hiking equipment and ended up hiking across the border.

Today I'm sitting on the front porch of my little house on Isle-aux-Coudres, in the middle of the St Lawrence River in

Quebec. It's smaller than Block Island but has the same sort of feel about it. Peaceful, as if nothing will go wrong here. As if nothing has ever gone wrong here. I don't know much about the island's history, except Jacques Cartier discovered it four hundred years ago and named it after the hazelnut trees. But since I don't need to know history or island stories, I am not seeking out the stories I needed on Block Island for my business. I'm learning the nuances of Quebecois and shedding some of my Parisian French so I don't stand out quite so much.

I am painting. A few small galleries here are selling my work, scenes of the island, of the rocks that jut out of the long, muddy shoreline at low tide, the picturesque tidy houses, the magnificent church that dominates one end of the island, the two tiny shrines that are nearly identical to each other, the windmill at the grist mill where the scent of fresh bread baking in the outdoor oven by the parking lot wafts along the breeze and tempts me to try my hand at bread baking. So far, though, I have only bought their bread, which is rich and thick and when I close my eyes I smell the freedom it's given me.

A ferry brought me over here after I spent a few days in Baie-Saint-Paul. My paintings brought me a few dollars and I bought a bike. I coasted down the long hill to the ferry dock, discovered it's free – Canada's taxes are high but I have found few discomforts – and planned to spend only a couple of days biking and exploring yet another island.

I found a house to rent the first day.

I do take the ferry to the mainland, however, borrowing a friend's car because the hill that's easy to coast on a bike is brutal on the legs going up. My paintings are popular; I have settled into life here easily. It is a true extension of my life before. Not the one two lifetimes ago, just the previous one. I have made a couple of friends. We drink beer and eat club sandwiches. There are no beaches here for swimming, but I've taken to kayaking. The shores on either side of the river are clear, and the sunrises are spectacular as the red globe peers over the horizon and spreads its pinks and reds and yellows and orange streaks into the sky. The gallery owners tell me these are the most popular of my paintings, and I keep them in stock, making enough money to support myself.

Winters are brutal, but I have learned to cope and take long walks along the lonely roads.

There are no cliffs here, but the flowers in spring are magnificent.

I have found another oasis, another place to reinvent myself.

My name is Susan McQueen.

I don't think they'll find me here. But I never say never.